TENANTS OF THE HOUSE

GILBERT PHELPS

TENANTS OF THE HOUSE

A NOVEL

BARRIE & JENKINS

LONDON

To Kay

Tenants of the house,
Thoughts of a dry brain in a dry season.

T. S. ELIOT: *Gerontion*

1

It was rent-day at Hugo's house—the "day of reckoning" as he always put it. Jocularly, of course, for Hugo prided himself on being on good terms with all his tenants. The better-off ones paid their rent quarterly by cheque or banker's order. But he always gave them monthly receipts, and called in person to deliver them. It was a little eccentricity that gave no offence: he was such a good-natured fellow and usually the tenants were pleased to see him—always at the same time, give or take a few minutes, on the first of every month.

The tenants on the top floor didn't use cheques and had probably never seen a banker's order. For each of them he had a neat little green rent-book—and on them, too, he called on the first of every month, although, their rooms being furnished, their agreements—where anything so grand existed—were on a weekly basis. Often, indeed, they would have flitted before the first of the month came round, without paying any rent at all. But Hugo never did anything about it. He had evolved this system (he himself preferred to call it a "tradition") and he was a man to whom certain fixed points were a necessity: if they were removed, he felt, the whole house would come tumbling round his ears. So when one of these poorer tenants decamped he merely put another card in the window of the tobacconist's shop at the corner, and hoped for better luck next time....

Recently, though, he had taken to closing each room that fell vacant in this way. It was a large house, however, and apparently none of the tenants had noticed what was happening. There weren't enough gaps as yet to make any noticeable difference to the feel of the house: when you went in it still breathed softly and evenly; there were no bronchial wheezes down the stairways and corridors, no sense of gaping cavities hidden away somewhere, such as you get in most houses where a good number of the rooms are unoccupied.

It was not only a large house, it was also rather tall and narrow-looking, with so many windows (also tall and narrow) that sometimes, on smoky-yellow autumn days, it looked like a giant block of Gruyère cheese. Many people were surprised that it didn't fall down because of its peculiar structure and the multiplicity of the openings in it. It was, in fact, very solidly built, and in spite of the large number of windows it bore no resemblance to the typical inverted shoe-boxes of today, in which the small quantity of actual masonry looks like strips of adhesive tape designed merely to support the window-frames. Hugo's house was, on the contrary, one of those late-Victorian houses which look as if they were thrown together by undisciplined armies of workmen, but which are the despair of the demolition men because everything is so intricately and mysteriously jointed and mortised, like a Chinese puzzle.

It was, admittedly, an ugly house, made of a purplish, coal-like brick, so that from the outside it reminded one of the complexion of a sufferer from heart-disease or lupus, though it also had numerous "Georgian features" round the doorways and windows—and big impossibly rounded pillars, like giant sausages, supporting the portico.

The material of which these pillars, the window sills, and the various unlikely cornices, architraves, curlicues and pilasters were compounded had the property of absorbing huge quantities of cream paint and of quickly transforming it to a hideous ochre-yellow. Unfortunately Hugo, being a traditionalist, insisted on cream paint. At any rate there was always a lot of it—thick, sticky and shiny—so that the house never looked neglected. Inside too, everything was always freshly painted—and there the cream paint more or less retained its original properties. Hugo did all the interior decorating himself, for he was a handy, springy man of the kind that can tackle most household jobs.

But the adjective that most readily springs to mind in describing Hugo's appearance is "spherical". Everything about him was spherical. He had one of those round, shiny heads that, even when they carry a good growth of hair, suggest premature balding: and when they *are* nearly bald convey the impression of a bristly crew-cut: Hugo's hair fell somewhere between these two extremes. His eyes were round and blue: he had a round mouth and the lobes of his ears looked as if they must have been trained that way by having coins inserted under the skin in infancy. He was in the habit, whenever the weather permitted, of wearing either a singlet several sizes too small for him, or a very faded blue shirt whose short sleeves had shrunk well above the elbows; in either case the effect was to make the biceps protrude like snooker balls. As his arms were on the short side, the forearms, too, had an unusually rounded appearance. Both singlet and shirt strained over a barrel-shaped chest, covered with a coppery fuzz, which disposed itself in circular ringlets. It would not be fair to say that he had run to fat: he was a strong and active man and the various bulges were so hard and firm that they deserve to be assigned to an intermediate stage between fat and muscle. At the same time there is no denying that his hairy paps had a circular look, or that the jeans or dungarees he wore (also too tight for him) showed up a firm but spherical stomach, two spherical buttocks, two spherical calves, and two spherical, well-covered knee-caps. About the house, and also around the garden when it was not too muddy, he wore beach-shoes with rope soles, and he walked with a slightly rolling gait, balancing himself on the balls of his toes—themselves unusually round, like ball-bearings.

It would be wrong to conclude from all this, however, that there was anything at all suggestive in Hugo's build and appearance of the hermaphrodite. He was normal male—clubbable and even hearty among "manly men", and reasonably attractive to the opposite sex. It might, however, be permissible to say that he was a man in

9

whom sex was held in suspension, a phenomenon far more common than is usually admitted, as for example among certain types of adventurer and explorer and often, too, among sailors—a much maligned race. This state of affairs was really inevitable in Hugo's case: he lived for and through his tenants, who were, of course, of different ages, sexes and conditions: he had opened his house to them and he saw to it that it was kept clean, that the central-heating worked efficiently, and that the roof did not leak: he was, so to speak, the zone in which their respective climates operated.

As a matter of fact the reference to sailors is not without its relevance: with his rolling yet agile gait Hugo did look something like a sailor—or perhaps an undertaker, which is another neat and handy kind of man.

Except that his face was not determined enough for the one or lugubrious enough for the other. It was (of course) a rounded face, rather pale, but healthy looking. Its most remarkable characteristic perhaps was its smoothness. It was difficult to believe that Hugo ever shaved: nothing remotely resembling bristles ever appeared on his skin— and certainly never a sore or abrasion: only, occasionally, a shadow formed round the chin and jowls, but that, too, so smooth it might have been a flush or a birth mark. The excessive smoothness might have been due in part to the fact that Hugo used an electric razor. He could not stand the mess of ordinary shaving—the soapy, bristle-flecked deposit on the blade; the bits nicked out of the towel; and most revolting of all, the scum left in the wash-basin. So, he used an electric shaver, and used it at least three times a day. It was rather an old-fashioned model and its throaty hum was loud enough to reach from Hugo's own neat, clean, but rather sombre flatlet-cum-office on the ground floor (opening off the tiled hall) to practically every corner of the house. The tenants had grown accustomed to this hum: it seemed to them like the dynamo of the whole house: if for any reason Hugo omitted one of his thrice daily shaves they felt uneasy and found themselves listening intently for the next time. Life in that house seemed inconceivable without the hum of Hugo's shaver.

Hugo's own presence did not register itself anything like as forcibly as the throaty hum of the shaver. He was not a man of memorable facial expression, for one thing. The most usual one was an extraordinary blandness. There was nothing in the least insincere about this expression, but all the same it was almost too bland to be true: not a crease, not a line, not a wrinkle appeared on that smooth surface.

All this, of course, made it very difficult to calculate Hugo's age. He certainly did not look youthful: but just as decidedly he did not look old, and he was too bouncy to be judged middle-aged. He had a curiously unused appearance, as if his metabolism was quite different from that of ordinary people—as if, say, he were really living on a planet where each day was a month long by our time, and where fruit, leaf and flesh ripened by infinitesimal degrees. It is true, on the other hand, that this smooth, rounded look is typical of a certain type of man in his fifties—and "about fifty" was what most people would reply—but vaguely and doubtfully—if they were asked Hugo's age, though even the tenants who had been in the house ever since he first opened it to them—and that was a number of years ago—had never made a different estimate. Curiously enough the fact that he had apparently not changed an iota in all that time never seemed to occur to them. At the same time it would not be correct to say that they took his presence entirely for granted. He was always at hand, busy, amiable, helpful. The house was Hugo's house, and would not have been there but for him; the tenants would not have been there without him.

The difficulty of placing his age perhaps explains why it was also so difficult to place his nationality. True, this bouncy, boyish type is usually English. On the other hand, the spherical torso—especially when surmounted by a spherical head which carries with it an impression of hair *en brosse*—belongs traditionally (at any rate in English myth) to middle Europe. The original tenants had, in consequence, decided to place Hugo in this particular pigeon-hole. He was, they suggested, a refugee of some kind. Not from one of the major middle-

11

European countries like Germany, Austria, or Hungary, which had clear-cut associations (Hitler, Strauss waltzes, goulash and so on) but some fancy place like Herzegovinia or Bosnia, which were words left over from school history books or stamp collections, but which nobody could actually point to on a map.

About the same time a vague idea became current (it may, again, have had something to do with the spherical shape) that some time "before the war" Hugo had been a practitioner of one of the more obscure arts—a minor romantic poet, or an *avant-garde* painter on unlikely materials, or a choreographer, or a performer on some weird stringed instrument plucked with the toes and shaped like a rustic lavatory seat.

Hugo readily fell in with the general trend of these ideas. More, he elaborated them and gave them a local habitation and a name. When it was first reported to him that the accolade of "poet" (even though both "minor" and "romantic") had been speculatively bestowed upon him, he had hurriedly excused himself and retired to his own flatlet. If his informant had been able to follow him he would have been startled to see the smooth, bland visage suddenly crumple for a second or so—and puzzled to observe the guilty look which Hugo directed at the green baize door, studded with brass nails (which he kept carefully polished) at the far end of the room, which led, Hugo said, to his wine-cellar—though no one had ever seen it open because, he explained, he had been on the wagon for twenty years and more.

But the bland expression had quickly reasserted itself, as if Hugo had pulled over his face a mask of oil—his complexion was, in fact, slightly tacky, like the sweating of a tallow candle, though the perspiration of someone who was so neat and tidy, and who slapped himself so astringently under the cold shower (winter as well as summer) could hardly be offensive. Indeed Hugo had no odour about him at all, apart from those of his aftershave lotion (also very astringent) and of the talcum powder with which he dusted his chin. His equanimity restored, he had let it be known throughout the house by a series of smiling hints: first, that he did indeed hail

12

from Central Europe—though neither from Herzegovinia nor from Bosnia, but from Llubjliana, capital of Slovenia; and second, that he *had* once, in a happier clime and time, been a romantic poet, the ardent latter-day disciple of Slovenia's greatest bard, Frans Prěserěn.

Hugo had come across the name while skimming through a nineteenth-century encyclopedia (his favourite form of reading). In the first instance it was the curious curved accents placed above the first and last vowels like tiny cuticles, that had attracted him: then when he went on to read the article his heart warmed towards Frans Prěserěn. Not, however, because of the poetry itself— the encyclopedia quoted nothing in English (indeed it expended only ten lines on the poet altogether) and naturally Hugo (who in fact came from Bootle) knew no Slovene. It was the very obscurity of the poet and the language in which he wrote combined with the comparative smallness of his potential readership that stirred him. Somehow there was something heroic, noble, disinterested to an extravagant degree, about writing poetry—especially romantic poetry—in a language so little known that hardly anybody except a handful of one's compatriots would ever read it. And so he had decided that if he *had* been an immigrant (and a poet) it was to this ethnic group that he would have liked to belong. Somehow, he felt, it would have given to alienation an element of the bizarre, which (as it is generally a dreary state of mind, being and fortune) it usually lacked. There was, he argued to himself, nothing very wicked in this small deception. The distinction to which he laid claim was hardly one that brought him fame or fortune, and it harmed no one. On the contrary, it brought to himself and his tenants an occasional small glow of pleasure.

On the morning of this "day of reckoning", then, Hugo extracted the various receipts and rent-books from the pigeon-holes where they were stacked, beneath the Gothic-looking dome of his vast roll-top desk, and placed them in a shiny black Gladstone bag which he kept for the purpose. The bag itself he padlocked to his left wrist. At the top of the bag there was a leather flap which buttoned over a small rubber truncheon. These were other examples of his harmless eccentricity. The sums of money he collected from the tenants on the top floor were certainly not sufficient to tempt even the most desperate of thieves—and in any case Hugo—though quite handy with his fists when pushed—had a horror of violence and weapons of violence, while, for the sake of convenience, the key was always left in the padlock. But his tenants, it seemed to him, lived lives of such variety and incident (though they were always complaining of monotony) compared to his own that he didn't see why he shouldn't at least attach to himself some of the trappings of drama. In any case this particular morning, which on the face of it was no different from all the others, contained the promise of a special significance, the beginning of some new train of events.

Armed thus he left the office, carefully locking the door behind him. He decided to begin his visitations in the Annexe. This was the name given—by tradition—to a protuberance at the back of the house. It must have been added quite soon after the original building had been completed, for there was no way of telling that it was an addition. The outside brick had the same liverish colour as the rest of the house. From the road it did not show at all, so it did not in the least affect the symmetry of the structure as a whole—though "structure" and "symmetry" seem remarkably grand words to apply to the house that Hugo owned. Only if you stood some distance away from the house was the protuberance noticeable; and then it had a perfectly natural look, like the hump that appears on the shoulders of someone bowed by age.

The Annexe, though, played strange tricks inside the house. It seemed to draw it out and to extend it in all directions, so that it continually appeared to be altering its shape and size. Even the oldest of Hugo's tenants lost their way in the Annexe, or even forgot the way to it. This was partly due to the multiplicity of doors in and out, all of them in unexpected corners, and at unexpected

14

angles and levels, so that you entered or left the Annexe up a couple of steps or down a couple of steps, or up a slight incline, or down a slope that suddenly forced you to proceed by quick, little steps like a hobbled horse.

Hugo, however, decided to approach the Annexe this time by way of the garden. It was in fact large enough to deserve the plural, if not grand enough to be designated as "grounds"—and it suited the house exactly, being the kind of garden you do still sometimes come across in districts of London which were once semi-countrified suburbs for the higher-than-middle but-not-quite-as-high-as-upper-middle classes. In other words the remnants of extensive paths, lawns, rockeries, terraces, avenues and urns were still visible, while the trails of creeper and the great loops of rambler roses that over-grew them belonged to the same period, reminiscent somehow of the loosened tresses of former Edwardian mistresses with Pre-Raphaelite tendencies. Although now completely surrounded by steel and concrete (the nearest open countryside was a good hour's train journey from Liverpool Street or King's Cross) the garden managed to retain a certain vicarage-lawn aloofness. Only a band along the front was nibbled and stained by the detritus of the city—rusty tins, scraps of paper, empty cigarette packets, milk-bottle tops and discarded bus tickets (to mention only the less objectionable items) which no matter how hard Hugo tried to eliminate them drifted through, under, and over gates, railings and walls as remorselessly as the sands of the desert.

Hugo, in fact, had no wish to civilize the garden as a whole: he liked the picturesque wildness (as, he was sure, Prešeren himself would have done) and confined his gardening efforts as a rule to periodic assaults with a scythe, which (besides giving him a good deal of rhythmic pleasure in a picturesque posture) made the lawns pass-able but left them with if anything an even more savage look, like prairies bristling angrily again after a fire. All the same he wished he could have made more impression on that sordid fringe through which one had to pass on entering through the front gates before the illusion of Edwardian suburban rusticity reasserted itself.

It was evident that Roger Quincey, the ten-year-old son of one of his most respectable tenants, thought so too. Roger was standing just below him on one of the "lawns"—well, "plots of grass" would be a more appropriate description; but there were so many unexpected slopes and levels in the garden, so many bays, corners, alcoves and arbours that everything seemed bigger than it was, and the whole garden even more confusing in shape and size than the house itself. Roger, at any rate, peered across the square of mangled grass as if at immense distances. He was wearing khaki shorts, a khaki bush-shirt and a topi, many sizes too big for him which some ancient relative who had served east of Suez had given him. He was carrying a long bamboo pole, poised in his right hand, level with the shoulder: he stood with his knees slightly bent.

Hugo prided himself on his ability to enter into the skins of all his tenants: it was, indeed, inevitable: he flowed, like water rising into a network of channels, this way or that, to right or left, forward or backwards. So now he became aware of an anxiety to get the physical details exactly right: the grass at present was of medium height—therefore it was necessary to bend slightly at the knees so that the topmost blades could touch them: only thus would the balance between reality and fantasy be preserved and the imaginary drama have any validity ... Get only one of the physical details wrong and the imagination could not perform its purifying work... His mind and body ached as he strove to achieve the perfect point of equilibrium....

Roger himself, suddenly still, the bamboo pole poised, frowned slightly, but he gave no other sign of being aware of Hugo's presence. He was used to it. It was like the weather, subject to vagaries but, on the whole, a beneficent presence. The frown disappeared: once more he balanced the pole, moving his forearm up and down, like a weight-putter. A gleam of triumph, as at the re-discovery of some age-old sensation of self-sufficiency and control, shone in his eyes. Then he hurled the bamboo pole straight at the point where the pile of rubbish was deepest, in the triangle formed by the iron gate, where it swung open, and the wall to its right. He gave a hoarse cry, of mingled anger and fear, and drawing a wooden sword from a length of rope knotted round his waist, rushed after his spear and into the pile of debris, attacking it furiously with his sword and sending bits of soggy paper, peelings and trodden leaves flying in all directions. Then he bent down and, very slowly, his face screwed up in an expression of disgust, retrieved the bamboo pole and retreated backwards, one step at a time, making threatening movements with the pole as if daring dragons to overstep their confines. When he was a few yards from the plot of grass he turned and ran, leaping and laughing, half in triumph, half in terror. At the centre of the lawn, he turned again, an expression of relief on his face, sniffed at the fingers which held the bamboo pole and wiped them on his shirt. He hesitated a moment about a second foray, decided against it, threw down the pole and made his way across several other miniature lawns, each at a different level and each a different colour (according to the recency or success of Hugo's assaults with the scythe).

Hugo himself now emerged from behind the trellis where he had placed himself, not so much for concealment as out of delicacy for another's rituals, and joined him. Together they entered the orchard, which curved in a kind of crescent round the side of the house. They loved this orchard. It was not at all a well-tended one: age had turned the bark of the trees black and grainy, and as they had not been pruned for years or their fruit regularly picked (there were few children in Hugo's house) lumps and nodules of withered fruit, leaf and bud festooned them like barnacles. When Roger climbed into one of the largest, by means of a rope he kept suspended from the main branch (which served in turn as horse's saddle, elephant's howdah and ship's spar) his hands and knees were quickly streaked with soot-like marks. But it was a different kind of dirt from that near the front gates, and he sat there several minutes as if allowing this good dirt to exorcise the memory of the other. Then he shinned down the rope and rejoined Hugo. They wandered aimlessly to and fro, through the

17

long, tufty grass, every now and then scuffling their feet in the brown mash of decaying apples, sometimes even transfixing a whole one on the toes of their boots—treacle-brown spotted with fungus like castor-sugar, a perfect sphere which would nevertheless liquefy at a cough.

Along one side of the arc was a high brick wall surmounted by bits of glass and rusty metal, and on the other side lay the school which Roger attended (he was on holiday at the moment)—a squat building made of the same coarse brick as the wall (though not of the same liverish colour as Hugo's house) with long ecclesiastical windows, planted in a square of asphalt so desolate that it looked like a section of an abandoned runway. Roger kept his eyes lowered (so that they would not encounter the spiky top of the wall or be reminded of what lay on the other side) as they made for their favourite spot, a stretch of the wall where the sun fell most benignly and where the springy, straw-coloured grass was as soft as mohair. Hugo wriggled his back against the wall, like the fruit trees as grainy as a coral reef, until he felt the stored warmth of the sun run down his spine. As it did so he also felt Roger's thoughts and emotions run into his mind, but translated en route, as at some international conference, into his own idiom. He saw the shaven head of Mr Cartwright (the headmaster of the school beyond the wall), speckled like a cannon-ball, and longed to grind it under his foot, like one of the rotten apples. He felt Mr Cartwright's stubby fingers trying to poke knowledge into him, and a pain as if he were fingering his intestines. He began to sweat and mutter, to shift restlessly against the wall.

He came to with a jerk as Roger addressed him.

"Have you been to that basement of yours this morning?" Roger was saying.

"No," Hugo replied, his heart unaccountably thumping.

"Don't be stupid!" Roger said, looking at him indignantly. "You know very well you go there several times a day. You have to."

"Oh, you don't need to look after wine as carefully as all that," Hugo told him.

18

Roger regarded him with a slow, candid look which suddenly turned troubled. "I wish you wouldn't say that," he said.

"Why not," Hugo countered, speaking with avuncular gaiety. "That's what I always tell you!"

"You know it's not that," Roger muttered. Again Hugo felt his heart skip a beat.

"If it isn't wine, then what is it?" he said, with a forced, waggish grin.

"I don't know," Roger said, very seriously. "But I keep feeling I *ought* to know ... I know one day, soon, I *shall* know ... In a funny sort of way I know already, but I can't say it ... Do you know what I mean?"

Hugo nodded. He no longer felt in a bantering mood: not that he was in the least apprehensive that Roger would talk to the other tenants: but it had suddenly struck him that it was inevitable that Roger should be closer to his secret than anyone else.

They got up and proceeded through the orchard, skirting a high yew hedge (so high that only Roger, from his lookout in the apple tree, could see over it), then climbed down yet another short flight of overgrown brick steps and into the kitchen garden. This lay in a kind of well, and was remarkable for the extraordinary lushness of the greenery. This lushness was partly due to the predominance of vegetables like curly kale and the kind of root vegetables which as they plummet into the soil release parachutes of feathery foliage. But in addition the kitchen garden must really have been above a disused well or underground spring, for it was always moist and for some reason the temperature here always seemed several degrees higher than anywhere else in the garden. Everything, in consequence, grew to excess and everything had an exaggerated greenness, such as you see in the illustrations to a nurseryman's catalogue; even the brussels sprouts, on scraggy, elongated stalks like the legs of ostriches, were vivid green rosettes.

The kitchen garden was one which Hugo reserved for his own use, and was as well tended as the wilfulness of the vegetation allowed. At first sight it appeared to be a dead-end, finishing at a greenhouse, but in fact there was a narrow path, concealed by a water-butt, bulging with age but painted a green which Hugo, by dint of a painstaking mixture of different shades, had managed to match up with that of the vegetation.

Hugo and Roger took the narrow path beside the greenhouse, in single file—and found themselves, as if in some pantomime transformation scene, in the rockery. It was in fact not much bigger than a ping-pong table, but the bewildering criss-cross of miniature paths and the multiplicity of bays, shelves and projections produced (at any rate for Roger and Hugo) the impression of a lunar landscape, especially since the stones that had gone to its construction were large, blotchy and porous.

Emerging from the rockery they were at the back of the house—with the Annexe sticking out like a giant conservatory. There was quite an extensive piece of land here too, but whereas the gardens at the front and sides —cared for or neglected by Hugo, as the whim took him —had a certain picturesque unity, those at the back of the house presented an extraordinarily piebald appearance such as might have been seen on Common land during the Middle Ages. For Hugo had allocated them in strips to those of his tenants who wished to cultivate them. Some of them did so spasmodically, others dutifully or even passionately. Some were vegetable gardens, some were entirely devoted to flowers or shrubs, and others followed a mixed economy.

Sergeant Palfrey had succeeded in turning his into a traditional English allotment: it was perfect of its kind, though perhaps with a suggestion of standard Army issue. He had made maximum use of every square inch of ground. Lettuces and carrots grew in the avenues below the runner-bean sticks, in neat rows like wedding parties passing under a ceremonial arch. The sticks themselves were arranged in perfect symmetry, like a row of one dimensional wigwams—and exactly parallel, at a slightly lower level, the feathery plumes of a row of asparagus waved like so many Red Indian head-dresses. Parallel again were rows of garden peas—a difficult vegetable to keep tidy, though Sergeant Palfrey had some-how managed to do so—and rows of potatoes, like miniature long-barrows. The compost heap, studded with marrows like giant green slugs, was so firm and rounded that one suspected that the Sergeant with difficulty forebore from blanco-ing it.

The garden shed was separated from the rest of the strip by the inevitable bed of geraniums and chrysanthemums. Hollyhocks, sweet peas and honeysuckle grew round the shed and its attendant water-butt—according to the season, of course (though in Hugo's gardens one somehow did not think very clearly about the changing seasons, which seemed to run into each other according to purely local laws) their scent blending with that of fresh tar. Hugo walked across the little plot of grass in front of the garden shed—Roger unaccountably hanging back—and peered through the window. The interior was as neat and orderly as the allotment itself. Spades, forks, hoes and other gardening implements, their blades gleaming as if they had just come from the ironmonger's, were stacked behind a padlocked bar like rifles in a rack. Balls of green twine and bast, tins of screws, nails and staples, boxes of bulbs and various other objects, all neatly labelled, were ranged along the spotless shelves. Insect sprays and artificial manures were conspicuous by their absence: old Palfrey had a horror of "chemicals". A small table, covered with patterned oilcloth stood in one corner of the shed, with a tea-caddy, a teapot covered with a hand-knitted woollen cosy, cups and saucers and a biscuit tin bearing portraits of the Royal Family of a generation ago on a tin tray decorated with equally highly coloured pictures of the Royal Residences.

As he turned away from the window Hugo's foot struck something hard and metallic. Stooping down he saw that it was Mrs Palfrey's gardening shears—the square of grass in front of the shed (together with the flower bed) was her special province: it was much too small to manoeuvre a mowing-machine, and in any case Mrs Palfrey liked to get down on her hands and knees, working away with the shears, inch by inch, as if they were a carpet brush, sweeping away bits of gravel, dried mud and the tougher stalks of grass with her hand every now and then, until the surface was as smooth as baize.

To leave the shears out in the open like this—the blades unwiped too—was completely out of character. As he stood staring down at them he remembered that Roger had been silent since they left the orchard. He raised his eyes and encountered those of his companion fixed on him with a defiant but troubled expression.

"Old Mrs Palfrey," Roger said. "Something has happened to her." Hugo experienced in his own body that odd sensation of guilty horror that belongs especially to childhood—not so much a leaping of the heart as a swirling sensation that sweeps heart and stomach together ... Not only childhood, though—it was the same sensation that attended the memory of his own private horror of twenty years ago, and which, he reflected, must be a constant presence in the basement below his office....

"Tell me about it," he said to Roger.

"She was cutting the grass—you know, the way she does—peering at it and stroking it—then ... then she sort of toppled over..."

"Yes?" Hugo prompted.

"She lay there, breathing in a funny sort of way..." Roger was having difficulty in keeping his voice steady: his eyes avoided Hugo's.

"She tried to get up," he went on. "But she could only ... roll ... perhaps she's broken her back." He shuddered.

"Where was Sergeant Palfrey?" Hugo asked.

"He was there—by the compost heap. Then when he heard the funny noise she was making he came running over.... He just stood for a bit, looking down at her ... I don't think he saw me..."

"Then what happened?"

"She ... she wanted to pick up the shears..." Roger took a deep breath, then hurried on. "But her hand—it wouldn't ... it didn't ... seem to work." He looked up at Hugo, his lips trembling. "It kept going sideways ... her hand ... like a spider!"

"But Sergeant Palfrey?"

"Well, suddenly he gave a kind of sigh; then he bent down and picked her up. He carried her a little way, to the path—where there's a kind of bulge—*there*." He pushed Hugo impatiently, making him look in the direction of his out-stretched finger.

"But she was too heavy, so he put her down. He was very careful ... She lay there like a bundle of old clothes..."

"What happened then?"

Roger gave a wild grin. "I ran away," he said, "but I stopped once and looked back..." He spluttered; and then, his eyes growing wide with dismay, he began to laugh.

"He ... he got the wheelbarrow!" His laughter came tumbling out in gulps that screwed up his eyes. "He got the wheelbarrow ... then he ... he lifted her up ... and put her in it ... and ... and wheeled her away!" The laughter surged up. "She ... she looked like a guy!" he managed to get out. Sobs blended with the laughter.

"I have an errand for you!" Hugo said, so abruptly that Roger stopped laughing and stared at him. "I want you to go to the corner shop and get me some tobacco. You know the kind I smoke." He fished in the hip pocket of his dungarees, where he always carried some loose change, and produced a handful of coins. Roger took them, and walked away. After a few yards, however, he stopped, turned round and looked back at Hugo with a puzzled expression.

"You can keep the change!" Hugo called out after him, in an indifferent, even rough tone of voice. He could feel by the way Roger turned on his heel that he had offended his sense of propriety. After all, who knew better than Hugo that horror can best be dispersed by dispersal? He had split his house among his tenants so that they should be his whipping-boys: it was only right that from time to time he should perform a similar function for them.

When Roger was out of sight he turned and hurried towards the Annexe. It was quicker to reach the Palfreys' flat by way of the Music Room. He extracted the key from the large bunch—which he usually kept in the little Gladstone bag (so that it would, even when empty of coin, make a clinking noise) and opened the french windows. He drew aside the heavy velvet curtains, entered, and locked the french windows again. Then he rearranged the curtains and, his eyes accustomed through long practice to the semi-darkness, stepped briskly across the room. As always it smelt sweet and fresh. Although it was unoccupied it felt the most lived-in room in the whole house. Perhaps it was the grand piano which stood glowing in the centre of the room. Hugo let his fingers glide along its polished surface as he passed, noting with satisfaction that they registered not a single grain of dust and reminding himself that the instrument was due for its weekly tuning tomorrow. Hugo did not play himself. The piano was kept locked except during the visits of the tuner. But it was a condition of Hugo's being to keep the piano in perfect trim, against the day when it would be needed again. His feet making no sound in the thick carpeting he reached the far door, unlocked it and locked it again behind him. He and the piano-tuner were the only ones allowed to enter the Music Room. It is doubtful whether any of the tenants knew of its existence. In this room he did all the polishing and cleaning himself.

The door to the Palfreys' semi-basement flat was almost opposite the Music Room. Hugo knocked loudly, but both the Palfreys were hard of hearing and when he received no reply he pushed open the door and entered. At the bottom of the short flight of steps he called out again, but there was still no reply. He could, however, hear a shuffling and gasping coming from the direction of the bedroom at the end of the corridor.

When he reached it he found Sergeant Palfrey bent over the bed. He was holding a chamber-pot in one hand; his right arm was round his wife's shoulders, and he was struggling to get the pot under her buttocks. He was so intent on his task that he did not notice Hugo, who turned quietly and ran back to his own flat. From the vast ceiling-height cupboard he took a porcelain bed-pan—he was an inveterate hoarder, but one who always knew where he had put his treasures. He ran back to the Palfreys' flat. The Sergeant was still manoeuvring with the chamber-pot. This time he heard Hugo enter, and came towards him still holding the pot. He gestured with it awkwardly towards the big, high bed. "The wife," he said. "She's been taken poorly." He had that odd grin, part-grim, part-apologetic you see on the faces of long-service soldiers or old servants. "The rent-book," he added, "it's on the dresser." Then he saw the bed-pan in Hugo's hand and looked at it in a puzzled way: he had arranged the pillows behind the old lady's back, but as soon as he moved his arm from around her shoulders she rolled to one side, inert, like a rag doll. She made a faint tut-tutting noise. She tried to raise her eyes towards them, but the pupils too rolled away, exposing the whites, like small fish. She tried to smile: one corner of the mouth lifted grotesquely.

The Sergeant lifted her again, rearranging the pillows. She made an attempt to move her right hand, staring at it unbelievingly when it refused to do her bidding. But she managed to raise the left hand, very slowly, squinting at it out of her crooked eyes, as if a heavy weight were attached to it. When the hand was level with her husband's face she patted his cheek, then with a guttural sigh let the hand fall back on the counterpane.

Hugo handed the bed-pan to the Sergeant. Again he gave him his odd sidelong grin, as if apologizing for "the turn of events" and at the same time defying him to say how it could have been avoided. A single tear suddenly appeared on his cheek, prominent against the grainy skin, which had the appearance of pumice stone, and much the same dirty-grey colour, the result of the gassing he had suffered in the First World War. He didn't feel the tear until it touched the edge of his waxed moustache; then he brushed it angrily away, as if it were an insect. He was still wearing his gardening clothes: corduroy trousers tied at the ankles, so that the tops of the old Army boots stuck out like the lips of inverted bells: a striped, collarless flannel shirt, open down the front, and an old black waistcoat, also unbuttoned but held together by a heavy silver chain from which hung various coins and medallions, a penknife, a small propelling pencil and a battered cartridge case. Forearms and chest were tattooed, but it was impossible to make out the designs because of the wiry, iron-grey hair: only a few faint blue marks showed through, like those on a miner's skin.

During the few minutes Hugo had been away fetching the bed-pan he had managed to undress his wife and put her into her night-dress, a voluminous flannel tent, yellow with age; the neck and yoke were threaded with pink ribbon but the Sergeant had failed to tie the ribbon in front, so that the night-dress hung awry, revealing, with a grotesquely girlish effect, one bare, skinny shoulder.

The old man was having difficulty with the bed-pan, struggling at one and the same time to support his wife, get the bed-pan beneath her, and keep the bedclothes decently draped round her. He threw a desperate look in Hugo's direction. Hugo went round to the other side of the bed. Between them they lifted the lower half of the old lady's body. As they slid the bed-pan under her hips the night-dress rucked up. Hugo was astonished by the appearance of the parts revealed—youthful, dewy, somehow innocent and unused. The lower stomach was soft and smooth, the skin pearly white. There was very little pubic hair. It might have been the body of a young girl: it seemed to have no connection whatsoever with the torso above, with its bulgings, protuberances and shrinkages, or with the blotchy, wrinkled face....

The defiances of the human body ... Hugo struggled to hold back a memory, but it burst through. He remembered the day he entered Belsen with the first detachment of British troops ... The wasted, skeletal bodies and even the corpses of the women had full, rounded breasts. "It is Nature's way," a R.A.M.C. Captain had explained, in a dry, clinical voice. "The last particles of fat go to the breasts." Later in the day some of the guards, who for some reason had not been disarmed, fired into a group of prisoners who were brandishing their puny fists. Hugo himself had immediately had the guards placed against a wall and shot, the only firing-party he had ever known to be conducted with alacrity. It was the only memory of violence he could recall without guilt.... And indeed quite another episode from the past was struggling to reach the surface. Hugo quickly suppressed it. He had no intention of having both tenants and guilty memories.

Mrs Palfrey's left hand was making vague, scrabbling movements: a whimpering sound came from her. The Sergeant, suddenly realizing what she was trying to do, pulled the rucked-up night-dress down and arranged it round the bed-pan. "There's my girl," he said in a gruff voice. She gave him a lop-sided smile, which somehow managed to be intimate, excluding Hugo for the moment. Then she jerked her head in his direction. There was a pleading expression on her face: Hugo leaned over and kissed her on the forehead: the skin was moist, with an acrid smell: but the furrows smoothed out, as if her sense of decorum had been restored.

They removed the bed-pan, rearranged the pillows and bed-clothes. She made a guttural, protesting sound and her husband, again reading her thoughts, carefully lifted her arms out so that they lay outside the counter-pane.

There was no telephone in the Palfreys' flat. "I'll ring the doctor from my place," Hugo told the Sergeant.

The old man darted a cunning look at him. "The doctor?" he said. "The old girl's nearly eighty. I'm two years older," he added, straightening his back.

"It's all right," Hugo assured him. "It's a doctor I know. Don't worry: she won't be taken away."

"Thank you—*sir!*" Sergeant Palfrey barked, as if he were on a parade ground. He went briskly over to the dresser and picked up a small heap of coins. "The rent!" he said.

"Never mind about that now," Hugo replied.

"Sir!" Sergeant Palfrey shot the word out indignantly. He thrust the money into Hugo's hands. Hugo took it meekly, and sitting down at a side table entered the amount in the Palfreys' rent-book. When he had finished he showed the book to the Sergeant who, taking a battered case—the leather long since disappeared, the metal smooth and polished with use—from one of his waistcoat pockets, extracted a pair of steel-rimmed spectacles and carefully hooking the ends over his ears, studied the entry. "Correct!" he said and handed the rent-book back. Hugo replaced it in his Gladstone bag: realizing it was still fastened to his wrist he unlocked the padlock and

27

returned that too, together with the chain, with an expression of disgust on his face.

Sergeant Palfrey gave the spiky end of his moustache a tug. "Thank you," he said. "We shall be able to manage now." Hugo turned to go, but an indistinct noise came from the bed.

Hugo went over to it. Mrs Palfrey's eyes were fixed on him with an anxious, urgent expression. She was trying to tell him something: her lips were moving as if she were chewing something with her front teeth. He bent down, bringing his head close to her lips. She spoke a few slurred words. At first he could not distinguish them. Then suddenly they registered. "The shears, the shears," she was saying, over and over again.

"I'll put them back in the shed," he said. She went on repeating the words.

"Yes, I'll clean them first." Her face relaxed.

"That's a good boy!" she said, with sudden distinctness.

2

Another "day of reckoning" had come round. By late afternoon Hugo had made all his calls but one. The Proudfoots—he begged their pardons, the Proudfoot-Lorns (though at this time of the year they used only one of the barrels)—were, of course, among the tenants who paid by banker's order; but Hugo's visits on rent-day were an accepted part of the routine of the house: in a sense it was built round them. In any case today was one of the two red-letter days in the Proudfoot-Lorn calendar, and therefore in Hugo's own—the day of Colonel Arnold Proudfoot's return from his latest anthropological expedition to the more inaccessible regions of South America. Hugo had a special part to play, for it was he (being something of a Jack of all Trades) who worked the home-movie apparatus on which the Colonel gave a preview of the film he had made on the expedition to a select group of friends.

So Hugo collected the bits and pieces of the equipment —which were also kept in the vast cupboard—and carefully checked them. Then, staggering rather under the load, he made his way to the Proudfoots' apartments—they were really too grand to be described simply as a flat. He was not at all sure that he was in the right mood for the encounter and his heart sank as he reached the floor which the Proudfoots insisted upon calling the mezzanine.

With some difficulty he managed to disengage a finger and rang the bell. The door was opened by Eunice Proudfoot. "It's you," she said, in her flat, listless voice. She held the door ajar and he squeezed through with his equipment. The atmosphere nearly drove him out again. He had forgotten how bad it became during this phase of the year. He had forgotten too, how complete would be the transformation undergone by the woman who now called herself Eunice Proudfoot. It always came as a surprise; but even greater was the surprise to find himself seized by a spasm of irritation. It was the first time such a thing had happened. As a rule he more than tolerated the vagaries of his tenants: he indulged them: he encouraged them to sprout in unlikely directions, even if they were only along a single plane.

Eunice must have noticed something, for she darted a puzzled look at him: it stirred her features momentarily, but then the flash of animation was smothered by the heavy jowls, and the stubborn, sullen expression returned. Her eyes seemed to sink back into cushions of fat. Her complexion was pasty and slightly moist, as if the greasy food she crammed into her body at these times oozed out of the pores. Her skin smelt of stale breadcrumbs and rancid butter. Other odours emanated from the shapeless mass of clothes she wore, the top layers of which consisted of a long grease-stained navy-blue serge dress, like a maternity gown, and a shawl of fine wool which had once been plum-coloured, but now looked as if it had been trailed in coal dust. Her bare feet, incongruously white and shapely beneath the puffy ankles, were thrust into down-trodden mules, the swansdown trimmings coagulated with dirt. Only the mass of hair, lustreless and bedraggled but defiantly thick and strong, and still recognizably honey-coloured, showed that she was still a comparatively young woman, and, potentially, a handsome one.

"The film's arrived," she said, pointing to two circular aluminium containers, resting bright and clean on the dusty carpet. She drew the back of her hand across her mouth, sniffed at it and wiped it on her shawl. "I'll be ready when I'm needed," she said. "You know where to go: you know what to do." She lumbered down the dark corridor and out of sight.

Hugo looked around him, curious but not surprised. The thick, embossed wall-paper, mercifully of a dark chocolate-brown, was practically obscured by the skins of lizard-like creatures of varying dimensions. The lamp-shade, too, was made of some kind of animal skin, far too opaque for its purpose. What small light there was rested on the circular containers. Hugo took a deep breath, shifted his burdens to a more comfortable position, and pushed open the door of the drawing-room with his knee.

It was in darkness, the heavy, maroon-coloured curtains tightly drawn. Hugo, however, knew every corner of his house like the back of his hand. He deposited his apparatus on the hearth rug, and then struck unerringly across the expanse of carpet (occasional slippery softness underfoot causing an involuntary shudder) in the direction of the three tall windows. He reached his objective with no other mishap than that his foot struck one of Eunice's discarded tins: during her brother's absences these were to be found, together with various bags and packets, scattered all over the flat. They were never completely emptied, and part of the stench came from the decomposing scraps of food they still contained.

The drawing-room was also permeated with an odour of a different kind, a musty itch, such as one might encounter in an abandoned museum, of matter long past the stage of simple decomposition, blended with the heavy sweetness of stale formalin and taxidermal spices. The Colonel's collection, in fact, looked even more neglected than it had on the last occasion, Hugo thought, as he pulled back the curtains, gritty and slightly sticky to the touch.

It was a large room which Hugo thus disclosed— indeed the flat was quite the most handsome in the house, occupying practically the whole of one side. With its imported Adam fire-place and finely moulded ceilings, its heavy crystal chandelier, the thick satin-covered chairs and settees, and the pieces of real Hepplewhite and Sheraton the room might have remained elegant, in spite of the layers of dust and grease, if it had not been swamped by the detritus of the Colonel's travels, like the silt deposited by a tropical river that has overflowed its banks.

31

Dead things, animal or vegetable, predominated: shrunken heads (whether human or animal it was not always possible to tell), stuffed lizards, snakes, and various nightmarish animals unknown to our own hemisphere; various skins, pelts and furs, which looked as if they had been inefficiently scraped and cured but were nevertheless as hard as washboards; numerous stuffed birds, feathered headdresses, mats and baskets of plaited reed interwoven with feathers, a multiplicity of dried leaves, nuts and gourds—all these were presided over by a huge stuffed black cayman, suspended from the ceiling, tilting awry and partially blotting out the chandelier. Scattered everywhere, on all the available surfaces, were clay pots of various shapes and sizes; but these too had a deep, heavy stillness of matter that had once been organic, but had long passed beyond the stage of any conceivable molecular structure. All these objects were dead, Hugo felt, with a deadness that defied chemical analysis. And what was curious was that the more exotic and highly coloured the object, the more beautiful it had been in its natural state, the deader it now seemed. The brilliant plumage of the stuffed birds, for example, like the glitter of their artificial eyes, merely served to emphasize the deadness.

Hugo would have liked to open the windows, but if he had done so he was convinced that everything in the room would have crumbled away, as a vampire's body is said to crumble in the light of day, and overwhelm him and his house in an annihilating ash. He had to content himself with sniffing at the gardenia which he wore in his button-hole—for this was one of the rare occasions when he wore a suit. This suit was made of a good serviceable serge, but in the dyeing, what was intended to be navy blue had come out several shades lighter: somehow, though, this increased rather than diminished—perhaps because it suggested the effects of distant winds and suns —the impression of nautical rotundity about Hugo's person. As for the gardenia, it was a present from Sergeant Palfrey. Hugo was now putting in an hour or so every day on the Palfreys' allotment, and his stipend was a daily gardenia, which the Sergeant insisted on cutting himself, with a special blade of his knife which he had shaped for the purpose.

In the Proudfoots' drawing-room the gardenia wilted: but it still smelt remarkably fresh, and the petals shone like miniature haloes, contrasting with the faint phosphorescent glow which came from those stuffed birds in which some deterioration of the taxidermist's materials had caused the plumage to turn a greenish black.

Hugo glanced at his watch. The preview party would be arriving soon. He fetched the canisters of film from the hall, collecting various toffee papers and banana skins en route and depositing them in those of the waste-paper baskets that were not already filled to overflowing. Then he cleared away several small pieces of furniture in front of the fire-place and set up his screen and projector. He opened the canisters: he liked their clean tinny smell almost as much as that of his gardenia. He threaded the film into the projector and switched on, in order to check his apparatus. There was a dry, whirring sound: it seemed as if the scales and feathers of all the dead creatures in the room sighed and stirred: the dry matter rustled and dust circled slowly in the fetid air: it was like the winnowing of a tomb. He glanced at the scene projected on to the screen: a canoe slithered down a creek: branches swayed: an animal, surprised at a water-hole, stared into the camera with lemur-like eyes: a group of naked savages danced, plumes nodding, naked breasts and genitalia swaying. Everything was a dull, muddy sepia: the obliterating slime of jungle rivers flowed into the room: apart from the whirring of the projector there was no sound ... the movements on the screen, jerky, galvanic, took place in a silence so intense that they became disgusting, like the stirrings of maggots.

Hugo switched off the projector. His throat was dry, his eyes ached as if he had been watching the film for hours. This would be the last time, he suddenly decided, that he would perform this particular service. Well, the last time but one: six months from now it would, of course, be Eunice's turn—a Eunice transformed, or rather, transposed.... Then the cycle would be complete and, Hugo resolved, he would be free.

The front door-bell rang, like a chink of light from the outside world. A few moments later the preview party entered. They nodded to Hugo, and then stood, their noses wrinkled, looking round them in distaste. Mrs Vaisey made for the windows. In her black suit with its squared shoulders, dazzling white blouse, gold-rimmed spectacles and gun-metal coiffure with its stiff wings of blue-grey, she was as neat and sharp-edged as a cut-out.

"It's no use," Hugo reminded her, as she stood before the windows. "They won't open." Although she had not touched them, Mrs Vaisey carefully examined the tips of her long white fingers before she returned to the centre of the room and seated herself on a straight-backed chair, first dusting the seat with a minute lace-edged handkerchief.

"It's more like a morgue than ever!" Susan said, her soft, pink lips pouting. Everything about her was soft, pink and pouting: she seemed to have no outlines: she reminded Hugo of a strawberry sundae—but a warm one, if that were possible—melting in the sun.

"What a place for *him* to return to!" she continued. "Poor Arnold!"

"Arnold, eh?" Hardiman queried.

"Susan thinks Arnold is going to take her with him on his next expedition!" Mrs Vaisey explained, tartly.

"Is he indeed?" Hardiman enunciated each of the words as if he were a conjuror producing balls from his mouth. He studied Susan with his piercing blue eyes, as if balancing the strawberry sundae in the palm of his hand.

"I'm tired of merely being secretary to the Society," Susan explained. "I want *my* share of adventure!" One of Hardiman's frost-white eyebrows shot up sardonically. "The real thing!" Susan added, not knowing whether to be angry or uncomfortable. It was the effect Hardiman had: nobody knew how to take him. He was, in fact, simply dirty-minded, converting everything into a *double entendre*; but it was impossible to believe, in the presence of the distinguished carriage, the stark, stoical expression like that of a martyr on the rack, and, above all, the far-away blue eyes that gazed at a point above one's head, so blank and unfocused that they looked like sections of a snowscape seen through binoculars.

"But why in God's name does Arnold put up with it?" Susan continued.

"They're very close, he and Eunice," Mrs Vaisey said.

"Close?" Susan cried. "How *could* they be?"

"They are twins, don't forget," Mrs Vaisey reminded her.

"But hardly identical!" Hardiman said, grinning inwardly at some innuendo he had managed to extract, but looking as if he had uttered a tragic truth.

"Well, they say that twins *are* very close," Mrs Vaisey said. Hugo, his back to them as he bent over his apparatus, smiled.

Hardiman was wandering round the room, stooping whenever he passed under the black cayman, whose tail had become detached from its fastening, examining the various exhibits.

"There are some new things here," he said.

"He brought them back last time," Mrs Vaisey told him.

"Interesting in their way—this, for example." Hardiman had picked up a wood carving of a grotesque crouching human figure. He turned it this way and that, then peered at its underside. "Female—I think.... Not my kind of thing, of course. Not *clean*—like mountains."

"Or sand!" Mrs Vaisey said. She was a desert traveller, as neat and clean-cut in her rather old-fashioned khaki outfit—a long skirt, not shorts—as in her tailor-made.

"Everything's dirty here!" Susan said. "What can you expect? I don't know why Arnold bothers to bring all these things back!"

"They are presents for dear Eunice," Mrs Vaisey said.

"Then she should look after them!"

"You don't understand," Mrs Vaisey told her. "These things mean nothing to Arnold—now. No more than used postage stamps."

"No, of course!" Susan cried. "It was the getting of them that counted!"

"Ah what a mountaineer he would have made!" Hardiman sighed. Tired of his wandering he made for the vast greasy-green couch and seated himself in it, abruptly, as if he had snapped himself in half like a jack-knife. Even seated he looked unnaturally tall: a fluffy halo of yellowish-white hair accentuated the mahogany of the forehead: the wide blue eyes stared as if scanning snow horizons. But gradually a puzzled expression stole across his face, causing the mouth to turn down in an even more pronounced arc, and the clefts at the sides of his lean brown face to deepen.

"What's the matter?" Mrs Vaisey asked.

"I . . . I think I've sat on something!" he said.

Susan shuddered. "Animal or vegetable?" she quavered.

"Good God!" Hardiman exclaimed. He had risen to his feet and was gazing down at a cardboard wreckage in the corner of the settee. "It's a box of chocolates!" And then wrathfully, "soft centres!" His eyes rounded as he fingered the seat of his trousers. Hugo, ever helpful in such little emergencies, stepped forward, scooped up the broken box of chocolates and began searching for a waste-paper basket that was not too full to receive the remains.

"Oh poor Arnold!" Susan cried once more. "What a terrible life. No wonder he has to get away from it all!"

"Alone!" Mrs Vaisey added caustically.

"He would hardly want to take *her* with him!"

"They both disappear every summer," Hardiman said.

"Perhaps he has to take her away somewhere—to nurse her or something."

"Or something," Hardiman agreed, his eyebrows twitching.

Hugo continued his search. "I'll take those!" Eunice said sharply: she had entered unseen, in surprising silence considering her bulk. She took the remains from Hugo's hands, selected a squashed chocolate and put it in her mouth. "Arnold will be here soon," she announced. Her voice was firmer. She had made a desultory attempt to tidy her hair, and she was wearing a different shawl, almost clean. The door-bell rang.

"Aren't you going to let him in?" Susan asked.

"He has the key," Eunice said softly. The pupils of her eyes moved for the first time.

They heard the hall door open and close: someone strode briskly down the hall: the drawing-room was flung open, and Colonel Arnold Proudfoot stood framed for a moment in the doorway, before advancing across the room, on feet as quick and dapper as those of a mountain goat. The feet were shod in beautiful dove-grey suede: from head to toe he was impeccably dressed, in silvery grey double-breasted suit, gleaming white shirt, and a bow tie—blue, with polka dots—whose ends bristled in unison with the waxed points of a small moustache. Moustache, hair, eyebrows were all of a preternatural whiteness. They did not suggest the normal fading of pigmentation; they seemed made rather, of nylon thread or filament that sparkled and crackled. The glitter of the eyes, too (bluer even than those of Hardiman) was not that of age but of minerals—mica or jet. As he smiled disclosing sharp white teeth, sparks seemed to fly off him. Eunice regarded him with a sleepy smile.

The Colonel looked from one to the other, raised his arms then let them drop to his sides, whether in a gesture of benediction, mockery or despair it was impossible to tell. He advanced first upon Mrs Vaisey: his feet hardly seemed to touch the ground: rather he seemed to roll on invisible castors or like a ball of fire. Eunice followed in his wake, drawn after, almost as fast and as soundlessly. In front of Mrs Vaisey Arnold gave a jerky bow, seized both her hands in his and gazed into her eyes, head slightly to one side.

"Arnold!" she cried, her pale face flushing. "Arnold, it is so good to see you again!" The head described a half circle, in order to incline to the other side. "I hope all went well?" The head was absolutely still. "But of course —another of your triumphs!" The Colonel nodded his head rapidly several times, smiled, squeezed her hands, dropped them, turned swiftly and arrived in front of Susan. He clasped both her hands too, this time bending slightly from the hips, the gesture conveying an additional degree of solicitude. His eyes darted over her face, in a circular movement; she blinked, drew back; her face, too, began to talk, softly but very fast.

"Arnold—I wrote to you so often. Didn't you get my letters?" Arnold's shoulders jerked, ruefully. "Ah, yes, I do understand, of course.... You had so many things to

37

think about? So much to do? Perhaps my letters got lost? Or perhaps they were waiting for you when you got back to the coast?" She paused. Head, eyes, moustache, hands, shoulders, described a bewildering variety of shrugs and twitches. "Yes! Yes! I see!" Susan continued, "You were in danger? The Indians attacked? You had a fever?" He smiled more ruefully, pumped her hands up and down, let go of them, and turned to Hardiman.

"Arnold, old man!"

The slight incline of the hips disappeared: the Colonel seized Hardiman's hand in a simple, manly grasp.

"You had me worried once or twice," Hardiman said. "Addison came back with some rather disturbing stories.... You know Addison?" Pause, while Arnold nodded briskly. "Met him in Iquitos, I expect?" Another nod. "He had some tale about your going through the Tihuanac initiation tests yourself?" Arnold nodded several times, grinning delightedly. "Including the, ah the—"—Hardiman lowered his voice—"including the sexual ones?" Arnold broke into a soundless laugh and nudged him in the ribs. "Phew!" Hardiman exclaimed. Arnold gave him a thump on the shoulders and pivoted round to face Eunice. He pointed to Hugo, with raised eyebrows.

"Yes, of course, Arnold dear," she said. "We are all ready."

During the Colonel's perambulations Hugo had been busy. He had arranged a semi-circle of chairs around the screen and at a comfortable distance from it. To the right, and slightly behind the chairs, he had placed a lectern-type desk, equipped with a strip of neon lighting. And to the right of the screen itself he had placed another chair.

The guests took their seats. It was Eunice who stood behind the lectern. She placed a sheaf of notes before her. It was always a mystery how and when she prepared these, and even more of a mystery how she knew the contents of her brother's film before it was shown: Hugo had in fact wondered whether she had a secret projector and screen of her own, installed, perhaps, in the larder.

"Quiet, please," Eunice called out, her voice unexpectedly firm.

"Friends," she continued in the stillness that had descended. "Once again we are privileged to be the first to see the film of my brother's latest expedition among the Tihuanac Indians of the upper Xingo region. As you know, my brother drives himself on these hazardous ventures to the limit, and when he returns he is quite, quite exhausted. As always on these occasions, therefore, I shall be deputizing for him during this, the first showing of his new film. Lights, please!"

Hugo turned off the switch. Only the strip of neon on the lectern remained lighted, illuminating the script and Eunice's fingers. The rest of the room was in darkness, but as Hugo switched on the projector an overflow from its beam rested on Arnold's face to the right of the screen.

The images danced at the end of the beam, in a kaleidoscope of dots, stabs and blotches. The Colonel was no cameraman. Before his films reached the television and cinema screens they were subjected to the ministrations of a horde of technicians. Even then little could be done about the jerkiness of the pictures or the sombre quality of the lighting. The producers, however, making a virtue of necessity, had exploited the defects to such an extent that Arnold's films, presented in the style of the early Chaplin films or the Keystone Cops, had become a craze, while the multiplicity of naked bodies, displayed in the most bewildering contortions—and protected by the label "educational"—had guaranteed an enthusiastic mass audience.

If it comes to that, Hugo was no projectionist; so that in one way or another the film that appeared on the Home Movies screen (itself of an off-white colour and defaced by innumerable folds and creases) was a confusion of branches, canoes, and an inexplicable brandishing of tattooed nipples and buttocks, and of penises—free-ranging, grotesquely skewered, or swaddled in what looked like old sacking.

Eunice and Arnold began their duet, synchronized, more or less, to the flickerings on the screen. Hers was the voice, issuing from the patch of dim light where she

39

was stationed—a voice stronger and more confident every minute, but academically neutral in tone—and his was the face, in its bright circle of light, upon which the import of the words registered, now twitching, now smiling, now grimacing; now expressing sorrow, now joy, now pain and now triumph: a Friar Bacon's head, with the voice issuing from an unexpected direction.

The film was nearing its climax. The atmosphere was tense and stifling. Beads of sweat formed on Hugo's forehead as he crouched over his projector, like a medieval torturer over his grid.

"And so the hour of my ordeal approaches." Eunice's voice came from the gloom: Arnold's face set into a mask of sorrowful and slightly smug resignation. "I stand waiting," (Eunice was now using the first person) "waiting for the moment when I shall become not only the first white man but the first stranger of any kind ever to attempt the terrible rites of the 'second initiation', unique to this small sept or clan in this remotest corner of the Upper Xingo. I must admit to a certain transitory sinking of the spirits," (Arnold winced) "as I watch my tribal 'cousin' M'atashi led away from the ritual circle. . . . You see that his lips are drawn back like those of a dead dog, his eyes staring with the horror of his recent experience. . . . After all" (Arnold's lips pursed in an expression of rational self-questioning) "he is a younger man than I, born into the tribe, accustomed since birth to the idea of the crisis which one day, in common with all his fellows, he would be called upon to face. He had, of course, already, six years previously, passed through the by no means neglible initiation tests that mark the transition from puberty to manhood. And yet here he is . . . look! You see the muscle twitching at the side of his mouth? . . . here he has failed to pass the 'second intiation', unable to accept the 'kiss of the hornet', as the Tihuanacs call it. . . . Yes, here he is being led away by his companion. . . . They're having quite a job with him!" (a whimsical smile, containing perhaps a touch of manly scorn, crossed

40

Arnold's features) "I should explain, by the by, that there is no particular disgrace attached to M'atashi's failure. It is very rare indeed" (Arnold lowered his eyes modestly) "to pass at the first attempt. The majority, indeed, never pass at all" (the lids of Arnold's eyes descended even farther) "and those who do succeed have usually hardened themselves over the years by successive attempts and failures, as well as by all sorts of preparatory exercises ... Ah, here you see they are laying M'atashi in his hammock —poor fellow! ... Now this is a shot of the band of 'true initiates', as the Tihuanacs call them—those who have actually passed the 'second intiation'. They sit apart from the rest of the tribe in specially carved chairs. They are, in effect, the elders of the tribe, except that with the Tihuanacs age has nothing to do with it: there are some who pass the test when they are comparatively young men, and others who only do so late in life: it would really be better to describe them as the 'élite'.... Ah, yes this is interesting—the women you see here are pre-paring the special mixture of palm-oil, fish-paste and honey (mixed with various sacred herbs) which will shortly be clapped on my naked manly chest," (Arnold's mouth pursed and his head bobbed in silent mirth) "not that it's any laughing matter!" (Eunice's voice was stern: Arnold's expression grew solemn, the lines along his jaw tightened: the audience stirred uneasily.) "There is a point about these women which I must explain." (Eun-ice's voice resumed its equable lecturing tone.) "They must be blood-relatives of the 'élite'. It is considered that some of the latter's 'virtue'—in the Latin sense—has rub-bed off on to those nearest and dearest to them, so to speak. As for the élite—you'll see they are now passing round the calabash containing the sacred drink (made from fermenting the milk of ant-eaters) which belongs to them alone—the Tihuanacs no longer regard them as nor-mal human beings. The agonies they have endured, the Tihuanacs argue, so far exceed all conceivable pains and punishments, human or divine, that they have been car-ried across the barrier which separates good and evil, so that now they can do no wrong. Yes, there is a close-up of one of the élite: note the remote, withdrawn expression

41

—god-like in the view of the Tihuanacs, ennobled by what they call *ankh*—the 'ultimate experience'.... And this is another member of the élite calling for the calabash to be refilled.... Yes, the Tihuanacs say that the courage the élite have displayed during their 'second initiation' is so much greater than the sum total of virtue that any normal man can be expected to exercise in a lifetime that they have 'paid' for good and evil—and now they are above both. They are 'changed men'. And so the 'freedom' of the tribe is theirs in the fullest sense of the word (ah, one of the women is returning with the calabash).... All the tribe's possessions, including, of course, the women, are theirs for the taking. In time of famine they are fed even before the infants, and if the famine continues so that all reserves of food are exhausted they supplant the infants at the mothers' breasts.... Here you have a close-up of the 'sacred mixture'—a nauseous brew, is it not?" (A grin split Arnold's face from ear to ear and the blue eyes twinkled in avuncular merriment.) "Yes, the 'sacred mixture' has now arrived at its correct consistency, and now, you see, I am being led forward to receive the 'ritual annointing'. My clothes, of course, have been removed: only the *tik'le*—the 'ritual garland'—is still about my neck." (There was a deprecatory lowering of Arnold's eyes as his pudenda joined company with those around, like a group in a school photograph.) "I can't pretend I was as calm as I appear in this shot," the commentary proceeded (the ends of Arnold's moustache stirred in a soundless chuckle) "but I had to keep the proverbial stiff upper lip, don't you know? After all, the issue was simple; I just had to go through with it. How else was I to win the confidence of the tribe? ... Ah, now here you see one of the élite spreading the 'sacred mixture' on my chest, to the accompaniment of the usual chants and dance-movements from the rest of the tribe— confined, needless to say, to the area outside the 'sacred circle'.... To continue—how else was I to learn the innermost secrets of this strange people, *except* by getting into their 'top set', so to speak? Remember, here was a tribe hitherto completely unknown: here was the only people in the history of mankind, as far as we know, to

42

practice a 'second initiation'. . . ." (Arnold's face took on an expression of owl-like gravity, which was accompanied, as it happened, by a darkening of the screen that reduced everything to an obscure and confused writhing.) " 'The second initiation'" (Eunice's voice, too, was grave) "is, the Tihuanacs believe, one which adds a mystic 'seventh stage' to their normal 'cycle of being'—birth, infancy, adolescence, adulthood, old age and death— Ah now, look!" (a perky look appeared on Arnold's features) "the first layer of the 'sacred mixture' has been rubbed in and now my skin is soft and supple: the pores are open, exuding the sweet honey-and-human smell that will shortly" (Eunice paused dramatically) "drive the hornets into a voracious frenzy!" (Arnold looked comical and smacked his lips.)

"No, oh no Arnold!" Susan moaned, mistaking the gesture for a premonitory grimace of agony. A shocked frown furrowed Arnold's brow: Susan bit her hand: Eunice's voice did not falter. "The moment of my ordeal approaches." (The frown on Arnold's face was replaced by the smug, slightly sulky expression.) "I knew I must endure, come what may. I had to show them that I was man enough, for one thing," (Arnold's chin jutted aggressively) "and for another I had to show them that I was a scientist, an *anthropologist!*" (Eunice's voice shifted to a more solemn key, then quickly brightened.) "Ah, this is a most unusual shot of the *gu'na*—the 'mat of the hornet'. You will see that it is made of reed—a very tough variety—very intricately plaited, and arranged in several layers." (The object on the screen was turned this way and that, a thumb, presumably that of Arnold, appearing at the left-hand corner, but the screen was still too dark to obtain more than a vague impression of something oblong in shape, somewhat like an outsize Shredded Wheat, dotted with black marks which might have been currants.) "These various layers are so arranged that although the hornets have freedom of movement, it is impossible for them to stretch their wings, and so escape . . . not that they are likely to want to" (Arnold's moustache was again agitated and his head bobbed up and down in a particularly hearty access of

43

soundless laughter) "with such a tasty meal in prospect!"
Eunice paused. The audience stirred uneasily. "With
such a tasty meal in prospect!" she repeated angrily: a
ragged, quavering laugh proceeded from the half-circle
of chairs. "I should explain, by the way," Eunice continued, "that these hornets have been imprisoned in this
way for some time, so that they are not only hungry but
exceedingly angry. Yes, they are active little fellows by
now! ... not so little, if it comes to that, for they belong to
an unusually well-developed species that inhabit the
swamps nearby, and which have been known to reach
the dimensions of, say, a small mouse. And now the
moment approaches. The mob on the other side of the
'sacred circle' fall silent. The women-folk of the élite,
wearing only their ceremonial *aug'ites*" (an exclamation,
quickly converted into a sneeze, proceeded from Hardiman) "take up the strange, trance-like steps of the dance
which, from time immemorial, has solemnized these
occasions. The musical instruments you see here—
played, according to custom, by the oldest members of
the élite—are of a pattern unique to the Tihuanacs.... I
have, by the way, brought back a number of these as
presents for my sister, together with several of the hornet
mats...."

"Thank you, Arnold," Eunice said, momentarily interrupting her commentary, but not in the least altering the
tone of her voice. "The drums throb, louder and louder,"
she went on. "And now, you see I am being led into the
very centre of the 'sacred circle'. Two *va'ii*—members of
the élite chosen to stand by me in my hour of need—take
up their positions on either side. Their task is to support
me if I should turn faint, to hold on to me if I should
become too violent in my agony, to do all in their power
to encourage and sustain me—in fact, to bring me all
comradely succour short of actually detaining me should
I display unmistakable signs of being unable to endure
my torments any longer and indicate that I should
prefer to rush screaming from the scene.... And here
you see they are marking out the 'inner circle' within the
'sacred circle'. For this purpose they use a paste made of
river clay and the ground viscera of the *pa'li-p'ali*, a

44

species of ground-sloth—I have brought a specimen back with me, stuffed, of course, though not very expertly, I fear: it was done almost immediately after my ordeal.... Ah, now you see I am being conducted into the 'inner circle' by my *va'ii*. The *p'wua*—that is, the two oldest members of the élite—advance. In their gnarled old hands they bear the *gu'na*—that is the 'hornets mat', you will no doubt recall?" (Arnold's face looked severe, as if he were conducting a seminar of rather dull students.) "The *p'wua* draw closer.... The *va'ii* take hold of my arms just above the elbow, but I shake them off." (Arnold's head jerked in an imperious gesture.) "I shake my head." (Arnold did so.) "The *va'ii* stand aside, with expressions of the deepest respect (nay, of awe) upon their faces. The *p'wua* hold aloft the *gu'na* impregnated with the *fu'uon* ('sacred mixture') and slowly lower it— closer, closer ... towards my naked chest.... Closer ... closer ... closer still...." (Eunice's voice had gradually been gathering strength, now it was full and vibrant.) "Closer and closer ... Now!"

Susan let out a scream. The others sat absolutely still.

"I keep my arms straight at my sides." (Arnold's head sagged.)

"I throw my head back defiantly." (Arnold's head jerked back.) "I have to endure for a full five minutes.... The pain is excruciating ... it is diabolical.... Surely, surely it is unendurable?"

Again Susan screamed. Eunice paused. This time it was she who frowned: in the few seconds' interval Arnold's face relaxed, becoming absolutely blank and expressionless. Then as she resumed; "*Can* I endure? Alas, even I cannot control the rictus of agony that momentarily distorts my features." (The left side of Arnold's face rose as if Eunice had jerked a string.)

"Soon, though, I regain my composure." (Arnold's face did so.) "My *va'ii* make an involuntary movement towards me, inquiry, compassion and admiration struggling to gain the uppermost on their dark, expressive features. I shake my head." (Again Arnold did so.) "I clench my fists." (As it was only Arnold's face that was visible within the beam of light, it was Eunice who obliged, raising her two hands aloft, spreading the fingers, then slowly closing them.) "The pain grows worse. Still three minutes to go. The whole village, you see, have crowded as close as they dare to the periphery of the 'sacred circle', watching, silent and intent. Even the élite, inured to such sights and usually bearing an expression of stoic indifference, lean forward in their ceremonial chairs.... Beads of perspiration form on my forehead. I dare not raise my hand to dash them away. The smallest superfluous expenditure of energy might be the last straw to crack my resistance. The drops form a trickle down my face: they lie salt on my cracked lips...."

And the audience gasped as drops of sweat did indeed appear on Arnold's face, like icing squeezed out of a tube; but a moment later the vision disappeared, for Hugo had switched off the projector. He had come to the end of the first roll of film. No one seemed to notice, however, and Eunice continued with her commentary as if nothing had happened. Only Hugo was concerned, and he was all fingers and thumbs as he undid the second container, took out the film, and threaded it in the projector. He made such good speed that within three minutes the film was again whirring through the projector, the screen was again flickering, and Arnold's disembodied head was again illuminated. But nobody seemed to notice, either, that the film had started again, or that by now Eunice's comments, naturally, bore no relation to the actual images on the screen. It was just as well, though, Hugo reflected, for in his haste he had put the film in upside down. He did not bother to correct his mistake: the vague sepia waverings looked much the same anyway.

"Still I endure!" (Eunice was crying. Her voice had continued to gather strength and variety. In her person, too, she looked oddly changed: her body seemed more close-knit; her hair cleaner and softer; there were flecks of light in her eyes.) "At last the end is in sight! A stir of expectancy runs through the seated élite; it communicates itself to the watchers beyond the 'sacred circle'; the stir gathers strength, like a wind through the jungle.... The hornets roar like lions: my flesh feels as if it were being

46

devoured, morsel by morsel: it is as if a thousand lighted torches were held against my naked breast, a thousand vials of acid poured into the wounds. And yet I hold on; I hold on. I am 'the captain of my soul' etcetera.... Still my face shows nothing, but nothing!" (An expression as wooden as a Maori carving fixed Arnold's features.) "Only two minutes to go! I exert the last ounce of my resolution. The élite are exchanging murmurs of wonder and approbation. My two *va'ii* exchange looks of joyous expectancy...." (And Arnold's face remained fixed: it was strangely flat, eyeless, as if he had donned one of the masks that decorated the walls. Now it was Eunice's voice alone that carried the whole burden of the accompaniment. It rose and fell; twisted, turned; it took on a hundred tones, levels and vibrations; it had become fluent, supple, adaptable, cunning and alive.)

"The ordeal is nearly over!" she announced, in a husky, tender contralto. "The moment of my release approaches. As you see, the women (wearing only their *aug'ites*) are working hard over the soothing unguents that will soon bring some measure of relief to my pain-racked body. You will note that they are hurrying over the last stages of their preparations. If truth be told they had never expected that they would be called on to complete them. But now they work with a will.... Only fifteen seconds to go! These last seconds are the worst.... I fight down a mad impulse to rush screaming from the 'sacred circle'. My jaws fall open like a snake's," (Arnold's face, however, remained static) "and yet no sound issues forth ... Six seconds! ... Five! Four! Three! Two! One! Zero! It is over!" And Eunice's voice rose to an ecstatic climax.

"Yes, it is over," she continued after a short pause and in more muted tones. "The *gu'nas*—hornet-mats—are snatched away from my lacerated flesh. My two *va'ii* embrace me. All the members of the élite crowd round me to congratulate me! The whole tribe erupt in a riot of shouting, cheering, dancing, clapping, waving, laughing, weeping!" (Arnold's head suddenly came to life again: it described a bewildering variety of movements: it jerked to left, it jerked to right: it leaned forward, it

47

tilted backwards: the eyes flashed, danced, swam; the eye-lids screwed up, then sprang apart like the lids of snuff-boxes; the lips twitched and trembled, turned upwards and downwards.)

The film, Hugo reflected, had become less necessary than ever—and, again, it was just as well, for ominous scars and stripes rained across it, and there was a note of anxiety in the whirring of the projector, like that of a blue-bottle in an inverted jam-jar. In addition, patches of almost complete darkness appeared, as if the film were entering a series of closely spaced tunnels.

Eunice at least appeared to be aware of the fact. *"Here you can see,"* she announced in a challenging voice, "the two *va'ii* have taken me by the arms to lead me away. Firmly I disengage myself from their well-meant offices. Unaided, I make my way out of the 'sacred circle', while the élite actually stand up to applaud, an unheard of honour, I may add. My step is as steady, my carriage as upright as when I first entered the 'inner circle'—how long ago? Can it be only a quarter of an hour? It seems a lifetime! Yes, I have lived through a lifetime of pain. Yes, I have endured, and I have won!"

The little audience broke into discreet but enthusiastic applause. Arnold's head bobbed up and down in acknowledgement. Eunice's eyes, there could be no doubt about it, shone. Susan dabbed hers with a handkerchief, smeared with pink lip-stick. Mrs Vaisey was thoughtfully stroking the razor-sharp pleats of her skirt. Hardiman was leaning forward, staring with a puzzled, slightly truculent expression on his weather-beaten face. The projector whirred, uncertainly. The screen flickered; Eunice resumed her commentary.

"Still upright, then, my shoulders squared, my jaw set, I walk unaided towards the *p'o'pui* or 'hut of atonement', as it is called, where the virgins of the tribe await me with their soothing unguents—hastily transferred thither by the women-folk of the élite in their *aug'ites*—and, of course, their adoring caresses." (Arnold's head lowered modestly.) "As you see," (Eunice once more stressed the words) "my *va'ii* are so overcome by emotion that it is they who stumble, and it is *I* who put sustaining arms round *their* shoulders! ... We reach the *p'o'puı*, 'hut of atonement', you will remember. At its doorway we pause for a moment. My companions and I spend a few minutes in manly embraces, gestures, and guffaws—with what import I leave to your imaginations...." (Arnold's eyes twinkled naughtily.) "Somewhat reluctantly my companions depart, and I enter the hut.... The virgins are naked except for their ceremonial *tu'alas*, or 'necklaces of maidenhead'." (Hardiman was shifting more uneasily in his chair.) "I am to stay here for seven days and nights, forbidden to leave on pain of being seized by the tribal demons, not to mention losing all my hard-won privileges. Now I should explain," (Eunice adopted the tone and stance of the seasoned lecturer) "that the seven days and nights that are to ensue are regarded by some sections of the tribe and by a certain group of élite as the 'second stage' of the 'second initiation'.... For the first few hours, however, I have to confess, I was prostrate, suffering from the delayed shock of my ordeal, no doubt, barely able to raise my head, my neck like a lopped stem." (Arnold's head dropped forward as if he had just been decapitated.)

"After a good, healthy sleep, however, the 'second stage' of the 'second intiation' began in earnest—the 'ordeal by women', as it is called. I had often wondered" (Eunice's voice became informal, almost chatty) "how it was that the 'elect' who had survived the 'kiss of the hornets' appeared to get through the sequel—a sequel, moreover, that ensued within so short a space of time—without any signs of undue distress. On several occasions, in the course of my scientific investigations, I had observed them emerging from the Hut of the Virgins at the end of the seven days and nights with firm and jaunty steps and with expressions of equanimity, nay, of positive contentment upon their faces.... Now I was to learn this secret too. To my surprise—and initial alarm—I discovered that something in the chemistry of the hornets' stings (or perhaps it was the acuteness of the pain itself) had a powerful stimulating—not to say aphrodisiac—effect ... I fear I must apologize at this stage for the poor quality of the film you are about to witness." (Hardiman's chair creaked more loudly and he muttered something unintelligible.) "I cannot begin to describe to you the difficulties I had to encounter—the taboos I had to circumvent, the prayers and sacrifices I had to offer up, the wearisome ceremonies I had to undergo, the plausible explanations I had to invent, in short, the lies I had to tell, in order to obtain permission from the élite to have my automatic camera installed in the Hut of the Virgins —well in advance of the initiation, of course, and carefully camouflaged by various creepers and banks of hibiscus-like blossom—indeed, I would not have succeeded, even so, had I not bribed the Senior Virgin with a good half of my remaining store of trinkets. During the actual 'second stage' itself, needless to say, the camera had to be left to its own devices, although on one or two occasions when the virgins, or rather *quondam* virgins," (pause while Arnold executed an exaggerated wink) "were in a condition of temporary listlessness, I was able to slide from their embraces and attend to the camera and even operate it myself for a short spell—as in these delightfully relaxed shots—at the same time, if truth be told, taking a momentary refuge behind the hibiscus, still luxuriant as you see, though the petals have wilted somewhat.... But you will appreciate that the interior of the hut was dim, apart from the faint phosphorescent glow that arose from the petals of the hibiscus and our tumbled bodies alike—and in consequence these pictures are not quite what I had intended, or, indeed, what an occasion of such unique anthropological importance merited."

And indeed the film at this stage grew darker than ever: all that could be discerned, and that only vaguely, was the suggestion of a tangle of limbs in varying degrees of motion, reminiscent of the well of a trawler after the nets have discharged their contents. Everybody craned forward. Hardiman's chair was close to collapse. He cleared his throat. Then suddenly he roared at Hugo: "Damn it all, man! You've got the bloody film on upside-down!"

Hugo, blushing, quickly switched off the projector. But something else must have been amiss, for there was a rending, tearing sound and film flew out in all directions, then settled round Hugo, draping him from top to toe, so that he looked like a chubby Laocoön.

It was not for nothing, however, that he also resembled a sailor, and with a number of dexterous movements he disentangled himself and stepped neatly out of the coils, which subsided on to the floor with a hiss.

"Can you repair it?" Hardiman asked in a husky voice, seizing him urgently by the arm. Hugo shook his head. "The spool is broken," he said. He turned on the lights.

"It is the *spell* that is broken!" Eunice exclaimed, in a tragic voice. But at that moment Arnold skipped down from his chair and advanced into the centre of the room, his face tilted back to catch the light, an anticipatory smile lying on his face, and his arms dangling loosely, the palms of the hands turned outwards as if begging to be grasped. Immediately, as if the snap in her voice when she addressed Hugo had been the snapping of a spring, Eunice sagged, and going over to the couch sank into it: the earlier sullen, flaccid expression returned, swelling her cheeks as if they had been stung by one of Arnold's hornets.

The others crowded round Arnold himself, seizing his hands and pumping them up and down, peering ecstatically into his face.

"Magnificent!" Mrs Vaisey cried. "An outstanding contribution to human knowledge! You are a true martyr to Science!"

"Arnold, you were *heroic!*" Susan whispered, her mouth and cheeks dimpling with a ripple effect.

"What a marvellous film it will make!" Hardiman exclaimed. "Eventually ... when it's the right way up...." He took Arnold aside. "That second part of the initiation," he said in a hoarse whisper, "did you really ... ?" The ends of Arnold's moustache bristled: his teeth, too, as white as the moustache, seemed to bristle: he nodded his head vigorously. Hardiman examined his face carefully. "Pow!" he suddenly exclaimed.

Suddenly Eunice spoke again from the couch. "My brother is tired now," she said.

Arnold showed no sign of it, as still nodding, grimacing, grinning, bristling, bridling and teetering up and down on the balls of his toes, he ushered them to the door. All except Hugo, who was engaged in packing up his equipment. When the door was closed Arnold came over to him, clapped him on the shoulder and raised one eyebrow.

"Very nice," Hugo said, and then added, on an impulse that caught him unawares, "but I should have liked to know what kind of things they grew, and what kind of food they ate." He was astonished. It was the first time he had ever ventured a criticism on these occasions, and he was ashamed that when it did slip out it should have been of such a naïve nature.

Arnold stared at him unbelievingly. His jaw sagged as if a pin had been pulled out of it. He tottered over to the couch and sat down beside his sister. He turned a stricken face towards her.

"Poor Arnold," she said. "Now it is your turn to rest."

Shouldering his equipment. Hugo tiptoed out of the room.

3

Yet another "day of reckoning". Hugo collected the rent-books for the tenants of the top floor, put them into the Gladstone bag, hesitated about the padlock, felt irritated and slightly disturbed because he had hesitated, snapped the pincers round his wrist and set out.

As always when he ascended to the "upper regions" (as he jocularly referred to the top floor) his heart was beating faster than usual, with a mixture of pleasurable anticipation and apprehension. This time it was he who felt like an explorer. This top floor was the only part of his house which he could not visualize clearly enough to have made a plan, accurately to scale. It consisted of a warren of smallish rooms under the higgledly-piggledy roofs, tucked in among the rafters and the masonry as if bored by out-size rodents. There were so many beams at so many angles; so many nooks, crannies and alcoves; so many pipes, tanks, and cisterns; so many gaps opened up or bricked in; so many inexplicable heaps of stone and timber (which Hugo never dared to move for fear he might bring the whole roof down) that the whole of this area had the frantic, provisional air you sometimes find at the top of a medieval castle or cathedral—as if the armies of workmen had been suddenly dispersed at the last moment by plague or invasion.

As the rooms at the top of the house were the cheapest, they were inhabited by the young, and the young of this generation, of course, had none of the passion for the ship-shape which had seemed so vital to Hugo's own self-respect at the same age. It was a circumstance he regretted but did not deplore. He turned a blind eye to all the boxes, crates, cases, bundles and packages scattered over the rooms and corridors of the top floor, while doing his best to clean round them from time to time with mop and broom. He delicately forebore to use a vacuum-cleaner because he knew that on this floor, at any hour of the day, an appreciable proportion of the tenants would be in bed for one purpose or other—the most common of which was, surprisingly, sleep.

He mounted the short flight of stairs that led to the "upper regions", opened the green baize door (installed for sound-proofing) and then, behind it, the main door, made of a timber so tough and heavy that it would be impossible to make use of it for fire-wood, and entered. He stood for a moment; his ears, tensed for the usual cacophony, quivered in mingled surprise and relief: by a curious coincidence all the tenants (those who were awake, that is) had chosen this moment to play record-ings of radiophonic effects, and although it could hardly be said that the result was more restful, it was at least more uniform. His nostrils, too, were quivering, but not in any particular alarm. The atmosphere, certainly, was not fresh, yet it did not arouse in him the same revulsion as he encountered, for example, whenever he entered the Quinceys' apartment, in spite of the expensive furnishings and Mrs Quincey's passion for cleanliness ... he hated the blend of Continental cooking, bath-salts, medicine bottles and Sunday colour supplements.... But then, of course, there was also the gin, particularly before or after their quarrels ... the beads that oozed from their pores on such occasions he found peculiarly nauseating ... strange, one would have thought that gin, being a spirit and colourless, almost clinical in appear-ance, would have had an antiseptic effect.... The Palfreys, of course, also smelt. They belonged to a genera-tion which believed that too many baths weakened the constitution; their bathroom was their pride and joy, but it was usually kept locked in order to preserve its spotless condition, especially when, during the winter months, the more delicate plants were stored there.... Still, Hugo did not particularly object to the Palfreys' smells: it was quite true, old people did smell like apples in a loft.

And, needless to say, the smell of the "upper regions" did not bear comparison with that which impregnated the Proudfoots' rooms at this season ... There was in it, it is true, a good deal of stale sweat proceeding from a variety of unwashed armpits, crotches and socks. It was, indeed, sufficiently robust to be described as a stink. And yet it produced no revulsion.... Perhaps it was because of the variety of supplementary sources: cigarette smoke; lighter fuel and the oil used to lubricate record-players; turpentine, paint and canvas (some of the tenants, needless to say, were artists or would-be artists) and the spirit-gum used for sticking the components of models; burnt sausages and saucepans caked with bakedbeans; the soapy scum flecked with bristles that adhered to rusty razor-blades; cheap perfumes, lotions and shampoos; damp garments hanging in bathrooms; scorched cloths under forgotten irons; snippings of materials; much-thumbed magazines; and above all that pungent odour from the hair-combings of young girls ... Yes, one returned to the physical factor. Perhaps, Hugo reflected, his tolerance was merely a matter of association.... He *knew* that here the bodies were young: the effluvia, being human, were perhaps identical, throughout the house, but here they hadn't had them so long ... perhaps even the smells were the same as those that proceeded from the Quinceys reconciled in gin, but the contrast between firm and sagging breasts, between lean and flaccid abdomens, made them seem different.... Still, he had heard it said that countrymen could tell how old the occupants of a stable or a cow-shed were from the smell alone, without a single glance at the teeth....

As Hugo picked his way along the first corridor a door opened and a girl of about seventeen came out and nearly banged into him. She was carrying a sponge-bag and towel. Her hair and eyes alike were tousled with sleep. She was wearing a nightdress so transparent that her nipples and a wedge of brown pubic hair, plump and springy, were clearly visible. Hugo modestly averted his eyes ... after all, as far as the tenants of his house were concerned, he was a large, bland and sexless Nanny.

The girl had, apparently, been long enough in the

house to think so too, for as she stepped aside and he, never having seen her before (not that this circumstance caused him any particular surprise), raised his eyebrows in inquiry (admittedly not a very intimidating gesture, as they were practically non-existent) the only response was a slight creasing of the smooth forehead. Then as she passed him she looked into his face with a mixture of pity, condescension and withering contempt. It was really astonishing, Hugo thought, how these soft, unformed features, the line from ear to chin as unbroken as a pod, could register, at such moments, a range of expressions more appropriate to some middle-aged matron with a jutting jaw, rouged cheek-bones and a body so uniformly rotund that it was impossible to tell whether she were corseted or not.... Where did they learn the expressions? Did they suck them in with their mother's milk? ... But when she had swept past him, heading with deliberately unhurried steps to the nearest bathroom, Hugo saw that her back was held so straight that the shoulder-blades stuck out like chicken's wings, and that there was a red flush exactly in the centre of the nape of her neck.

He knocked on the door of Number Two. A voice immediately responded with a peremptory "Come!" It was a very gruff voice, with a kind of gravelly boom as if dredged up from a mine. It was a source of constant fascination to Hugo to hear these preternaturally deep voices issuing from frames still so willowy and unplaited: it was as if some large but improvident god had chosen for his oracle a cave several sizes too small for him.

One of the reasons why Hugo was, on the whole, tolerated by the young was that he always appeared to be hanging on their every word. In consequence, stretching out their legs luxuriously, they would lecture him by the hour on the ills of society and the measures that were needed to set them aright. They did not realize that Hugo was hanging on their words in a quite literal sense: his air of rapt attention (though of course out of politeness he would nod from time to time and even grunt) was auditory and visual rather than intellectual: it seemed to him that he actually watched the sounds as they came booming out of lips that had not yet lost the pout of childhood, as awe-struck as if the Oracle had indeed spoken. The young women made a similar miscalculation, assuming that his grave demeanour was a tribute to their maturity, a respectful acknowledgment of charms he was still able to appreciate aesthetically but was, naturally, too old to think of enjoying; whereas in fact he was marvelling that creatures so little removed, it seemed to him, from the schoolroom could with such ease run through the whole female scale from vibrant contralto to shrill soprano. . . . What a miracle the human voice is! he would tell himself, that even at this age it can register a whole life-cycle of desires, aspirations and emotions. And, equally, how miraculous is the human ear that it can pick up and imitate all the sounds of adult experience at a time when experience itself has barely begun!

He pushed open the door of Number Two and entered. "Good morning, Mr Sturmer," he said. He always made a point of addressing the tenants of the top floor in this formal fashion, even when, like Mr Sturmer, they had not yet reached their eighteenth birthdays. They would reply irritably, "Call me Joe!"—or Jack, or Harry or George: but it seemed to please them, especially as they made a point of calling him by his Christian name.

"Hello, Hugo," Mr Sturmer replied now. "No bread for you today, man."

"Pardon?" Hugo asked.

"*Bread*—dough, lolly—what was it you called it in your day?" (with a passable imitation of a nineteen-twentyish accent) "sponduliks?" Mr Sturmer gave a grin, part derisory, part patronizing, as if he were addressing a child or a lunatic. Hugo was not in the least offended by the jest or the tone in which it was uttered, though a little hurt by the implied miscalculation as to his age, and by the failure to realize that he was quite *au fait* with the term "bread": which, indeed, had frequently been addressed to him by Mr Sturmer's fellow-tenants in a similar context. But he merely nodded, being of the opinion that it was good for the young to be given as many opportunities as possible for feeling superior.

57

Mr Sturmer scowled and fell silent: but Hugo knew, by the way the young man stretched out his legs, that neither the scowl nor the silence was a signal for him to depart; past experience told him, in fact, that Mr Sturmer was aching to impart to him something that would either impress or shock him. So he, too, sat back at his ease and passed the time by covertly examining Mr Sturmer's get-up (he begged his pardon, "gear")—for the uniforms of the young fascinated him almost as much as their voices.

It was a hot day, but Mr Sturmer was wearing thick corduroy trousers (of a hideous ginger colour) unzipped for several inches at the top—Hugo could see the head of the safety-pin inserted to keep the zip in this exact position. The bell-bottoms of the trousers, as floppy as cabbage leaves, drooped over soft leather boots: on the upper part of his body he wore a winter-weight American Army tunic—which, he had informed Hugo on the occasion of their last meeting, he had acquired from a G.I. deserter with conscientious objections about Vietnam —which was now festooned with a variety of loops, braids and frogs of startling colour and exuberance, and various insignia and buttons bearing legends of a pacifist, revolutionary, or ribald character. In addition he had donned two pieces of equipment of a particularly crippling nature. The first of these was a wide khaki belt (aquired perhaps from the same American benefactor) of many pouches, each of them bulging to capacity, the whole so heavy that it stayed on his hips with difficulty, and had to be buckled so tightly that the lower part of the tunic (which was in any case several sizes too large for him) stood out below the waist like the *tutu* of a ballet dancer. The other piece of equipment was a guitar, slung across his back by a multi-coloured sash, and banging against the back of the chair whenever he moved.

He detected a gleam in Mr Sturmer's eye, and hastily shifted his gaze away from the belt. He already knew by heart the treasures it contained: rolls of bandages; a tin of dressings; a bottle of aspirins; a bottle of iodine; a cigarette-rolling machine, a packet of cigarette papers and a tin of wispy, straw-coloured tobacco; a bottle-opener

58

and corkscrew; a compass and a thermometer; a set of spanners; a card of fuse wire; various screws and nails, and a miscellaneous collection of bits of wire. Mr Sturmer walked through life dreaming of emergencies for which only he would be prepared; but though Hugo had welcomed his aid on several occasions when odd jobs needed doing about the house, he did not wish to have another exhaustive demonstration of the contents of the belt.

Mr Sturmer looked so disappointed, however, that Hugo obligingly glanced at the guitar. Glad, no doubt, to be relieved of the obstruction at his back, Mr Sturmer swung the instrument round and on to his lap.

"I have found some new chords," he announced. He strummed away for a few minutes: the new chords were not very successful, partly because Mr Sturmer had not learned to play the instrument, and partly because the back had been split open during some party or similar fracas and was now stuck together with bits of Sellotape. But his face, surmounted by a mop of frizzy hair (like that of the young Schubert), framed in an inverted halo of side-burn and mutton-chop whisker as soft as lambs-wool and decorated by a pair of steel-rimmed spectacles (also reminiscent of the young Schubert, though in Mr Sturmer's case the lenses were tinted, as if he were about to watch an eclipse of the sun), was so solemn and intent that Hugo was absorbed—for he found the expressions of the young just as fascinating as their uniforms and their voices.

The door opened and a young woman walked in. It took Hugo several minutes to recognize her as the girl she had encountered in the corridor half an hour earlier. She was now wearing a long-sleeved black silk shirt, under a kind of surtout of soft black leather; boots, also of soft black leather, reached halfway up her thighs. Round her neck she wore a chain, reaching nearly to the waist, with links big enough for a chain-gang; suspended from it was a medallion the size of a dinner plate. Her hair was piled on top of her head in a kind of elongated gossamer coil, like the strange diagrams, formed of innumerable intersecting ellipses, which one sees in books

59

of astronomy. She was using a very light face-powder; her eyes were ringed with mascara: the eyelids were darkened: her face had the look of a mask in a Japanese Noh play. Except for her mouth, which seemed to consist of two lumps of ghastly pink flesh, as if the lips had been removed in an operation. An extra layer of white powder on the small, rounded chin drew attention to the pimple it was designed to hide. It was the schoolgirlish eruption that restored a youthful prettiness.

"Pat," Mr Sturmer announced, with a nod in the girl's direction of such extreme nonchalance that Hugo guessed that she was the phenomenon he had been waiting to display. Hugo rose to his feet, executed a jerky old-fashioned bow, at the same time directing at her a look of humble elderly admiration. "Do?" she said, slumping into a chair, picking up a magazine and studying it intently. Mr Sturmer looked pleased. "She works for Shelter," he said, and swept his fingers across the guitar in another unsuccessful chord. He told Hugo all about Shelter, at the same time seizing the opportunity to educate him in other matters. Hugo, however, was so absorbed in the sound of Mr Sturmur's voice that the words and phrases that did from time to time impinge upon his consciousness—"system", "them," "Che", "demo", "revisionist", "Rosa", "Chairman Mao", "re-revolution", and "force forces force to reveal force"— were like the punctuation marks that catch the eye when it glances down a page it has no intention of reading, although every now and then, true to the romantic image he had created for himself, Hugo murmured "bliss was it in that dawn" (causing Mr Sturmer and Pat to exchange looks of mingled exasperation and pity). From time to time, too, by way of friendliness—and perhaps also in the hope of mitigating the over-all impression of senile idiocy—he interjected a question—"violence?" "chaos?", "democracy?", "principles?", "compromise?" and so on. A single word was more than enough, and usually it was Pat who answered, lowering her magazine impatiently, and speaking in tones of weary contempt.

Eventually Mr Sturmer finished his harangue: he swept his fingers once more across the guitar with discordant but vaguely triumphant effect, glanced quickly at a vast portrait of Dr Ernesto which covered practically the whole of one wall (and which, Hugo thought, bore a remarkable resemblance to the late Clark Gable, with whiskers) and turning to Pat began to debate with equal heat and passion which café they were going to have their supper at. Hugo got up and tiptoed to the door, but before he had opened it Pat called out: "Hey, you, Hugo!" Hugo turned and faced her. "You're all right!" she said: she threw him a small smile, quickly cut off. Mr Sturmer got up from his chair, kicked aside a pile of clothes recently brought back from the launderette, and went over to the dresser by the door. He opened a drawer, extracted some coins from it and pressed them into Hugo's hand. "The bread, man," he said, with a smile of the most frank and unaffected charm.

Hugo (having made the appropriate entry in Mr Sturmer's rent-book) went on his way. His calls on these occasions tended to be rather random: he chose them entirely to suit the mood of the moment: one consequence was that a number of his tenants in the "upper regions" found themselves living rent-free for months at a time. Now it was a sense of duty that assailed him, as he climbed a steep flight of stairs at the far end of the corridor that led to the Studio. Hugo's house at this point rose to a narrow peak, something like that of a tent, and the Studio occupied the whole of this peak— an oddly shaped room, itself resembling a bell-tent, lit by a series of skylights. It was not this feature, however, that had given it its name, but the fact that it was traditionally occupied by an artist—penniless, needless to say, and usually ineffectual but at any rate committed to an artistic avocation.

Hugo knocked several times; then, receiving no reply, pushed open the door and entered. His nostrils wrinkled; this time there was no way of romanticizing the stink which penetrated even through the stale fumes of paint and turpentine. The room was in semi-darkness, the blinds over the skylights drawn—though a few shafts of sunlight, as painfully brilliant as laser beams, broke through the edges where the blinds did not fit properly, and there were small golden constellations where the material had worn thin.

Nothing happened when Hugo tried the light-switch, so he released one of the blinds: it recoiled with a sound like a pistol-shot, and Hugo's eyes quivered in the sudden flood of light. Those of the young man who lay in the narrow bed, his head half propped up by filthy pillows, regarded him, unwinking. They were almond-shaped eyes, the pupils very black, but with an oddly metallic appearance. They looked as if they had been inserted in the dead white face as an afterthought: the down-curving eyebrows, too, looked like black incisions. The hair on the narrow, elongated head was so even and smooth that it resembled the black paint on the heads of wooden dolls. As Hugo wandered round the room, too appalled at the moment to know what exactly he ought to do, the black pupils in the white face followed him, as if pulled by magnets: Hugo fancied he could hear them clicking like beads, until he saw that the sound was caused by the acorn-shaped head of one of the blind cords, which was tapping against the wall. Or, rather, against one of the canvases, for most of the wall space was taken up by paintings. They were all studies of peasant women of some unspecified country, though vaguely Slavonic in appearance (perhaps that was what had originally induced Hugo to take in their creator). All of them were squat, ungainly, with lumpy foreshortened arms and legs; the faces, too, were lumpy and dough-like; the backgrounds were of a uniform dark green, almost black, like linoleum which has been constantly polished but never scrubbed. Another painting stood on the easel: it was barely begun, but the same lumpish features were beginning to emerge.

The racks of canvases and frames were covered with a fluffy dust, like grey snow. Brushes and spatulas were thick with coagulated paint. Other brushes stood, their bristles stiff as wire, in jars from which the turpentine had ebbed, to leave a hard, multi-coloured crust. Paint-streaked cloths lay in the corners, as stiff as fragments of chain-mail. Uncapped tubes of paint squelched under his feet among scraps of discarded sketching paper. A can of

62

yellow, solidified glue stood on the cold iron stove.

Hugo returned to the bed, carefully skirting a chamber-pot, almost overflowing, in which floated used match-sticks, and cigarette stubs, bloated and disintegrating into gingerish threads, like wire-worms. He looked down at the occupant of the bed. The black beads shifted their position, looking at him from under lowered eyelids: the lids, too, had a metallic look, like slivers of white tin.

"It won't do, Mr Smith," Hugo said, marvelling for the hundredth time at the mundane surname. "No, it won't do at all." Hugo shook his head, more in sorrow (literally, given Hugo's pacific personality) than in anger. "You know the rule of the house," he said. "This room is a studio and it cannot be let to idlers." The black pupils changed momentarily, taking on the appearance of glittering mica. "I do not question you as to the results of your artistic activities, but activity of some sort I *do* expect—activity, I mean, of an outgoing nature—even if it is only *talking* about work. Not to mention," he added, "the little matter of rent."

The slivers of white tin descended, giving the long, sallow face, with its black stubble (that, too, smooth and uniform as if shaded in charcoal) an expression of icy disdain.

Hugo took hold of the young man's shoulders. He neither resisted nor assisted but, remaining absolutely limp, allowed himself to be dragged from under the sheets, and out of the bed, his heels banging on the floor, and then to be stood upright, bent slightly at the waist, one shoulder raised. He stood there for a moment, swaying, his eyes tightly closed. He was wearing a painter's smock, torn and paint-stained; his bare legs, very smooth and slender, were covered with black, silky hair. Then, as Hugo gave him a shove, none too gentle, he lowered his shoulder, half opened his eyes, and subsided into a chair; he fumbled in the pocket of the smock, produced a cigarette end, sniffed at it and placed it, very carefully, between his lips. With a sudden jerk, like that of a spastic, he swept a pile of paint tubes, brushes and mixing jars off the top of the table at his side, disclosing a sodden book of matches. Holding it close to his eyes he tore off

63

the tiny strip of cardboard and tried to light it. It was too damp, and the oblong of sandpaper had disintegrated; he went on drawing the match along it, with intent, pernickety gestures as if he were threading a needle, long after the head had worn away. Hugo took out his lighter (a metal affair, such as sailors use, with a wind-shield so large that it suggested a brazier at which one might roast potatoes). Mr Smith seized his wrist in a grip like a vice and held the flame steady. At the first whiff of the cigarette end he released Hugo's wrist: the lids of his eyes suddenly sprang wide open, and the black pupils fixed themselves on Hugo: the rest of his face was expressionless. A bottle of turpentine had broken when he cleared the table: the liquid had formed a pool which reached his feet: he wriggled his toes, but did not attempt to move them. Hugo returned to the bed. He carried the chamber-pot to the nearest lavatory and disposed of the contents, using the flush twice and employing the interval while the cistern was filling to sprinkle disinfectant into the pot. Then returning to Mr Smith's room he began to strip the bed. The sheets were stiff with stale semen. Clean ones, he assumed, he would have to fetch from his own quarters, but when he opened the top drawer of the chest he found a pile of them, unironed and smelling of mildew, but reasonably clean. Hugo made the bed in his usual shipshape fashion; he pulled the cover over it, and arranged a few cushions on top; the cushions had been used for wiping paint brushes, but they gave the divan a reasonably cheerful day-time appearance.

When he had finished he turned to Mr Smith—who was regarding his unfinished canvas with the same expression of icy disdain he had bestowed on Hugo.

"And that," Hugo said, "is the last time I shall perform that particular service for you." The black pupils flickered in his direction: Mr Smith was as startled as Hugo himself: Hugo had spoken in tones of unaccustomed irritation and even firmness.

Although the reasonably well-to-do tenants paid by

bankers' order Hugo called on them too on the first of every month. He usually did so immediately after his tour of the upper regions, and usually he began with the Quinceys. It is true they were probably not as well-to-do as the Proudfoots (or Proudfoot-Lorns) but *they* observed a calendar peculiar to themselves: the Colonel's latest film, after the innumerable technical processes to which it had been subjected in order to make it more or less visible, had achieved its customary "way out" success— and the Proudfoots (or Proudfoot-Lorns) had disappeared on one of their mysterious vacations, the secret of which was known only to Hugo. In any case the Quinceys suited Hugo's mood on these occasions. They themselves were convinced that after his foray into the dirt and disorder of the upper regions—which they themselves, of course, had never seen, though they sometimes imagined in their nightmares that they had been banished to that dark continent—Hugo yearned for the discreet aromas of their own smart establishment. It was true that Hugo welcomed the contrast, but not in the way the Quinceys supposed: for contact with their ambience, he found, quickly restored his faith in that of the other (in spite of Mr Smith), no matter how sorely tried it had been by his monthly ascent (especially to Mr Smith). Besides, the Quinceys did not know that their deodorants were powerless against that sweetish, upper class odour of gin distilled into sweat drops.

Mr Quincey was a tall, baggy man in his early fifties. His suit was not, *de sui generis*, in the least baggy, but that could not hide the fact. He had a long, loose frame that sagged in unexpected places; his shoulders and wrists, for example, looked as if they were permanently dislocated; he could bend in several places, alternately or all at once, as if he had a whole series of waists. The way in which the suit, like a ramrod sergeant in charge of a squad of abnormally awkward rookies, grimly struggled to hold out against the shape to which it had been condemned was, indeed, a notable tribute to its West End creator. The same could not be said of Mr Quincey's skin, which was badly in need of various tucks and gussets. These large areas of loose skin, which were of a

65

sallow, unhealthy colour (surprisingly, in view of the fact that their owner played a good deal of loose-limbed, tweedy golf) were particularly noticeable when Mr Quincey smiled. Being a Senior Civil Servant he had a professionally humorous expression, something like that of a bishop crossed with the poet W. H. Auden: when he smiled, therefore (which he did a great deal), creases ran up and down the length of his long face, like those round a boa constrictor when it is swallowing (or perhaps regurgitating) its prey: so that it was difficult to tell whether it was the mouth, or the neck, or the chin, cheeks or forehead that were smiling.

It was possible, Hugo reflected as he sipped the gin and tonic which Mr Quincey had slapped in front of him as soon as he had seated himself in the peach velveteen-covered wing-chair, that gin had something to do with this phenomenon too ... no doubt it caused the inward parts to shrink away from the outer, as when a taxidermist is too lavish with his pickling fluids (memories of the Proudfoots). Not that either of the Quinceys actually came into the category of "alcoholics": they were not temperamentally capable of anything so positive as an insatiable craving; they never indulged in sudden and spectacular "blinds"; it was simply that they absorbed a regular quantity, day in and day out, year after year— so regularly, indeed, that they knew to a fluid ounce what their intake was, and exactly how much to budget for it.

The other outstanding feature about Mr Quincey was the large quantity of lank, flat hair which flopped about like a detachable scalp. In his twenties this hair must have been blond; then a hair here and a hair there had turned grey. The invasion had gone no further, with the result that for the past twenty years the top of his head had suggested a kind of dusty khaki camouflage.

Mrs Quincey was a small, dark woman of about the same age as her husband, who still retained the vestiges of her earlier status as a *jolie laide*. The frizzy hair, dyed black, the darting light-brown eyes, the long, knuckly fingers still gave off an impression of vivacity, heightened now by mascara, rouge, ear-rings, bangles, pendants, numerous rings with big stones in big, dramatic settings, and a profusion of bows and tassels and other details about her clothes that danced and dangled whenever she moved. The passage of the years, however, had made the forehead and cheek-bones more prominent, the eyes more bulbous, the lines, sweeping as distinct as a Chinese mandarin's moustaches from the long upper lip on either side of the mouth to enclose a small pinched chin, more pronounced: the upper part of her face, in consequence, now looked more simian, the lower more frog-like. The compact little body had also grown skinny: the shoulder-blades had a sharp cutting-edge; the knee-caps, beneath the expensive nylon, were as hard and shiny as snooker balls.

"We went to the theatre last night," Mr Quincey began, like a player in one of those complicated strategic games, cautiously pushing forward a pre-emptive piece, "to see the new Osborne." There was a pause during which husband and wife regarded each other warily.

"A good production?" Hugo himself ventured, when he could no longer endure the suspense.

"The tempo was all wrong," Mr Quincey said, shaking his head mournfully, while the creases contracted and retracted. "You see, the crisis should have been a frantic gabble—instead, it went like a funeral. The whole point about Osborne is..."

"I can't stand these non-communication plays," Mrs Quincey interrupted. Expecting you to read all sorts of things into these long pauses! And I'm *so* tired of having to look at basements and dust-bins and so on...."

"It was an *Osborne* play we saw, my dear, not a Pinter," Mr Quincey said, with a particularly bland smile that started up new waves of creases until he looked like the Michelin Man. "As I was saying just now, the whole point about Osborne is that..."

"Personally I think that Pinter..." what she had to say was quite interesting in its way, apart from the fact that it came from the wrong band of the wrong record. Was she secretly aware of the fact? Hugo wondered.

When she had finished, with a toss of her *petite* head that set all the ornaments and tassels dangling and tinkling, and a flash of her well-known *gamine* smile (she had three new fillings, Hugo noticed) her husband (after re-filling the glasses) tried again.

"Did you read about the Dimsey Report?" he ventured, carefully addressing his question to Hugo, though the bland smile, curled slightly at the edges, was presumably for his wife's benefit. He cast a hasty glance in the direction of the despatch case, rolled umbrella and raincoat still lying on a chair by the door; Hugo, following suit, saw a corner of the evening paper protruding from the raincoat pocket. Mrs Quincey stared straight ahead: but her chin quivered: she seemed to be hugging herself.

"The Dimsey Report?" she said, softly.

"Yes, my dear ... You know, my dear fellow" ... again studiously addressing Hugo ... "the investigation into the differences between the behavioural patterns of ten year-olds in the Home Counties and the provinces..." The Quinceys were readers of the *Guardian* and *New Statesman*, and therefore *au fait* with such matters ... "It appears that the differences which emerged were significant—ah, highly significant. You see, the whole point about them is that..."

Mrs Quincey burst in triumphantly. "There was a discussion about it on Woman's Hour this afternoon—I heard it, and..."

"But," Mr Quincey said, and refilled their glasses. He did not succeed in diverting his wife: she managed to sip and talk at the same time.

"I wouldn't agree with you at all that the results were significant—let alone" (mimicking her husband's voice) " 'Ah, highly significant'. On the contrary, the report showed that school results up to the age of ten..."

"But, you see, as I was about to say, the whole point..."

"...hardly differed at all. In fact, it seems much more likely that..."

But Mr Quincey was studying the *Radio Times*. "My dear," he said, beatific smiles undulating from neck to temples, "*you* are talking about the Andrews Report...!" But Mrs Quincey was not in the least abashed. "Naturally," she said, "it is much *more* significant!" Mr Quincey gave a long sigh and (after refilling the glasses) sank back into his wing-chair (rust-coloured velveteen): the Bond Street suit held severely aloof.

An hour later Hugo reached the hall (dark green wall-to-wall Wilton). He was slightly tipsy: gin was not his drink: he preferred Lamb's Navy Rum: the Quinceys displayed no apparent effects, apart from perhaps an increase in volubility.

"Oh, by the way," Mrs Quincey said, "we've lost our char. Do you think the old lady could give me a hand?"

"Which old lady?" Hugo asked.

"The wife of that sergeant person over in the Annexe."

"Mrs Palfrey? She's ill. She's had a stroke. Perhaps *you* could give *her* a hand?"

"Oh..."

"Don't you remember?" Mr Quincey said: the smiles writhed triumphantly. "Roger was talking about it yesterday."

"Yes, of course." The corners of Mrs Quincey's mouth drooped.

"Some nonsense," Mr Quincey continued, with a quick glance at his wife to see if she had rallied, "about it being 'his fault'."

"His fault—yes...." she murmured, sulkily; and then with a spurt of defiance: "What nonsense!"

A crash came from the room on their right.

"He's in there now." Mr Quincey said.

"Roger's play-room," Mrs Quincey added, throwing the door open. They entered. Roger was kneeling in the middle of the floor, in between two rows of toy soldiers, guns, tanks, and fortifications, scrambling from side to side doling out the fortunes of war. The largest of the forts was in ruins: it had not simply been toppled on to its side, but smashed to smithereens.

"Really, Roger!" Mrs Quincey exclaimed. "That fort was practically new: I bought it at Selfridge's...."

"Harrod's," Mr Quincey murmured.

Roger stopped his game and stood up, in that docile, waiting attitude common to only children who have been born to parents later in life than usual.

"Aha! A battle in progress, I see!" Mr Quincey exclaimed. He leaped over the nearest battle-line (knocking over one of the tanks) and pranced about in no-man's land, shouting "Bang! Bang! I've deaded him!" Roger, regarding him warily, returned to his kneeling position: he removed several.of the recumbent soldiers out of the way of his father's suede-clad feet. "Bang! Bang!" Mr Quincey cried again, and gave another jump, joints creaking, arms and legs flying in all directions: a row of sharp-shooters subsided: the suit seemed almost to groan aloud. Then suddenly Mr Quincey stopped, and mopped his forehead. He gave a shame-faced grin, stepped gingerly out of the circle, patted his son awkwardly on the head and hurried back to the gin. For once he was not smiling. Roger stared after him, with an expression half tender, half pitying. Mrs Quincey, who had watched her husband's cavortings without a word, also stared after him. Then, stepping over the half-dismantled battle-line, very carefully, as if it were many times higher than it actually was, she took her son's head between her hands and pressed it convulsively against her stomach. Roger submitted patiently. Suddenly she let go, gave a lop-sided grin, and also hurried from the room: like her husband she had apparently forgotten Hugo's presence. Silently Roger indicated a point on the circumference of the farther battle-line. Hugo knelt down, and, still without speaking, the two of them rearranged the pieces. When they had finished, Roger looked inquiringly at Hugo. Hugo nodded and Roger fired the first shot from one of his mortars. The pellet bounced harmlessly off the shield of one of Hugo's guns. He rubbed his hands and took aim. But Roger did not explain why he had told his parents that he believed Mrs Palfrey's stroke to be his own fault. Hugo bided his time: in any case he was absorbed in the game.

Mr Skidmore had also just returned from work when Hugo called. His coat, hat, despatch case and rolled umbrella were neatly stowed away in the tiny entrance-hall. His large bed-sitter was also very neat: the green cover over the divan was stretched so that not a single crease was apparent, and pulled down so that it would hide the legs: the cushions were arranged so that the bulge of the pillow beneath the cover would not show. The books were stacked in their cases according to sizes and pulled forward so that they stood exactly to the edges of the shelves. The drawers of the tall mahogany chest were carefully pushed in. The curtains were drawn to meet exactly, hem-on.

Normally, Hugo would have approved of such habits, but in Mr Skidmore's case they were not a reflection of personality. It was simply that he was devoured by an overwhelming desire to remove from the room all traces of his presence, and, indeed, every wrinkle or particle that pointed to human occupancy of any kind. The room, in consequence, had an unlived-in atmosphere. Perhaps it was because there were no lingering smells of cooking or of the aerosols meant to disperse them. There was a neat kitchen-alcove, with gleaming aluminium sink, pots and pans, and a spotless electric cooker, concealed by a green silk screen, but Mr Skidmore never used them: he would not even boil a kettle, and he had all his meals, including breakfast, at a near-by restaurant.

He was seated on the edge of an arm-chair staring into a blank television screen. "Listen," he said, the moment he was aware of Hugo's presence. "You remember I told you how Matilda suddenly walked out on me?"

Hugo nodded and quietly sat down in the chair facing Mr Skidmore, who frowned when he took several seconds to rearrange the cushions more comfortably.

"Three months ago tomorrow she left me," he continued, emphasizing the words as if to warn Hugo that he expected no further interruptions.

"A right turn-up for the book!" His voice had the flatness of extreme fatigue, a flatness somehow accentuated by his fondness for turns of phrase that normally demand exclamation marks. "Matilda of all people! The last person you'd expect to behave in that way! ... It's not as if she was—is, I mean—an excitable type ... Rather solid ... square-looking really—d'you know what I mean? ... She was always inclined to be plump, of course—plenty to grab at when she was young, eh?"

71

He made a noise that was meant presumably to be a laugh, but which sounded more like the wheeze of an asthmatic: it stirred the ends of his large, ragged brown moustache. Oddly enough he was not at all neat in his personal appearance: his tweed suit was baggy and unpressed: his collar was frayed: the old Fair Isle pullover he wore under his jacket was snagged into innumerable loops and loose ends.

"Yes, she got squarer as she grew older," he went on, "especially on the hips, you know? Her face seemed to get bigger too—heavy, sort of, round the jaw.... She was always very quiet.... Big eyes in that pale, big face...." He focussed his hot little eyes on Hugo's face. "You know the type?"

Hugo nodded. "As for me, well, you can see, I'm the easy-going type...." He paused for confirmation.

"Yes, of course," Hugo agreed, a few seconds late on his cue. He could quite see, however, that in his normal frame of mind Mr Skidmore *would* be an easy-going man; the curly brown hair and moustache, the slightly florid complexion, the wide mouth with the full, ruddy lips spoke of a clubbable, even a hearty, man. Now, it was true, he looked rather like a painting in which the colours have begun to run ... perhaps it was the eyes: they were pale blue, with the wide irises that usually denote a frank and manly gaze, but now they were bloodshot, suffused, as if from conjunctivitis.... Eyes and voice were somehow linked: it was as if the flat monotone, and that alone, held the eyes in equilibrium and prevented them from overflowing....

"Never a cross word," Mr Skidmore repeated, "popular with the neighbours—both of us ... played golf ... Matilda always used to come with me to business lunches and that kind of thing. She was very quiet, of course. 'One of us is enough!' she used to say. I was always the life and soul of the party, you see.... Always got on well with people: made friends quickly—had to, really, because we were always moving about.... Don't know why, but we never seemed to settle down properly.... We used to take a liking to a house, move in, slave like navvies to get it all shipshape ... you

72

should have seen the roses I grew! ... Matilda hated gardening, though ... it would have been nice if she could have taken an interest—both of us bending over the plants, you know—yes, I would have liked that.... She was wonderful about the house, of course: could do anything—carpentry, wiring, the lot: and she'd do the decorations, top to bottom. Wonderful cook, too— though she lost interest towards the end: I quite liked cooking myself, in those days—nothing fancy, you understand; roast beef and two veg (Yorkshire pudding as well, of course)—plain, but good.... She never complained ... neither did the kids—ate whatever I put in front of them...

"I travel for a family business, you know—I'm a partner really—dog-biscuits, mostly—old established firm. So you can see I can choose where I want to live, within reason.... Funny, I never really *wanted* to leave any of those houses, though I was just as keen as she was to move on! ... Do you know, when all the furniture was taken out we used to wander for hours round the empty house, up and down the stairs, from one room to another.... I used to look at the bits and pieces in the grates; the bits of fluff left on the tacks where the removal men had yanked up the carpets; the patches on the walls where the pictures had hung; the marks on the mantelpiece where the ornaments had stood; and the bits of old crayon and pencil in the kids' rooms.... Matilda never said anything; her face used to go stiff, sort of, and there was a swelling under her eyes...

"I'll tell you another funny thing—I never forget any of the houses we've lived in. Sometimes I have to drop whatever I'm doing, get into the car and drive off to one of them.... There I am, driving very slowly along the old road.... Then I stop outside the house, pretending I'm lost or looking for a number.... Sometimes, if the people are away, I get out of the car and go into the front garden and look in through the windows.... It's *horrible* how different everything is! ... Still, there's bound to be *something* I can recognize—a fire-place, a boiler, a radiator, the door-knobs.... When that happens

73

I rush back to the car and drive about like mad for an hour or so (I've got a Jag—but, as you can imagine, I'm a good driver).... I tell you what, though—once I pretended I was inspecting the electric wiring for the council! Yes! I got right inside; went all over the house, even up into the loft where the water tank is.... Christ! Do you know, I found several old bits of wood that *we'd* left there? ... And even the leg of a doll ... wonder how that got up there? ... it was like a horrible pink slug.... Didn't do that again, though: made me too angry. The people kept looking at me too—I thought they were going to send for the police! Haven't been anywhere near that house since ... Dreamed about it last night, though—there I was, back in the living-room. It was a long, oblong-shaped room, with one wall nearly all glass.... We had an old couch, very long, which Matilda had bought at a sale—she'd covered it with a brown moquette that had big flowers all over it—stood along that wall. Now, we had four kittens when we were living in that house—Mitzi's, of course: she'd had eight, but we'd given four away (hated doing it, but enough's enough, eh? ... had her doctored later—of course). These kittens used to love that couch! It was snagged all over from their claws but we didn't mind.... Matilda was house-proud, of course, but even she didn't mind about the couch—it *belonged* to the kittens, if you know what I mean? ... They were quite house-trained, by the way. (Trust old Mitzi for that!) ... But this dream—You see these kittens had a special trick—they used to get *under* the couch, one behind the other, lie flat on their backs, and then, one after the other, drag themselves along by their claws! You should have seen them! They kept on doing it—the sacking under the couch was hanging in shreds before they'd finished! And the speed they got up! We used to watch them for hours on end—me, Matilda and the kids—and even Matilda used to laugh—out loud—at those kittens! All the neighbours knew about it, and *they'd* come in to have a good laugh! ... Mitzi didn't like that much, though (she didn't mind us, of course). When the neighbours were there, laughing their silly heads off, she'd walk about for a bit with her tail

74

in the air (a great bushy tail it was—lovely markings on it), purring. But then, suddenly, she'd get cross—as if she'd decided that they were taking the mickey out of *her* kittens, you know—and she'd dash under the couch, take them up in her mouth, one after the other, jump on to the window sill and then out through the window into the garden and to a special secret place she had there. One after the other, all of them wriggling and squealing in her mouth and, honest, they were all of them nearly as big as she was herself! ... She was one of those cats with such a lot of fur that they look bigger than they really are—when you stroked her or held her tight in your arms your hands would sink right through the fur, and you'd realize that she was really quite small ... a dainty little creature, in fact—lovely markings, too, lovely markings...." Mr Skidmore stopped abruptly: leaned forward, hands on knees, staring sightlessly, though every now and then the ends of his moustache stirred, as if he were muttering to himself. The minutes ticked by.

Then quite suddenly, in an irritable, almost hectoring tone of voice, he said: "Have I told you about me and animals?" Despairingly Hugo shook his head.

"Must have done!" Mr Skidmore said, glaring. Again Hugo shook his head.

"Well, I've got a way with animals," he announced: He paused as if daring Hugo to contradict him. "Yes, both Matilda and me were fond of animals," he continued, "not in any sloppy, townee, way, though. The contrary, in fact. We're both country-bred, you know— we both *know* about animals ... all kinds of little things that you townees never think about—things like ... let me see, now ... yes! That you can always make hens lay better if you stroke them every day— Bet you didn't know that?" Again he glared at Hugo, who hastily shook his head, feeling unaccountably guilty.

"Thought not!" Mr Skidmore said, with a jeer. "Well —you do now!" He tugged irritably at the ends of his moustache. "Of course the neighbours used to pull my leg a bit about those hens. Suppose I *am* a bit of a crank where animals are concerned! ...

"We had a budgerigar once ... Joey ... yes, Joey....

We had a real understanding, that budgie and me." His voice was husky; he spoke so softly that Hugo had difficulty in hearing him.

"We used to let him out of his cage, you know.... But instead of flying round the room as you'd expect, he used to make straight for my head and perch on top of it. He'd stay there for hours—in fact I used to walk about the house with him there! (This was before Mitzi of course.) And he'd keep lifting up strands of my hair in his beak! Matilda used to say it was just instinct—that he was looking for material to build his nest.... Yes! But if that was the case he'd have had to be a 'she'!— God! I wish I'd thought of that at the time!—that would have put Matilda in her place! Matilda didn't have much patience, of course, with my ideas about animals and birds—'empathy' and that kind of thing, you know (I'm a great believer in empathy, personally).... We nearly broke our hearts when that damned budgie took sick—a chill or something (we never seemed to have much luck with our pets, for some reason).... He was as perky as you please one day; then the next, he was all ruffled up—off his food, too; then he got so weak he couldn't stay on his perch and he fell off, on to the floor of his cage. He just sat there, all huddled up like a broody hen. Matilda and I talked it over. She wanted to send for the vet. But I don't think much of vets—me having this special gift, you see— and Matilda agreed after a bit that *I* could do as much for Joey as any vet! ... She always gave in quickly if you argued with her (not that I ever threw my weight about or anything like that, you understand?). She'd shrug her shoulders, and give that funny little smile, that just dented the corners of her mouth.... So I decided to give Joey a drop of brandy every now and then—only a tiny drop, of course. I found an old eye-dropper in the medicine cabinet (sterilized it first, of course), spoke to him so that he would open his beak to cheep, and, hey presto! in went the drop of brandy! Joey gave a kind of surprised 'cheep'—very loud—shook himself— and jumped up! It was fantastic! We really thought we'd done the trick. But after a bit he weakened again....

Matilda and me took it in turns all that night, every three or four hours, to go downstairs and give him another drop of brandy. He'd buck up every time, too, for a few minutes, but it was no good. I gave him his last drop at six o'clock in the morning, I remember. We both got up just after that and went downstairs to the living-room—and there was poor old Joey, lying flat on his back at the bottom of the cage with his legs stuck up in the air.... Honest, he looked for all the world like a midget turkey on a poulterer's slab!"

Mr Skidmore made a huffing noise and agitated the ends of his moustache. "Funny, really, when you come to think of it!" he said. "Well, Matilda took one look at Joey, and then—do you know what?... Women! She opened her hand-bag and took out her powder puff and compact and started powdering her nose! She always did that if she was upset. She had rather a small nose—button-shaped I suppose you'd call it—and she'd bang away at it with the powder puff—I wonder she didn't hurt herself sometimes! Anyway, that's what she did now—slap, bang, slap, bang, with the bloody powder puff. 'Perhaps we ought to have sent for the vet after all?' I said, but she only looked at me ... the funny thing, though, is that her eyes were shining and she looked quite beautiful ... now, I wonder why that was? ...

"Then the kids came down. You should have heard them! They were so upset it was no use letting them go to school. I'd have liked to stay home myself, to tell you the truth—I was really fond of that budgie.... What worries me now is that I might have killed him myself! I mean, a drop of brandy, every three hours ... and, after all, he *was* only a tiny thing! ... It would be rich, wouldn't it? if it wasn't the chill at all—if the poor little perisher died of alcoholic poisoning!"

Mr Skidmore went off into another mirthless laugh. "Still," he said, cutting the laugh short with a champing motion of his jaws, as if he had bitten off a mouthful of chaff. "Perhaps it was just as well. I don't expect Mitzi and Joey would have taken to each other at all—and Mitzi is a special case. Yes, a very special case." He darted a sidelong look at Hugo. It was a very odd look, Hugo thought; part-suspicious, part-frightened, part-cunning. Mr Skidmore's face, too, looked odd: it had gone the pale, tacky colour of someone suffering from a sudden attack of food poisoning: it made the veins of his cheek and of his rather fleshy nose stand out in a livid red tracery, like a cluster of ripe elderberries.

"Have I told you about Mitzi?" he asked in a soft, almost insinuating voice. But Hugo had taken advantage of the pause this time: he was already half way to the door. "Another time, Mr Skidmore," he said, "another time!" Mr Skidmore left his chair with surprising alacrity.

"Of all the bloody nerve!" he cried. "I was just coming to the important part!"

"I ... I'll come back," Hugo said closing the door quickly as Mr Skidmore advanced on him, his jaw working.

4

It was "tumbling time" in Hugo's garden. It was the term he coined for the kind of sultry late September which sometimes follows a wet and windy spell. At such times, he used to point out, one invariably jumps to the conclusion that the slide into winter has begun early, and gives up all attempt at keeping growth at bay, with the argument that the frost will soon see to it, and the excuse that it is too wet to get out anyway. Then, suddenly, an Indian Summer begins—and one realizes that during the past few weeks grass, plant and weed have stealthily proliferated.

In Hugo's garden now they spread everywhere in great clumps and clusters. In the beds tall weeds half smothered the late yellow and purple pansies. The dahlias and chrysanthemums were more like shaggy sheepdogs than ever, and their buds stood out in vivid green carbuncles. The soil, churned up by the earlier rain and wind, caked into coarse clods in the sudden heat. The sun seemed to have sucked up all the bits of stone and gravel and deposited them on the surface of the soil. Tiny flies, slender and delicate as bits of aluminium, buzzed over the fallen petals and leaf-mould, which were still steaming. There was none of the freshness of spring: the atmosphere was close and enervating: there was a fetid smell, as of a premature resurrection.

Hugo, in fact, nearly did tumble as he made his way down the garden paths; for everywhere they were obstructed by the rambler roses that had been blown down from the pergolas and now lay in coils as thick and spiky as barbed wire—and by the strands of bind-

79

weed, thin and spindly but almost as tough, which grew with extraordinary vigour: no matter how carefully Hugo probed down for its vicious little roots, like rats' teeth, the bindweed came surging back as soon as his efforts relaxed, stifling the plants, breaking through the cracks in the walls, climbing up the topmost branches of the fruit trees and even festooning the drain-pipes. Hugo had the fancy that the whole of his house and garden were held in a kind of basket of bindweed: so strong was the fancy, indeed, that he was fearful of too drastic an onslaught on the roots, in case house and garden should collapse and disintegrate in a cloud of dust and debris.

Ensnared with bindweed, then, Hugo nearly did fall on the grass—but saved himself in time, when he saw that this particular square of lawn was already occupied by Mr Sturmer and Pat. They had spread out an old plaid travelling rug, for although the tops of the longer blades of grass formed a limp, dry fringe, lower down they were yellow and so wet that each might have grown out of its individual spring of water. At the same time, there was so much grass that the rug seemed to float as if on the topmost branches of a tree or the crest of a wave.

Mr Sturmer and Pat lay on their sides, facing each other, but several feet apart, finger-tips touching, in such still, formal attitudes that Hugo was reminded of effigies on a tomb. Their eyes travelled over each other's faces, up and down, to and fro, round and round, very slowly and delicately as if they were tattooist's needles. They paid not the slightest attention to Hugo's blundering approach. He was, admittedly, an easy man to ignore; but being also of a sentimental—or at any rate, a minor-romantic—frame of mind, he preferred to think it was because they were too absorbed in each other. They paid no attention, either (he could not help reflecting) to the rank smell of damp earth, rotting leaves and petals, or to the fretful Indian Summer insects, or to the late wasps which, irritated by the unexpected heat, and feeling, perhaps, that they should already be moribund in the first frosts, stung at the least provocation.

Hugo backed away, mopping his forehead as he went:

it was indeed a strange heat, that produced a perspiration like oil, and made one uncertain, too, whether it was sweat or damp that made one's clothes and skin so clammy.

Through an overgrown archway, down two overgrown paths, as tricky as one of the Army assault courses of Hugo's war days, and he came to another lawn, where the grass was also thick and rank, but of a very deep, blackish green. This lawn had little scallops and bays in it, formed by flowering shrubs of various kinds. A group of children were playing cowboys and Indians, in a rather half-hearted manner, wilting in the muggy atmosphere, fiery red bands round their foreheads where their head-dresses had slipped, beads of perspiration, like small blisters, on their noses and upper lips. Hugo had watched them carefully skirting Mr Sturmer and Pat, their giggles and sidelong glances more conspiratorial than derisory, acknowledging a kinship.

But now as they came upon another recumbent couple, beyond a fringe of shrubs, they stopped, and stood staring in disapproving silence. To Hugo's middle-aged eyes Mr Venner and Mrs Bradbury looked every bit as charming as the admittedly far more youthful Mr Sturmer and Pat. They lay in much the same postures: their eyes were just as busy. But clearly the children experienced some sense of incongruity. They kept glancing at each other inquiringly: their lips smiling, as convention demanded, but the giggles suppressed. After a while their expressions grew more solemn. They emerged from behind the bushes, advanced a few feet, stopped, advanced again: at length they stood in a semi-circle looking at the two lovers, still oblivious of their presence. Then they joined hands, and crept forward again, very slowly, a step at a time, like sparrows prospecting for crumbs in a park. When they were only a few feet away, they stopped again, and cocked their heads to one side, trying to peer into the side-turned faces beneath them in order to gauge their expressions, their own doubtful and troubled.

One of the children sneezed. Mrs Bradbury sat up with a jerk. Mr Venner followed suit: he blushed, then scowled. The children stood, silent, rather sullen, demanding something that would restore their sense of propriety. Mrs Bradbury looked from one to the other, very carefully, aware that she carried a responsibility.

At length she gave a slow, comfortable smile. "Hello," she said, "very hot for the time of the year, isn't it." She patted the grass beside her. Immediately they crowded round her, sat down, and started chattering noisily. "Guess what," a girl of about seven said, "my tortoise is woken up again!" "He never went to sleep proper," a small boy said, with withering contempt. "Yes, he did!" "No he didn't!" the other chorused. Mr Venner ventured a timid "Hello". They ignored him, drawing closer to Mrs Bradbury. The smallest child, a boy, dumped himself in her lap. The girl caught hold of her left hand, opened it out, turned it over and began studying the fingers. She came to a big, old-fashioned ring with a cluster of garnets. She raised Mrs Bradbury's hand to examine the ring more closely, screwing up her eyes like a jeweller. "Pretty," she said. Then in a loud whisper, "Did *he* give it you?" pointing to Mr Venner as if he were a tree or a garden seat. Mrs Bradbury nodded. Mr Venner ventured another "Hello". The girl gave him a haughty stare, and turned back to Mrs Bradbury: "That's all right, then," she said. She guided Mrs Bradbury's left hand round her own shoulders. The small boy gave her a shove. "Of course he doesn't really know *anything* about the habits of tortoises," the girl assured Mrs Bradbury. She sat upright, stretching herself so that she could see over the intervening shrubs to the other lawn where Mr Sturmer and Pat still lay entwined. "Of course I expect *you* were just sun-bathing," she said. Mr Venner scowled.

Hugo tiptoed away. He had intended to ask Mrs Bradbury and Mr Venner if their respective divorces had come through. Not that he was a nosy-Parker: it was simply that they had promised to let him know so that he could make what arrangements he thought fit about their rooms when they married and moved on to a place of their own.

He continued his tour of inspection, noting, with distaste, the gardening jobs that were accumulating and which he supposed he would have to tackle—unless this unseasonable muggy spell ended and the frost jumped in first after all, like a naked man throwing off a stuffy red cloak—wondering, too, if he would have much difficulty in coaxing the rather temperamental motor-mower into life. It occurred to him that he had not see Roger among the group of children with Mrs Bradbury—though of course he was rather too old for them, he supposed—and, indeed, that he had not seen him for several days past. He came across him, however, in the orchard: he was seated astride his apple-tree steed, the reins hanging listlessly from his hands. Since Hugo had last been that way Roger had improvised a pair of stirrups out of the inverted brake-forks of an old bicycle, attached to the branch by lengths of string. He kept rising in these stirrups, as high as he could reach, and after a moment Hugo realized that his main purpose in doing so was to get a good view over the hedge.

Unseen by Roger he took the narrow path round the yew hedge and made his way through the kitchen garden and the rockery to this part of his domain. For the most part it was a wilderness of weeds, tangled pea-sticks and tumble-down bean poles; some of the tenants had not even bothered to pick the final crops from the latter, and the runner-beans, coarse, bloated, and blackened along the edges from the brief early snap of frost, dangled obscenely in clusters as long as one's forearm. The Palfreys' strip, however, was still an exception. Having started from perfection, it had had farther to decline; during old Mrs Palfrey's illness Hugo had managed to keep it in reasonable trim—and then at the beginning of the hot spell the Palfreys themselves had re-emerged. A good half of the strip was now back to its former state. At the moment Sergeant Palfrey was busy with his hoe: he wielded it so swiftly and dexterously that the bits of stone on the surface of the soil tinkled like goats' bells and threw off occasional sparks.

When he saw Hugo, he winked, smiled his mocking grin, exclaimed "Sir!" wincing as his hips ground their gears, managing nevertheless to bring his hand to his forehead in a smart salute. He was in his gardening regalia, complete to waistcoat, Albert and medallions. Waistcoat and flannel shirt were open to the waist. Drops of sweat, like glycerine, clung to the iron-grey hair. But the Sergeant himself appeared to have shrunk and the strip of hair, from throat to navel, hung loosely, like the pelt of an animal: his ribs showed through; his collar-bones stood out like a yoke. His corduroy trousers were now too big for him: the army belt was buckled as far as it would go, with a good eighteen inches of "tongue" hanging loose. Even his ankles must have grown thinner, for the tops of his boots were like inverted parachutes. He had difficulty in keeping the shirt-sleeves rolled up above his attenuated biceps, and the flesh had fallen away from his forearms so that the muscles stood out in ridges. This shrinkage had the effect of bringing out the tattoo marks: for the first time Hugo could make out the dragons, serpents, naked maidens, army crests, and arrowed hearts under the wiry hair, like frescoes that emerge when the walls of an old church are cleaned. The Sergeant's face was thinner too: the skin stretched tight over the forehead: there were long clefts in the cheeks and the lower jaw (he had discarded his dentures, perhaps because they no longer fitted) looked as if it were hinged on with wire; the moustaches, waxed more needle-sharp than ever, seemed enormous. But the bright little eyes in the shrivelled face danced with pleasure.

"Back on parade!" he said, giving the ends of the moustaches a twirl. "Soon lick the little perishers into shape!" He directed a gaze, part ferocious, part fond, at the rows of vegetables and plants still smothered with weeds.

Mrs Palfrey was seated in a wheel-chair on the square of lawn between the flower bed (a dense mass of red, white and blue dwarf asters) and the water-butt. She raised her stick shakily and waved it. Hugo and the Sergeant went over to her. The Sergeant had recently retarred the water-butt: the tar, still tacky in the heat, gave off an aromatic smell that obliterated the dank odours which prevailed elsewhere. He had also repainted the shed dark bottle-green. It must have been a particularly hard

84

and quick-drying paint, unaffected by the rays of the sun which beat directly on to the front of the shed. For butterflies kept settling on the glossy planks on either side of the doorway, the frantically brilliant butterflies of an Indian Summer. At one point Hugo counted no less than five of them: two cabbage whites, the colour of clotted cream, their wings abnormally thick with powder: two gaudy Red Admirals, and a peculiarly beautiful butterfly with markings like those on a peacock's tail-feathers, which Hugo had never seen in his garden before and whose name he did not know. For a few minutes they hung motionless, as if they had been pinned there.

Whereas the Sergeant had grown thinner during the past few months Mrs Palfrey had become stouter. The spots on the pinafore which she wore over her dress in the garden seemed interminable: her legs in the brown woollen stockings had swollen to twice their former size: the ankles had practically disappeared: the bunions seemed to have grown too, bulging through the thick felt of her bedroom slippers. Her cheeks looked enormous, purplish across the cheek-bones, a grainy white beneath: her eyelids and the deep circles under her eyes were black and yellow like bruised pears, the pores as big as blisters. Her breath came in short gasps, as if she were snatching at the air. Her body exuded a sense of terrible, overwhelming fatigue. But she managed to give Hugo a lop-sided smile.

"They'll get up to their tricks again if we don't get started!" she said, pointing her wavering stick in her husband's direction. She took a deep breath, then called out, in a slightly louder voice: "Give them weeds what for!"

"Yessir!" Sergeant Palfrey called back, executing a little skip, and began wielding the hoe again. "Don't miss that chickweed there!" Mrs Palfrey cried, "it's skulking behind them lettuces! ... Ah, just look at that thistle over there, up to 'is tricks again! ... Look out, that dandelion's trying to give you the slip!"

"Well done!" she said, a moment later, as her husband rescued a row of beetroot, "My, they're looking quite chipper now!'" speaking in an indulgent tone of voice, as if they had just finished up their puddings or swallowed their opening medicine. And a little later, when her husband uncovered another plant that had been fallen under the weight of weeds, "Tha ... at's it—you'll do nicely now!"

In the intervals of her exhortations, she leaned forward in her wheel-chair and clipped at the arc of grass in front of her with a pair of long-handled shears. "Never thought I'd see the day when I'd do me work sitting down!" she told Hugo.

But Hugo was not listening. He had seen a head above the yew hedge, some two hundred yards away, as if propelled by a rocket, hang poised for a second, and then disappear just as suddenly. Half a minute later the phenomenon was repeated—and Hugo remembered Roger, astride his springy branch, rising up and down in his stirrups.

"I'll be back in a minute," Hugo told Mrs Palfrey. He retraced his steps through the rockery, across the kitchen garden, along the narrow path that skirted the yew hedge, and back to the apple tree. Roger lowered himself into his saddle and looked down at him warily.

"Wouldn't it be better," Hugo said, "to find out for certain?" Roger checked himself in another upward movement. He stared at Hugo unbelievingly. "How did you know?" the boy muttered.

"I have to," Hugo told him, somewhat cryptically. "I can't help it." With a rush Roger came scrambling down the rope that hung from his perch. In a rush, too, he began to speak. "I did it," he said, "it was my fault. I hid behind the water-butt, and I waited for her: when she was close I jumped out at her. No! It wasn't a joke, it wasn't a game—I enjoyed it, I wanted to frighten her! And she didn't say anything, she didn't scream! She wasn't even looking at me! She just grunted, and fell over, slowly, like a pile of bricks, toppling...."

"Look," Hugo said, "Mrs Palfrey had a stroke. People don't get strokes because they've been frightened, but because they are old and their arteries get clogged up."

86

"I know all about that," Roger said, roughly, "but I can't be sure! ..."

"Then you'd better come and talk to them," Hugo told him. Roger stood staring at his feet. "Oh, all right!" he said after a moment, in a peevish tone of voice, and then almost with a sneer, "You've got a guilty secret of your own, after all!"

"Yes," Hugo agreed, "we are in much the same boat." Immediately Roger's manner changed again. "Come on!" he said, "let's get it over with!" He led the way to the path that skirted the hedge. "Now I'll do something for you," he said, as they walked through the rockery. "When are you going to let out ... that wine in the cellar?"

"When you've all gone," Hugo told him.

"All of us! Do we have to go?"

"You'll have to, eventually."

"Has the house been condemned or something?"

Hugo reflected for a moment. "Yes, you could put it like that."

"Then you'll have to go too!"

"I'm condemned as well!"

"You?"

"Yes, to be here, in this house, alone...."

"Alone? But there's the wine in the cellar!"

"Oh, yes, of course! I mean alone except for that."

As they approached the Palfreys' allotment Roger hung back for Hugo to take the lead. The Sergeant was working close to the square of lawn.

"Turn 'em out! Turn 'em out!" Mrs Palfrey was telling him as he applied himself to another clump of weeds. "That's it! Give 'em a piece of your mind!" The black rings under her eyes had deepened: her lips had a bluish tinge: exhaustion was a huge weight, moulded to her body, pressing down on her from every angle, forcing her to the ground: she gasped under the pressure: but defiance still flickered in her eyes.

The Sergeant meanwhile had broken into a cracked, rasping song: " 'Good-bye Dolly, I must leave you... !' " He prodded away with his hoe in time with the music.

"Them young cabbages," Mrs Palfrey said to Hugo,

"they're looking poorly: plenty of fresh air and a nice drink of water, that's what they need." Then catching sight of Roger, "Hello, sonny, I expect you'd like a biscuit, eh? Go and get the tin."

Roger regarded her with surprise, but he went into the shed and returned a moment later carrying the tin with the portraits of their one time majesties George and Mary on the lid.

" 'Though it breaks my heart to go!' " Sergeant Palfrey was singing.

Roger placed the tin on Mrs Palfrey's lap. She tried to take the lid off, but before she could prevent it, the tin slid off her apron and on to the ground. Roger watched the ineffectual scrabblings of the hand with horrified fascination. Hugo retrieved the tin and opened it. "Go on," Mrs Palfrey said to Roger, "help yourself. You always like them chocolate ones, don't you?"

Roger stared at her. "Don't you remember?" he said.

"Remember what?"

"The last time I was here."

"No. Should I?" Mrs Palfrey looked puzzled. "My memory's not what it was...."

" 'For your king and your country need you so!' " Sergeant Palfrey finished the verse and stood for a moment, leaning on his hoe.

Roger looked at the biscuit tin and put his hands behind his back. He swallowed, then burst out in a challenging, almost hectoring voice:

"I hid behind the water-butt there. I jumped out at you...."

"Did you now?" Mrs Palfrey interrupted him: she gave him a shrewd glance. "Gave you a proper fright, I expect," she said. "Sorry I didn't see you, son. Not that I could have done anything about it. I'd been feeling funny ever since I got up that morning."

" 'Good-bye, Dolly, I must leave you,' " Sergeant Palfrey began again.

Mrs Palfrey held out the tin. Roger chose a biscuit and began to eat it, slowly, taking very small bites and chewing carefully. Mrs Palfrey steadied the tin on her lap with her good hand and raised the other to push back a wisp of stray hair. The hand fluttered in front of her face blindly, like a bat. Roger leaned forward and guided it to the right spot.

Hugo's face was as bland and unmarked as ever, but something was happening to him. The day he both longed for and dreaded was, he supposed, getting closer: soon he would have to come to a decision—letting the long past out and the small future in. In the meantime he could feel something growling inside him, like a train that had just entered its last tunnel. Even his little traditions suddenly seemed to have lost their force: he took to wandering round the house (the Indian Summer had ended in raw, damp fogs, like burnt brown paper) every two or three days: it was in his house, after all, that he could best observe the symptoms of internal change.

The tenants didn't like it at all. Some of them, assuming the first of the month must have come round again, absent-mindedly asked him for receipts for their rent, as custom dictated and he just as absent-mindedly gave them. A few were so put out that they gave notice and left. All were put out in one way or another: if it had not been for the fact that the electric shaver still purred as regularly as ever at the appointed times there might have been a general exodus—at any rate among the better-off tenants.

His unexpected return halfway through the month, to the "upper regions" (even though he did not take the Gladstone bag—and had discarded the handcuffs) produced consternation of a different kind. As he progressed along the maze of corridors and passageways, doors to left and right of him were flung open and strange faces peered out. Shadowy—and as far as he was concerned, equally strange—shapes scurried past him, or, at his approach, stared, and fled. The window leading to the fire-escape was open, and looking through it Hugo saw several figures rapidly descending. It was like a French farce or a scene from a Marx Brothers' film.

89

The presence of strangers did not in itself surprise him. He had long been aware that the tenants of this upper floor took in lodgers, on a casual basis, or gave shelter to a motley collection of refugees. He made no attempt to turn them out. All those who came to his house, he felt, had as much right to be there as he had himself: if the house chose to admit them, there was nothing he could do about it. He could do no more than trust to luck and take a few sensible precautions. As far as his "upper regions" were concerned—the vast majority of the occupants had so far given little trouble and had profited in one way or another from their sojourn under Hugo's roof. Those who had failed to do so in too spectacular a fashion were sent packing, together (if they happened to be casuals) with the regular tenants who had harboured them—and the rooms vacated were promptly locked, thus adding to the accumulating rows of keys on the green baize board behind glass doors in a corner of Hugo's office.

As for the "precautions"—he had of necessity devised a certain code of conduct. He would not, for example, condone the more obvious or demoralizing forms of drug-taking: a man who had spent so long waiting to live was not likely, after all, to approve of artificial stimulants. While, too, he never reported anyone to the police, except in cases that were absolutely unavoidable, or where failure to do so would jeopardize the house as a whole, he co-operated with them to the best of his ability (and within reason) if they sought his help. It could not be said that Hugo ran an orderly house; but he had, on the whole, justified his policy of trusting to luck. There had been a few wild parties and a few conflagrations, all of them quenched without too much difficulty; a few small-scale police raids; a couple of minor stabbings (hushed up and dealt with on the spot —Hugo, of course, held the Advanced Certificate of the St John's Ambulance Brigade); half a dozen or so abortions (the Certificate came in handy here too); and the occasion when Mr Smith had suddenly become violent and taken to smashing windows and doors, until Hugo took him in hand. It was on the latter occasion, that

Hugo had had the double set of doors installed at the top of the stairway leading to the "upper regions" (green baize on the outside, solid oak on the inside) and had also had soundproofing inserted into the ceilings—the respectable tenants, after all, also belonged to the house and they, too, had their rights.

The service Hugo had rendered Mr Smith was only an extreme example of the function he fulfilled in some measure for all his tenants. It would not be easy to say whether it was Hugo's face, figure or personality which qualified him in this respect. The face which looked as if time had written nothing whatsover upon it was the kind of face which you imagine when you first encounter it—with feelings of relief, cosiness and even a kind of retroactive nostalgia—that you have known all your life and which you will never forget, whereas in actual fact it slips out of memory like a pat of butter down the throat if you so much as go into the next room—though when you see it again, there it is: you know it as well as your own face in the mirror. In the same way, an absence of the shortest duration melted all recollection of the rotund, handy body, like a snowman melted in the sun. And his personality had the same amorphous quality. For his tenants that is: Hugo knew that he had a personality and even a future and a destiny locked away in the basement—but for his tenants he was variously a rubbing-post, a lamp-post, a salt-lick, a pillow or a teddy-bear, and these, he knew, were facilities which are in demand only at the proper time and in the proper place: he was not therefore, surprised that his present erratic and unpredictable behaviour imposed such a strain upon his tenants.

As he continued now along the corridor of the "upper regions" he heard a scrambling noise behind him, and, turning, saw two escapees converging simultaneously on the open window that led to the fire-escape. The taller of them, a thin young man in bell-bottomed trousers, Castro-type whiskers, steel-rimmed spectacles, and a long, gaucho-type waistcoat fringed with what appeared to be very ancient boas, was the first to get a bare foot on to the topmost rung. Behind him a girl waited impatiently for him to descend a few rungs. As she scrambled through the window her foot caught on the grill, and one of her sandals fell off. She hesitated a moment, glanced down at the young man, now making rapid progress (despite the bare feet) then at the sandal, then at Hugo, who had retraced his steps and was interestedly watching the young man's almost seamanlike dexterity on the narrow iron rungs of the fire-escape. Deciding, apparently, that the inconvenience of losing a sandal outweighed that of facing Hugo the girl climbed back into the corridor—though as he regarded the scrap of thin leather, cracked across the middle and as limp as a dirty dish-cloth, Hugo could scarcely feel flattered.

"You've caught me," the girl said calmly. "So what?"

"Wouldn't it be more convenient to leave in the ordinary way?" Hugo inquired politely, "by the door, down the stairs, and out of the front door—or by one of the back doors or side doors if you preferred it?"

The girl considered the proposition.

"On the face of it," she conceded, "yes. But someone shouted 'fuzz!' and we decided to beat it. A reflex action, I imagine."

"Is there any reason why you should be afraid of the fuzz?" Hugo asked, eager to show off his command of the argot of the upper regions.

"None that I know of," the girl replied. "But you don't stop to analyse a reflex action, do you?"

"I suppose not," Hugo agreed. He was aware of a strange sense of kinship. He looked at the girl more carefully. The extraordinary get-up had so far discouraged him from doing so, as if, like the protective colouring of certain plants and insects, it had been expressly designed for that purpose. But now, emerging like a spirit photograph out of a murky background, composed of a dusty, ankle-length black skirt, a plum-coloured cardigan riddled with holes, a jangling assortment of waist-length necklaces, chains and rosaries, a length of fur (round the neck) that looked like a polecat run over by a steamroller, a resurrected granny's shawl, hair like the stuffing of a scarecrow, and a moth-eaten green felt hat like an inverted soup tureen, with floppy edges

92

reaching to the shoulders (and a brighter band of green round the crown where a ribbon had once been) appeared the outlines of a slender, girlish body, a small, silvery-pale face, and a pair of large, very bright grey eyes. To Hugo's astonishment the sense of kinship now resolved itself round the ship-shape, orderly part of his being. Suddenly the explanation presented itself, as his eyes alighted on the girl's hands: they were clean and well-kept, with pink finger-tips and neatly trimmed nails. She felt his eyes upon them, closed her hands and retracted them into the ample sleeves of the cardigan. Glancing downwards, however, Hugo saw that the feet— one in its exiguous sandal, the other still bare—though far from clean, were also carefully tended, with properly cut nails instead of the horny excrescences usually cultivated by the young, about which, being a romantic soul, Hugo was particularly squeamish. The girl raised an eyebrow, and gave him a quizzical, lop-sided smile.

"Sharp, aren't you?" she said. "Putting two and two together?"

"You have parents?" Hugo asked.

"People do."

"Yes, but, I mean..." Hugo floundered.

"I've passed the age of consent, if that's what you mean," the girl volunteered.

"I was thinking rather of the age of self-support," Hugo said.

"Well, I did do a job."

"Let me see," said Hugo, looking at the toe-nails again (the hands still being out of sight). "Something not at all messy..."

"Like me, you mean?"

"Well..."

"Lovely, isn't it?" She withdrew her hands from the sleeves of her cardigan and shook herself, looking down admiringly as all the fringes, loose ends, and necklaces swayed to and fro. "Lovely, lovely squalor! But do go on with your quiz."

"Something ... quite orderly," Hugo said. "Dressing windows at a little boutique in Chelsea ... arranging flowers in an arcade in Knightsbridge—or" (growing quite excited as he followed the trail) "arranging books on shelves in a little shop in Greenwich—slim volumes of poetry...!" Then, recollecting that this is an imperfect world, he sighed and said: "Arranging files—I suppose that would be more likely?"

"Well done, Fido! Yes, you've sniffed that out—I used to work in an office," she said, fishing for the dropped sandal with her bare foot, finding it, and curling her toes up inside it.

"You didn't like it? Office work, I mean?" Hugo asked.

"Oh I didn't mind the job itself! As a matter of fact I was rather good at it. But then, you see, they moved us into one of these modern, healthy, air-conditioned, centrally heated glass houses, with wall-to-wall carpeting. swivel chairs, drawers that slid out like oiled eels, and electric typewriters that didn't make any noise and started working if you so much as picked your nose...."

"That was no good?"

"It was hell! I didn't mind that poky old office in the mews off the Charing Cross Road—but, God! have *you* walked round the new City Beautiful? You feel like something under a slide—inside the buildings or out of them! ... That poky little office, now ... you had to hang your coat and umbrella in a cupboard along with the tea things ... nobody gave a damn if you kept your make-up, and your love letters and a box of chocolates or a couple of half-nibbled sandwiches, say, in the drawers of your desk ... and you could brew up on the gas-ring whenever you felt like it."

"But wasn't *that* rather messy ... inefficient?"

"I used to get twice the work done there in half the time.... Do you know, in the chromium-plated morgue you had to go into a separate room to smoke; you could only get a cup of tea in the canteen; you couldn't pee in the loos because they had the atmosphere of deep-freeze plants (in spite of the central-heating); you had to put all your odds and ends in a special locker; and when you left your desk had to be as bare as a baby's bottom!"

"And so," Hugo said, knowingly, "you opted out?"

"Opted out?" the girl replied, scornfully. "Opted in, you mean! What was there to opt out *of*?" She shook

94

herself again and raised her arms. "Oh this lovely, crazy *mess*!"

"And how do you live now?" Hugo asked.

"Oh, I get along," and then, mockingly, " 'consider the lilies of the fields' ... or, if you prefer it, 'not a sparrow falls'—etc. etc."

"Your father's a clergyman?"

"How *did* you guess?"

"Well, *where* do you live?"

"Mostly here... But that's a damn fool question, under the circumstances—and in any case, what business is it of yours?"

"I'm sorry," Hugo said, apologetically, "but you see, I'm the landlord!"

"What! A filthy slum racketeer!"

"This house isn't a slum!" Hugo protested indignantly. "We do our best..."

"And as a matter of fact," Hugo coughed modestly, "I'm the owner as well...."

"A filthy capitalist! A member of the propertied classes!"

"Oh, come now! You flatter me!"

"As a matter of fact, you don't look like a landlord or an owner...."

"What do I look like?" Hugo asked, eagerly.

"A caretaker."

"Oh," Hugo sighed, disappointed. "Well, I suppose I am in a sense...."

"Still," the girl said, "I grant you that you had the right to ask a few well-chosen questions. Have you finished?"

"Where 'here'?"

"It's a clumsy question, but I think I follow ... I live here and there—mostly with Smith at the moment...."

"*Mr* Smith?" Hugo asked, aghast.

"I always call him Smith. Lovely squalor, yum! yum!"

"Oh well, I'm sure it's very good for Mr Smith," Hugo said, and having no idea how to conclude the conversation hurried on.

Mr Sturmer was at home, and Pat was with him.

"We were waiting for you," Mr Sturmer told him. "Why have you been so long, Hugo?"

"But your rent isn't due for a couple of weeks!" Hugo pointed out.

"What's the rent got to do with it?" Mr Sturmer demanded, shifting himself gingerly as the guitar prodded his back. "Why do these people *always* have to think in terms of money?" he demanded of Pat.

She shrugged her shoulders. She was wearing the same clothes as when Hugo had first been introduced, except that she had put on a new white chiffon scarf: she smelt as if on this occasion, too, she had just come from the bathroom: her thigh-length boots were freshly polished: her hair was piled up even higher than before, like moulded candy-floss: her make-up had been applied with particular care: the spot was completely obliterated.

Mr Sturmer, too, was partly washed: he had also put on a clean white shirt, the collar only slightly defaced by blood from a squashed pimple, and a new neck scarf: he had also bought a new Spanish-type bandolier for his guitar.

"I beg your pardon," Hugo said, humbly, "I shouldn't have mentioned the rent...."

"Forget it, man! Forget it!"

"The point is," Pat intervened, "we want you to do something for us."

"Yes?"

"Yes!"

"Well..."

"Will you or won't you?" Pat demanded.

"Couldn't I perhaps be told what it is first...?" Hugo ventured.

Mr Sturmer and Pat exchanged pitying glances. There was a pause. "Look," Mr Sturmer continued at length, "I'll put it in words of one syllable—will you marry us?"

"What?"

It was not often that Hugo's tenants succeeded in surprising him.

"What's biting you?" Pat asked, at the end of an even longer pause.

96

"Isn't it—well, isn't it rather unusual?" Hugo suggested. The "empathy" with the young on which he had so prided himself seemed to be rapidly evaporating.

Mr Sturmer and Pat began to laugh.

"Don't tell me you were going to suggest a *church*?" Mr Sturmer said.

"No, no! I wasn't thinking of that *old jazz!*" Hugo replied in a desperate attempt to regain his footing.

"Or a Registry Office?" Pat said, accusingly.

"Well ... I thought that ... perhaps nowadays...?"

"Rubber-stamped by the State! Is that what you think of us? I'm asking you man—is *that* what you want?" Mr Sturmer was even more angry.

"Oh no, no, of course not!" Hugo reassured him. "But you see ... well, I don't quite understand ... I mean ... well, 'is your journey really necessary?'" Hugo laughed wildly, remembering too late that he had reverted to the idiom of another era altogether. He had, however, been construed.

"Yes, it *is* necessary—for us!" Pat told him, in quite a different tone of voice.

"Nothing hymeneal, I take it?" Hugo said, still slightly hysterical: to his surprise this, too, was apparently understood.

"It's a little late for *that!*" Pat said, with a touch of asperity in her voice, which made Hugo feel that he was being reproved as a dirty old man. "But still, we feel we'd like *something....*"

"We've gone everywhere, and done everything," Mr Sturmer explained. "Now we want to—well, sort of *seal* it...."

"And we think—on the whole—that you're the right person to do it," Pat added.

This time Hugo really was flattered. He was also beginning to pull himself together. He remembered Prěserěn. More practically, he remembered that those tenants who had not taken him for a Middle European refugee poet had assumed he had once been a sailor—and, after all, ships' captains were entitled to perform marriage ceremonies, and it did not need too great a stretch of the imagination to see Hugo's house as a kind of ship pitching at anchor on London's tide. So he hitched up his trousers, and walking with a slight nautical roll, advanced to the centre of the room. He beckoned imperiously to Mr Sturmer and Pat, who followed him with surprising alacrity. He only had the vaguest recollection of the Christian marriage service, and in any case he did not wish to offend the susceptibilities of his new-found flock. For a moment he panicked again: seeing a small red book lying on the table he snatched it up, opened it at random and began to read: "It is the view of Chairman Mao that..." He was checked by an exclamation of disgust from Pat. "Really!" she cried.

"Look, man, you do *your* thing—and let us do ours!"

"Surely you haven't lost *all* sense of decency!" Pat cried. Hugo swallowed—but then suddenly inspiration came. He imagined that he *was* Prěserěn, and began to deliver an impassioned chant, full of the faded, romantic imagery of a bygone age. Gradually a peaceful, sleepy expression stole over the faces of his communicants. When he had exhausted the rosebuds, garlands, nightingales, bosky glades, nymphs, shepherds, shepherdesses, oaten pipes and roseate dawns, and run through all the names of classical deities he could remember, he brought in reserves of half-remembered passages of poetry, snatches of song from the days of his youth, quotations—more or less correct—from Buddha, Confucius, Lao Tse and the Vedantic philosophers, which somehow lingered over from an *Anthology of the World's Wisdom* he had been presented with as a boy, and (when all else failed) philosophical snippets from the *Reader's Digest* and mottoes from Christmas crackers. Hugo was quite carried away by his improvisations, and from the set, solemn expressions on the faces of Mr Sturmer and Pat it was evident that he had succeeded with them too. From time to time Mr Sturmer struck a chord on his cracked guitar: its assonance, no doubt as a result of the increasingly oriental provenance of Hugo's discourse, seemed perfectly in keeping.

Hugo was, however, at a loss how to bring his peroration to a suitable climax, and again panicking slightly,

98

he allowed more traditional elements to penetrate it.

"If there are any here, being of sound body and mind," he said, groping for the words, "who know of any just cause or impediment" (skipping a section) "let him speak now or forever hold his peace!" In the gathering dusk Mr Sturmer and Pat gazed round them, half truculent, half fearful. Hugo allowed the pause to extend to a good half minute. Then he made a peremptory gesture: immediately, as if they had rehearsed the scene half a dozen times, Mr Sturmer replaced the guitar at his back and took Pat's hands in his. Hugo swelled his chest. "By the authority invested in me," he said; then, changing his mind: "according to your most grave and solemn request, and the office which I have (not lightly or irreverently) undertaken I hereby pronounce you man and wife!" The bandolier round Mr Sturmer's shoulders suddenly snapped, and the guitar fell with a jangling clatter to the floor. Mr Sturmer and Pat still stood holding hands and gazing into each other's eyes. "And now," Hugo commanded, his forefinger raised aloft in a token of benediction, "you may kiss each other!" Mr Sturmer and Pat complied with the utmost docility.

"'Oh, for the wings of a dove!'" Hugo sang softly as he continued his rounds of the "upper regions", walking now not so much with a nautical roll as an episcopal waddle. He had not only enjoyed himself in his new role, he had also allayed his disquiet, and the evironment seemed to respond. He put his head round first one door and then another, and smiled: the bland features, appearing to dissolve in the haze of dust and cigarette smoke, left only a disembodied sickle smile, like that of the Cheshire cat, hovering in the doorway. And smiles floated up out of the haze in response, from every conceivable angle: from the levels of chair, bed, table, cupboard and floor, rising from the tangle of limbs, beards, tousled heads, fringes, tassels and shawls, dirty coffee cups, wine-glasses and beer mugs, laden ash-trays, scattered records: bright eyes and smiles like glow-worms and petals shining from the flank of a dark, smoky wood. A blur of beneficence and benevolence swaddled the upper regions of Hugo's house.

Cushioned on it Hugo continued his rounds. Last of all he knocked on Mr Smith's door, heard an impatient grunt which, he knew from experience, indicated that an artist within wished to demonstrate that he was too busy to be disturbed, but nevertheless wanted to provide visual evidence of the fact, and entered. His nose, which had instinctively wrinkled in self-defence, relaxed in surprise: the studio really was permeated with the workmanlike smell of fresh paint and turpentine, and with another smell, fresh and invigorating, which he could not place.

Mr Smith was seated at his easel, in his painter's smock, a palette and cluster of brushes in one hand, like a lop-sided coat of arms. His long, white fingers, with black caterpillars of hair along the backs, shook like those of an alcoholic, but somehow in the fraction of a second before the tip of the brush touched the canvas, they steadied. The black, lack-lustre eyes were fixed on the canvas; when he lowered them again to the palette, the lids came down like tiny shutters.

Seated, nude, on a stool to the left of the easel was the girl Hugo had encountered in the corridor by the fire-escape. The fair, shoulder-length hair was still spiky and unkempt; her legs were tucked under her disclosing the orange and grey soles of her feet; but the rest of the small body looked and smelled like a freshly peeled chestnut.

"Hullo!" she said, recognizing Hugo. Then, feeling his eyes on her, she gave a lop-sided grin, and glanced demurely at her body. "It's Art," she said. Mr Smith raised his head from the canvas and studied her intently; she shivered; goose-pimples appeared on her thighs. Slowly, as if carrying water in the cup of his hands, Mr Smith transferred his gaze back to the canvas—where the outlines of one of his lumpen peasant women were beginning to appear.

Hugo was so unexpectedly—and, he could not help reflecting, illogically—cheered by his encounter with Mr Sturmer and Pat that he felt strong enough to contemplate keeping his promise of a return visit to Mr Skidmore. On the way he was obliged to pass the Proudfoots' apartment. It was the scene of feverish activity. The doors were open and a small army of removals men were carrying furniture and dozens of tall crates, like upturned coffins, labelled "Handle With Care: This Side Up"—the latter, presumably, containing the Colonel's relics, specimens and trophies: indeed the tail of the cayman protruded from the corner of one of the crates, where several of the planks had been removed, swathed in corrugated cardboard. Another small army were carrying furniture and crates in; these in marked contrast to the outgoing ones which, impregnated with dust, formalin and Eunice, exuded a resinous, linseed odour. Yet a third army of workmen were busy inside the flat, stripping and fumigating the walls, burning off the paint and scouring the floor-boards. Of the Proudfoots, of course, there was no sign. The television and film series had, once more, been a tremendous success: the natural deficiencies of Arnold's film-making had been even more brilliantly exploited by a new psychedelic producer, who was also an ardent follower of Marshall McLuhan, and the sepia flickerings had proved compulsive viewing to young and old alike. The vogue for the old silent movies had no doubt helped. Arnold's films were written about enthusiastically by the critics of the high-brow Sunday papers. His narration—or rather, presentation—carried out entirely by means of facial gesture and dexterous play with a pointer—won special praise for its "mimetic originality". His face, in one or another of its manifestations, had become one of the best-known in the nation, gazing down from hoardings and appearing hourly in television commercials, in connection with a wide variety of consumer products, from patent medicines to male cosmetics—and even Mr Skidmore's dog-foods.

Hugo was not surprised by all the activity, and he did not enter the Proudfoots' flat: he knew they had already left and the new occupants would arrive, as they always did, in due course. Nevertheless he resumed his journey with some reluctance. Reaching Mr Skidmore's door he raised his hand and gave a knock which he hoped might be inaudible. But immediately Mr Skidmore's voice barked back: "About time!" Hugo sighed, and entered.

Mr Skidmore was sitting in exactly the same spot and in exactly the same posture, gazing into the blank television screen. Hugo wondered, indeed, whether he had left his chair at all since he had last called on him—except that Mr Skidmore was freshly shaved, though even that was not conclusive, for his jowls looked red and raw, as if he had scraped off the stubble with whatever instrument lay to hand, his penknife, say, or a bit of glass from a broken tumbler. He did not look up as Hugo crossed the room and even before he was seated, he resumed his monologue at the point he had left off.

"Mitzi was a stray," he announced. "She just turned up one day, out of the blue. Nobody had seen her about the neighbourhood, and nobody knew where she came from. Then one morning we woke up, very early. 'Can you hear it?' Matilda said ... We slept in single beds, by the way—rather nice ones, I must say, with tall quilted head-pieces and gold bedspreads (little lamps on bed-side tables, too; all that sort of thing) ... as a matter of fact I could tell you quite a lot about that bed-room...."

"Poor old Mitzi!" Hugo interposed cunningly, hoping to push the needle into the next groove. Mr Skidmore jerked as if he had been shot.

"Are you suggesting that we maltreated that cat?" he demanded truculently.

"No, no!" Hugo assured him hastily. "A manner of speaking, that's all."

"I should bloody well think so!" Mr Skidmore said. "... Anyway, when Matilda said 'Can you hear it?' I sat up in bed. To tell you the truth I couldn't hear a thing. I switched on the light at the side of my bed (it was a pretty lamp—had a pink shade of some sort of pleated stuff) and looked at my watch (never believe in wearing a watch in bed—the sweat gets into the works—did you know that?). It was five o'clock. I was just going to cut up a bit rough (well, it was early) when I *did* hear it! A very thin, high-pitched kind of sound—very plaintive, if you know what I mean—it was Mitzi's special sound as a matter of fact: never known another cat miaow quite like it...."

Mr Skidmore again stopped abruptly. He sat very still for several seconds, his head cocked on one side.

"It stopped after a bit," he resumed, throwing an odd, crooked look at Hugo. "We didn't think any more about it, and went back to sleep. Then when Matilda got up an hour or so later and went downstairs to bring in the milk—there was Mitzi sitting beside it, sedate as you please! She trotted after Matilda into the kitchen, her tail in the air (there was so much fur at the end of it that it looked as if she was waving flags!). She went straight over to a corner, just as if that had always been her special place (I was downstairs now, by the way) and looked up at Matilda as if to say: 'Well, what about it?' So of course Matilda gave her a saucer of milk. When she'd lapped it up she squatted down, stuck her back legs up in that funny way they have, and began cleaning her belly. Damned if I know why! The fur was already as white as snow—long and silky, just like mohair... Lick, lick, lick, she went, and then, nibble, nibble, nibble, as she went for a bit that had got knotted. Lick, lick, lick and nibble, nibble, nibble, and all the time purring away like mad! When she was licking the straight bits the purring would be a kind of even hum, like a dynamo; then when she was worrying the tangled bits (have you ever noticed, by the way, how lovely and pink the flesh is between the fur? ... Mitzi's was anyway) well, then the purring would come in bursts, as if someone was pressing up and down on her chest (you know, artificial respiration or something like that) ... As a matter of fact the kids had a funny name for it—'Mitzi's *rusty purr*' they called it—trust them to hit on something unusual like that! ... I've never heard a cat purr quite like it!

"Oh, by the way, don't jump to the conclusion that Mitzi was white all over—only on her belly, between her legs, on the backs of her paws, and on her throat and chest—a great sweep of white there, like those long beards you see on old men who are good at keeping themselves clean ... though the children had a special name for that too: they called it 'Mitzi's surplice!' Good, eh? ... And you should have seen the antics she went through to get her throat clean! She'd sort of bend her head back and then make stabs and darts at it with her tongue sticking out as far as it would go, for all the world like a snake striking! Yes, and purring away all the time! ... But apart from that she was all the colours of the rainbow..."

"A tabby-Persian?" Hugo suggested.

"Who told you that!" Mr Skidmore said accusingly.

"You did."

"Oh, I did, did I? ... Well, yes I suppose you *might* call her that: except that she had long orange streaks: well, not just orange: some of them were rust-coloured, some tawny, some almost yellow, like a primrose, and some of the streaks were such a deep orange colour that I don't know *what* you'd call it. But the tabby part of her wasn't that common sort of alley-cat tabby—you know all khaki and brown stripes like a shaggy old comforter! There was a patch on Mitzi's back, for example, just above the tail, that was a kind of chocolate. The top of her head, between the ears ... oh yes, I'd nearly forgotten, the insides of her ears were like brown Canterbury Bells or bee-orchises! ... She had those very dark brown bars round the tail too—though round her backside the fur was a fawn colour, like fluffy camel hair...."

Once more Mr Skidmore fell silent: he gazed at the television screen so long and intently that this time Hugo began to think that perhaps it was turned on after all, but with the contrast knob so badly tuned that from the angle at which he was sitting he could not pick up the image.

But suddenly Mr Skidmore was off again.

"God, we adored that cat!" he exclaimed. "Although she was a stray we clicked at once—all of us. Even Matilda. She'd take that cat on her lap and croon over her for hours! Mitzi would sit there, her eyes half-closed so that they were little yellow slits in the fur, purring away like a kettle on the hob! But if there was the tiniest change in the sound Matilda was making—if she gave a sigh, for example, or if there was a bit of a crack in the crooning noise, Mitzi's eyes would spring open at once, and she would gaze up into Matilda's face very carefully, as if she was examining it for something, and if she didn't start the crooning again straight away, she'd stand up in her lap and take a closer look: she'd make a funny little worried mew and lick the tip of Matilda's nose or her eyebrows, or even put out her paw and dab at her face: but as soon as Matilda made the crooning noise again, she'd sink back, her eyes half-closed, all humped up, the claws in the white part of her paws going in and out of Matilda's skirt like a baker kneading dough!

"And as for the kids, they *doted* on the animal, positively doted! Of course, being kids they were a bit rough with her at times: they'd squabble over which of them should have her on their laps, or whose bed she was going to sleep on, and sometimes each of the kids would have hold of one end of the poor beast and they'd almost pull her in two! She put up with it all though. Patient! You've never seen a cat as patient as Mitzi! She knew they loved her, you see, so she'd put up with anything... Oh yes, they loved her all right! I can tell you there were times when I felt quite jealous at the way one or the other of them would hold her tight, talking to her in a singsong voice, with a kind of burning, hungry look in their eyes, as if they wanted to eat her... Sometimes I'd notice Matilda watching them as they stroked Mitzi, with a faraway look on her face—and do you know, when that happened Mitzi would somehow or other wriggle away from the kids and come over to Matilda—and then when Matilda smiled at her (I do believe Matilda doted on that cat as much as the rest of us, in her quiet way) Mitzi would jump on to her lap and start making a terrific fuss of her—purring so loud you'd think she was going to rupture herself, and rubbing her head against Matilda's cheek ... funny thing, that cat had a way of pushing her whole head, very hard, against your face, so that her ears got pressed right back and you could feel the insides of them—very cold, by the way—gave me quite a surprise, that—and you could feel the inside of her lips (very pink they were), all wet and sticky against your face, and sometimes even the edges of her teeth....

"Normally I'm a doggy man myself (not surprising really, I suppose, me being in dog-biscuits) and I don't much care for cats as a rule (not a *man's* pet, I always say). But Mitzi was different. She'd do everything about the house a dog can do. She had a whole repertoire of noises, for one thing—one noise to let you know when somebody was at the front door; another one, quite different, if the telephone was ringing.... Do you know, I can see that cat now ... in my mind's eye, of course"— and Mr Skidmore again darted an odd look at Hugo— "yes, I can see her now, trotting down the garden path with her tail stuck up in the air, giving that special telephone miaow! ... You couldn't hear the telephone ringing when you were on the lawn in that house....

"As a matter of fact, although I suppose I oughtn't to say it (and needless to say I wouldn't have dreamed of suggesting such a thing to Matilda) but I believe that cat was more attached to me than to any of the others. I expect it's this empathy thing I've got with animals. What I didn't tell you was that this house was on a corner, so that the road ran along the side of the orchard. Now, as often as not I'd come home by car—and Mitzi knew, oh she knew all right! She'd be waiting on the roof of the garage for me. But if I came by train and had to walk along the road by the orchard, well, she'd know that too! Don't ask me how! But on those days she'd come running along the top of the fence to meet me. She had a special welcoming miaow, by the way, for these occasions.... Well, when she was level with me, she would look down at me, and then drop, *slap on to the back of my neck!*"

Mr Skidmore stopped, and stared challengingly at Hugo, who, not knowing what was expected of him, adopted the cowardly device of repeating Mr Skidmore's last words: *"On the back of your neck?"*

"Exactly!" Mr Skidmore responded, looking pleased. "*Not* on my shoulders, you notice!" He stood up and bowed his head.

"Now you will observe," he went on, his voice slightly muffled, "that at the very top of my back, just where it joins the neck, there's a kind of pad or shelf of muscle—go on feel it, feel it, man!" Hugo complied: Mr Skidmore, his face scarlet from his contortions, resumed his seat, and Hugo followed suit.

"Yes," Mr Skidmore said, "I've had that pad for a long time. Don't know what caused it—might have been golf: used to play a lot at one time—and I was always most careful with my putting... It's so broad, that pad of muscle, you can balance a pint-mug of beer on top of it (full, of course—done it many a time). It's an interesting 'physiological feature', that's what it is—sorry about the specialist jargon.... Yes, I can still feel it, that little thud when Mitzi landed on that pad of muscle—I'd walk about with her perched there for hours, purring away or even spreading herself a bit and washing herself. I even used to take her for walks like it—but I had to stop that because Mitzi was terrified of traffic.... The funny thing about it, in fact, was that she was terrified of practically everything and everybody, except us. She couldn't stand strangers—she wasn't too good, if it comes to that, with friends of the family, or even with blood relatives. She wouldn't let *them* stroke her or have her on their laps, and if they tried too long she'd let fly with her claws, I can tell you!"

As Mr Skidmore again showed signs of falling into a reverie Hugo ventured another nudge. "And how did Mitzi take your moving about so much?" he asked. Mr Skidmore nodded approvingly. "A good question," he said. "You are quite right, of course—Mitzi *hated* it when we moved. We always had a terrible job with her. She was like a mad thing. Even sleeping pills had no effect. The last time was the worst of all. As soon as the removals van drew up outside she jumped up out of her basket, gave us a wild, pleading kind of look, and then let out a dreadful caterwauling sound... We all did our best to calm her down, but it was no good. We couldn't

107

even smooth down her fur: it stood up all over her body in untidy tufts—and not a single purr out of her either—nothing but that pitiful, sort of *pleading* miaow.... Honest, it gave us the willies! Then when she heard the first of the removals men come down the garden path—you know what heavy tread removals men have—she started racing about the house as if she'd swallowed mustard—up and down the stairs, in and out of the rooms. Then when the front door opened—she was off like a streak of greased lightning. We guessed she'd made for her usual place at the back of the garage, and as we weren't moving all the junk there and I'd already backed the car out and moved the odds and ends we *did* need myself, we decided that the best thing was to leave her where she was until it was time for us to go.

"Well, at last everything was loaded up and the furniture van drove away. The kids were sitting in the back of the car, hugging their dolls and teddy-bears and that sort of thing, absolutely tired out the both of them and a bit tearful—you know, the way kids get when they're tired. Matilda wouldn't come back into the house this time. It surprised me because she had always come with me before on a last look-round.

"When I got back to the car, the garage doors were open, and Matilda was calling out to Mitzi. Usually it *was* Matilda who managed to coax her out and put her into her basket—Matilda had a theory that she was the only one who could understand exactly what it was Mitzi was feeling at these times, both of them being female. Well, it didn't work this time! She kept on calling and calling, until her voice began to get hoarse and she got back into the car, then the kids had a go, but still no luck: when they found she wouldn't come *they* began to howl too, so we packed them back in the car.

"And then I had an inspiration—or rather two inspirations! It's the most astonishing thing that's ever happened to me ... I tell you, it was positively uncanny: you see, suddenly I felt as if I was right *inside* Mitzi, underneath all that fur—I tell you, empathy's nothing in it: just for a fraction of a second I *was* Mitzi. And in that fraction of a second I knew exactly what was wrong with her—she was pregnant. You're not laughing, are you?" Mr Skidmore glanced at Hugo, his red-rimmed, watery blue eyes bulging: he hurried on without waiting for a reply: his voice had become husky. "I know it sounds daft, but I'm telling you the gospel truth! In that one flash I *knew* Mitzi was going to have kittens. I could *feel* that funny restless, excitable, half-crazy state a woman sometimes gets in when she's going to have a baby. What's more—and this is what I meant when I said just now that I had *two* inspirations—in some funny way I can't really explain, I didn't feel like this as a female, but as a male! I know that sounds even dafter than the other.... Perhaps I felt both things at once, I don't know.... Anyway, at the same moment that I knew what was going on inside that furry little hide I also felt big, strong, protective, sort of—if you know what I mean? I knew that what Mitzi needed wasn't another female—but something *male*! So I began to talk to her. I was absolutely confident about it. I don't think I've ever been more sure of what I was doing. I don't know *what* I said, that didn't matter—it was the *way* I said it, and somehow my voice went very deep, and quiet, and slow—all at the same time, and I had a funny feeling as if I was pouring into it all the best part of being a man, if you see what I mean? ... I'll start getting sloppy, though, if I go on like this— 'nuff said!

"Anyway, I talked like that for several minutes to the back of the garage—not a sign of Mitzi, you see, at first— and then there was a slight movement somewhere among all the old boxes and sacks and other odds and ends, and I saw two yellow eyes gleaming out of them. I went on talking, very calmly, in exactly the same tone of voice, and the next thing was Mitzi began to crawl out. There was a clatter as she pushed a cardboard box to one side, but I paid no attention, just went on talking, talking—and she came right out and jumped up into my arms. She was trembling all over and her head kept darting this way and that, but she lay quite still. I carried her back to the car, taking care not to hurry too much. I knew it wouldn't do to put her in her basket, so I told Matilda to move over to the driver's side, and I got in beside her, with Mitzi on my lap, still talking in that very quiet, almost lazy way. Matilda drove very quietly, being careful about sudden turns and bumps in the road. I wouldn't exactly say that Mitzi had calmed down; every now and then she flattened her ears and looked round her as if she was going to go through the roof; but all the time I went on talking to her and stroking her—somehow *willing* her to understand that *I* understood! ... All about leaving the old house, and the new one she didn't know anything about, and the kittens inside her, and how she'd already chosen a place to have them and now had to find another one and was in a tizzy about it—all that kind of thing.... And you've got to believe me, she understood it all! She'd dig her claws into my thighs (they were bleeding quite badly at the end of it) and then slowly let go, with a kind of sigh; and then after a bit she began to look up at me every now and then and blink at me—have you noticed the way a cat, when it wants to show you that it likes you, gets a little chink of gold in its eyes? She was much too worried, of course, to purr much, in her usual way; all the same, from time to time she'd look up at me and give a quick sort of purr—'Prrm!' that's how it sounded—and I'll swear she was telling me she knew what I was trying to do and was thanking me for it....

"The kids in the back of the car kept very quiet: they didn't fidget or squabble, but sat forward on the edge of the seat watching us—and every now and then they'd say in a whisper: 'Dad, you're a marvel!' And even Matilda looked at me once or twice in a kind of sad, thoughtful way, almost as if she was proud of me. ... And damn it all! I was proud of myself! It was the proudest moment of my life! ... Daft, I know—just a cat—but somehow I've never done anything before or since I've been able to feel proud of in that *thorough* way, if you know what I mean.... Usually when you do something you're rather pleased about there's a nagging feeling at the back of your mind as if there was

something not quite right about it—something under-
hand, crafty, phoney—know what I mean? ... But not
that time, oh no, not that time, and that's something I
shall never forget! "

5

The calendar (the calendar of Hugo's house, that is) had reached its halfway mark. The Proudfoots had been gone a week and the Lorns had taken their place. Once again Hugo was in demand as a projectionist. He knocked at the door, and pushed it open as a husky voice from somewhere in the interior bade him enter. He braced his nostrils against the assault of a new array of odours. Even after all these years they were startled by the sharpness of the contrast. Whereas during the first half of the year it seemed that his olfactory organs, as soon as the Proudfoot door was opened, turned and raced with their tails between their legs to the farthest recesses of their caves, during the first few encounters with the Lorn tenure it felt as if they were being dragged out protesting by the scruffs of their necks. Hugo recalled a line from Shakespeare (it was perhaps characteristic that it should be rather an obscure one from one of the least-known of the plays):

One fire drives out one fire, one nail one nail...

Something of the same principle, he reflected, was at work here. All traces of the old odours of human and animal decay had been obliterated by the strong resinous smells one associates with Swedish furniture, Austrian mountain chalets, Swiss cuckoo clocks, brand new comprehensive schools and office blocks, and the pews and vestries of ultra-modern churches. The hall in which Hugo was now standing was, indeed, reminiscent of all these. The Persian carpets that had once covered the floors—silky and valuable but so engrained with dirt and grease that they had looked as if they had been used to line the inspection pit of a garage—had been removed; the wood blocks beneath had been scoured, scraped and sandpapered, then treated with some light, sticky oil. The lower walls had been panelled in light wood and treated in the same way.

Normally Hugo loved the smells of timber. The corpses of trees, he argued, were the only ones to decay with dignity, declining from one state of beauty into another (for there was no such thing as an ugly tree). Trees alone locked up within them when they died a moiety of their living freshness: only in them were the effluvia of death as kind to the nostrils as those of life. Hugo, in fact, was something of a minor expert in these matters. He had had an uncle who was a picture-framer and as a child, had spent many happy hours in his workshop. His uncle had initiated him into the mysteries of the various woods. Hugo had collected the scraps left over in the workshop and arranged them in a box, one section for the 'natural' woods and another for the veneers. He could tell at a glance from what tree a particular piece of wood derived, whether in its natural state or made up into articles of furniture and clumsily disguised under layers of varnish or phoney veneers. With most of the English timbers, in fact, he could probably have told you from which forest, wood or copse in which corner of which county they originated. He had a special affection for those English woods which have now practically disappeared from the workshops— walnut, rose, pear, and blackthorn. He loved handling wood: he had a little workshop off his office with a bench and racks of tools. The one occasion when he really felt that his identification with Prešeren was justified (completely obliterating the itch of guilt) was when he was planing wood and the shavings curled up before the blade like miniature waves, doves about to take flight— or even the delicate rhythms and images, it seemed to him, of a romantic poem. When he had planed and then sandpapered the piece of wood upon which he was working—in fact he seldom actually *made* anything: simply working upon a piece of wood was usually enough for him—he would run his fingers along it with a sense of

113

satisfied achievement. It was one of the rare sensuous gestures of a purely personal nature that he allowed himself.

He was not at all sure, however, whether it was to his eyes, his finger-tips or his nostrils that these activities gave most pleasure. To his nostrils, he suspected: they knew the various smells even quicker than the other senses: all of them as distinctive and individual as those of human bodies—but *clean* bodies, for it was almost impossible to make wood really dirty: it retained something of its freshness even under layers of mildew and fungus. Above all, perhaps, he liked the smells of sawdust—that of simple deal or plane like wheat chaff; that of oak like snuff; that of mahogany like curry powder, and so on.

These light woods of the Lorns, however, constituted the one exception to the general rule: they were too yellow and sticky and their resinous smell was somehow repulsive: they were, in Hugo's view, farther removed from the living tree than the most blotchy and water-logged stump. It made Hugo feel guilty and disloyal; perhaps, though, it was something to do with the surrounding decor. The walls above the panelling were distempered in a pale green. In place of the pots, masks, mats, baskets, beads, and remains—human or animal—of the Proudfoot occupancy were series of vastly enlarged colour photographs of groups of Africans outside churches or mission halls constructed, apparently, of exactly the same timber that lined the lower walls of the Lorns' hall. The colours were of that simple, straightforward kind that one somehow associates with ecclesiastical art—or at any rate with that of the Church of England—flat, rounded expanses of brown, black, white, green and blue, with hardly any intervening shades. The glass over the pictures seemed of abnormal thickness and shininess, like the spectacles of the short-sighted. The frames were too narrow for the size of the pictures, and they too were of a chilly, light-coloured wood. The effect of all these factors was to remove from faces and bodies all semblance of animation. The wide smiles had less meaning than the rows of dentures in a dentist's black velvet-lined show-case. It had been quite unnecessary to drape breasts or buttocks: their rounded lines were no more suggestive than those of clouds or melons, more sexless than puppy fat. Even the distended bellies of the famine cases merely guided the eye on another meaningless switchback.

The whole of the wall space at the end of the hall, where all kinds of decaying matter, animal or vegetable, had once swarmed, like the jumbled floor of a tomb just disclosed by the archaeologist's spade, was now taken up by a huge crucifix. This, too, was made of a yellowish wood, slightly tacky, evocative of King Willow rather than of the King of the Jews: the Christ that hung from it was a mere lump of shiny metal: by contrast the canisters of film standing in a corner winked at Hugo like warm, pagan gods peering out of a thicket. He picked them up, with something approaching reverence, and, both arms now loaded, pushed open the door of the drawing-room with his knee.

The transformation within was even more complete. It was the windows that always struck Hugo first. The heavy, dusty hangings of the Proudfoots, with their grease-braided tassels, had been replaced by narrow curtains of a rather thin, sack-like material, hanging very straight and dyed a neutral dark blue: they revealed expanses of glass, also very highly polished and glinting like the pebbles of spectacles, in utter contrast to the opaque panes of the Proudfoot days (when these had been visible), streaked and grimed with the London dirt to a muddy brown like that of the jungle rivers of Colonel Arnold's films. There were pictures here, too, of our Brethren in Christ beyond the Seas, but the two main walls were occupied by huge blow-ups of the Lake District of Cumberland. The range of colours in these seemed just as limited as that of the other pictures: the greens of the rounded mountain tops; the darker greens of the trees; the light blue of water; the dark blues of the strips of sky; and the black stripes of shadow —produced the flat, static effect of railway posters. At the same time they dominated the room to such an extent that Hugo had the illusion that the cold, clear windows looked out on to identical scenery: the illusion was so strong, indeed, that for a moment he wondered whether painted boards (such as one finds sometimes in underground restaurants) had been placed behind the window-panes.

Along the other walls were ranged bookcases—made of the inevitable light yellowish wood, and with shiny glass fronts, containing books and pamphlets, neatly arranged according to size, and reminiscent of the porches of churches which specialise in supporting the missionary societies. The ecclesiastical motif was reinforced by the presence of various larger books bound in soft, crinkly black leather, from which protruded purple book-marks decorated with gilt crosses, carefully arranged on side-tables—and of a light-oak lectern on which lay a large modern Bible, open at the halfway mark, thus displaying two pages of print so large, black and distinct that they might have come from an oculist's consulting room.

The only feature that vaguely reminded Hugo of the former tenancy was the presence of several African carvings: they were, however, utterly defeated by their surroundings, their hard black wood somehow reduced to the appearance of clumsy cast-iron and their strength and terror to straightforward ugliness. Far more in keeping were the light-coloured wooden bowls, each with a silver disc at the centre, engraved with a crucifix and the names of the mistress of the house and of the devout donors—which always put Hugo in two minds as to whether he should deposit a coin in them or mix a salad.

Edgar Lorn was seated in one of the armchairs—large but uncomfortable, by virtue of the wooden knobs and other protuberances. In the interval of Hugo's reluctant progress from the front door to the drawing-room he had forgotten all about Edgar. He was slouched forward in his chair, his own arms stretched clumsily along those of the chair (the knobs, presumably meant for gripping, would only have fitted the grasp of a dwarf), snoring through the ends of his ragged, nicotine-stained moustache, his head tilted forward so that it displayed the freckled, dandruff-flecked bald patch. His feet in their thick grey socks, streaked with black where he had wiped the stems of his pipes, had trodden down the edges of his carpet-slippers. He was wearing a tweed suit of a fawnish-grey colour, with a herring-bone pattern, which had once been good but was now shabby and shapeless. One of the leather patches on the elbows dangled by a thread. Other loose threads surrounded the frayed button-holes and formed a fringe round the turn-ups of the trousers. The middle button of the jacket was missing: so were several of the fly buttons, and round the whole area of the crotch were yellow stains, such as one sees on the fingers of laboratory workers. A maroon cloth waistcoat, stained with egg yolk, was buttoned up incorrectly, so that the top part stuck out like a cloche. The knot of the thick woolly tie, also stained with food, had slipped down to reveal a large collar-stud, tarnished with verdigris: the edges and wings of the stiff old-fashioned butterfly collar (itself the colour of ancient papyrus) were frayed and spotted with blood. A dirty white handkerchief, spotted with ink-stains, dangled from the breast pocket. In the cold, harsh light shed by the blues and greens of the pictures, the glittering expanses of glass, and the interminable surfaces of yellow wood Edgar seemed to be slowly, lazily disintegrating as if all the cells of his body and all the threads of his garments were mouldering into a dry scurf, the particles of which danced round him to form a kind of dusty miasma or shadow image.

When Edgar continued to snore, Hugo dropped one of the canisters on the nearest area of sticky yellow parquet. Edgar woke up with a jerk, dislodging from his lap a fat, concertina-shaped file. It fell to the floor upside down.

"For God's sake!" Edgar exclaimed, in a peevish voice, "do be careful of the Work!"

Hugo retrieved the file and handed it back to Edgar, with the solemnity he always adopted in the presence of any form of creativity, even the most slender or putative —even, indeed, the phoney, on the grounds that there had at least been a wish to father a thought. It was a tradition of long standing that Edgar was engaged on a vast fictional family chronicle that would eventually outweigh even *The Forsyte Saga* by several hundredweight, and which was always referred to as "The Work". This had been in existence ever since a reviewer, in mildly praising Edgar's one and only novel (published while he was still an undergraduate at Oxford) had advised him to try and "exercise his undoubted talent" on "a somewhat less tenuous theme".

As Edgar now took the file from Hugo he continued to hold it upside down, so that it gaped open in a series of yawns; a single sheet of paper fluttered to the floor. Hugo picked that up too, and he did not scruple as he straightened up (his curiosity about the creative processes was inexhaustible) to cast his eye over it. He saw a bold heading, executed in Indian ink, with so many flourishes and curlicues that it must have been the work of many devoted hours—it read THE PERRETT FAMILY. Beneath this heading spread a genealogical table of such astonishing complexity that it made the traditional Tree of Life pattern look like a simple monkey puzzle, descending from the dense upper foliage of our own over-populated modern times, through the stout sustaining arms of the middle years, until it came at last to rest upon the acorn of "Baron de Perrett, c. 1040—c. 1089".

"This," Edgar explained, accepting the piece of paper from Hugo, "will be placed at the beginning of each volume (in addition, of course, to a Family Index at the back)." He returned the paper to the pocket of the file tagged with the letter G for Genealogy. He laid his hand lovingly on top of the file, which, as the air from the other compartments was expelled, let out a soft "pfffft".

Hugo, intrigued as he was by this glimpse at the scaffolding of a vast literary enterprise, could not help reflecting that although it was just possible that more people in these islands had heard of Edgar Lorn than had heard of Prešeren, the latter had the edge as far as bulk of output was concerned—although he hastily and guiltily reminded himself, Edgar was still a comparatively middle-aged man.

"What you have just seen," Edgar continued, "is an

entirely new reconstruction, completed less than a year ago. In it you will find that in 1657 old Sir Compton Perrett now marries Janet Ferris and *not* her cousin Joan Percy, thus bringing in the whole of the collateral branch of the Ferris clan, and thereby enabling me to deal with the problems confronting the minor Cavalier families on their return to England at the Restoration, after their years of exile in France and the Low Countries. In turn, this will lead me into...." Edgar's voice, surprisingly deep and sonorous in quality, but with a curious double-echo, such as one finds in old church organs whose pipes have cracked, was smothered in an equally sonorous yawn. He folded his hands over his egg-stained stomach and fell into another doze, while Hugo busied himself with the projector and screen, sniffing at the canister before he removed the first roll of film, and again relishing the clean tinny smell.

There was a knock at the door. It did not arouse Edgar, and Hugo paid no attention; he knew who the visitors would be and that they would enter of their own accord. Captain Truscott and the Reverend "Ronnie" Beddoes shared a bachelor *pied-à-terre* in Hugo's house, which they occupied during their periodic visits to London, to attend the numerous conferences and committee meetings connected with their various avocations. These overlapped a good deal, for Captain Truscott (R.N. Retd.) was Warden of the Excelsior Mountain Rescue School in Cumberland, one of the main centres of the Excelsior Movement, while the Reverend "Ronnie" was Chaplain-in-Chief to the Movement. At this time of the year, which was the open season for conferences, they occupied their *pied-à-terre* for a good six weeks at a stretch. A regular feature of this annual sojourn in London was a preview of the latest film brought back by Dame Alice Lorn, the famous missionary, from Darkest Africa—as she still insisted on calling it despite the advent of neon lighting—before it was shown at the Excelsior Cinema in Regent Street and then released for general distribution up and down the country (the backers of the Excelsior Movement were more than powerful enough to ensure that it made the circuits) and, of course, at the various Excelsior Schools of Fitness and Endurance. Dame Alice was one of the governors of the Movement and therefore attended many of the same conferences as Captain Truscott and the Reverend "Ronnie". In addition they were old friends who had known each other as children in Cumberland: Dame Alice indeed frequently visited Captain "Tim" Truscott's Mountain Rescue School in connection with the showing of her films.

The two men now entered, nodding to Hugo, and stood over Edgar, shaking their heads disapprovingly. "Poor Alice!" they murmured in unison. At the mention of his twin sister's name, however, Edgar suddenly sat upright.

"Soon, soon," he said, and indicated the sofa, also stiff, hard-backed and decorated with knobs in the most unlikely places. Captain Truscott and the Reverend "Ronnie" seated themselves. They made an extraordinary contrast. At first sight the Captain did not look in the least like a former officer in Her Majesty's Royal Navy. He was small and dapper; his face far from being masterful or weather-beaten was thin, finely drawn and pallid. When you looked closer, however, you saw round his eyes a network of tiny lines, too mobile to be called wrinkles, that suggested those "long years of focussing upon distant objects" so beloved by the writers of sea stories. Since leaving the Navy he had, in fact, led a number of polar expeditions, besides achieving a reputation as a mountaineer.

The Reverend "Ronnie" looked much more like a sailor than his friend. He was a tall, broad-shouldered man of about fifty, with chestnut and blond hair, a ruddy complexion, big lips and chin, pale blue eyes under bushy eyebrows, and thick wrists covered with wiry gold hairs which looked as if they ought to have a tattooed anchor lurking among them. He smoked a short, stubby briar with strands of tobacco dangling from it.

Whereas Captain Truscott gave no clear impression as to his dress—apart from the fact that it was neat, clean and grey—the robust presence of the Reverend

Beddoes was accentuated by a very furry, light-coloured and rather loud sports jacket, startlingly set off by black clerical trousers, black "front" and an unusually wide and gleaming white dog-collar.

Edgar had fallen into another doze. Tim Truscott's eyes kept darting irritably in his direction, and his small hands made delicate clutching movements at the knees of his trousers, as if he were longing to seize Edgar by the shoulders and hustle him to the top of a mast or a mountain. His gaze alighted on the air-bulged file on Edgar's lap.

"What's that?" he snapped.

"The Work," Edgar replied, opening one eye.

"*Work!*"

Edgar opened both eyes. "The Perrett Saga," he intoned.

But Captain Truscott's eyes had glazed over. Suddenly he began to speak, the voice still sharp and incisive, but the tones somehow dreamy and far away.

"We brought off a rescue last Saturday, the boys and I," he began. "This old fellow, he'd lived in Cumberland as a boy, climbed all the mountains, thought he knew them like the back of his hand...."

Edgar paid no attention. Easing himself out of his chair he shuffled over to a filing cabinet, pulled out one of the drawers and flicked his fingers across the closely stacked cards. He raised one of them slightly and read: " 'The Operation of the Tithe System in Eighteenth-Century Cumberland.' "

"He was a fool, of course," Captain Truscott continued, unaware of the interruption. "He should have realized that one can *never* get to know a mountain completely...." At the end of each sentence he fell silent, his mouth slightly open, his eyes vacant.

"I am picking them at random," Edgar said. "Here's another—'Thoughts of Sir Humphrey Perrett on the Eve of his Execution'." He rummaged through the row of cards.

"This old boy took three of his pals to the top of Handy Tor: they were decently fit of course—self-respecting types, and this old fellow had them properly roped together. But they were getting on a bit, and they'd been living in cities for years. . . ."

"Here's another—'Colonel Fulke Perrett in the Peninsular Wars'. . . ."

"A mist came up, as it so often does—not a very thick one, you know, nothing dangerous in itself, but cold, clammy, like corpses' fingers, one of the boys said!—and of course it made the rocks slippery—the ropes difficult to hold. . . ."

" 'Dame Madge Perrett at Osborne Castle'. . . ."

"Well, on the way down one of them came a cropper. The old boy knew *what* to do—and he did his best: dug his heels in and lay back. But he couldn't hold them, and down they came. . . ."

" 'Sir Oscar Perrett and "Teddy" at Ascot'. . . ."

"One of our look-outs spotted them—we have posts manned day and night—and reported back to us. You know our system—the instructors and I form the nucleus of the rescue teams, but it's only a tiny nucleus, it's the boys form the bulk, it's the boys we have to rely on. . . ."

" 'Some Notes on the Advent of the Aeroplane'. . . ."

"These boys of mine—an absolutely new intake, came to us straight from the towns—they're mostly apprentices you know; the farthest most of them had been from the factory floor was the local park. . . ."

"Yes, a factory of the creative imagination. . . ." Edgar said.

"I beg your pardon?" Captain Truscott sat up with a jerk. Hugo, whose head had been swivelling from one to the other (he had set up the projector and screen), uncertain which should command his attention, now went over to the filing cabinet eager for a further glimpse back-stage, but Edgar blocked his view, nudging him aside with his shoulder. Disappointed, he returned to his place by the projector, as the duet recommenced.

"Absolutely inexperienced," Captain Truscott said, "never had to face a physical test in their lives. Only been with us a week. We'd hardly got them used to the 'assault course'—climbing ropes, then swinging on them to tiny platforms (we've got a sawn-off tree—excellent for the purpose), walking along rope cat-walks and poles, that sort of thing—though I *had* liked the way this new intake shaped up to it..."

"It's an entirely new method of composing a fictional *magnum opus*," Edgar said, "revolutionary, really. Every character and incident indexed and cross-indexed..."

"You should have seen the way those boys behaved! When we got to the foot of Handy Tor—blood everywhere ... bits of flesh ... bones sticking out ... groaning ... —the boys went pale, of course, but not a trace of panic—just carried on as we'd taught them..."

"Not only each separate character and incident, though, but a detailed 'provenance' for each—a network of creative meaning..."

"Picked up the bodies and laid them on the stretchers —only one of them still alive though—even picked up the bloody pieces..."

"Twenty years work..."

"One of the boys went behind a rock and spewed his heart out—but he came straight back, carried on as if nothing had happened—a skinny little runt when he first arrived..."

"A long time, I know. But what's twenty years for a task like this? You can't break entirely new ground in less!"

"It was an experience those boys will never forget. They learned something about disaster, something about pain, something about themselves.... It has changed their whole outlook on life..."

"In a month?"

"Eh?" Captain Truscott sat up with a jerk, staring at Edgar in astonishment that his dialogue had momentarily impinged on his own.

"A month," Edgar said. "That's how long your Excelsior courses last, isn't it?"

"Long enough to show them what life's really about," Captain Truscott replied. "In their towns and factories they think it's all a matter of smoke and noise and crowds of people and cafés and discotheques—then they come to us and find that life isn't muddled and mindless after all—that it's more like the countryside they've come to: mostly open spaces, often cold and often monotonous, but punctuated here and there with a sudden burst of hunger or danger or challenge or pain, like the gorse breaking into flower..."

"There's challenge here too," Edgar said, indignation muffled in a yawn.

"A man driven back on his own resources ... a few comrades ... That's when you begin to recognize the essentials. Everything else falls away..."

"I prefer the adventures of the imagination..."

"Danger—that's the catalyst! And danger—that's what we give them. Not artificially created, I mean, as in these violent sports like hunting or rugby football where the rules of the game thrust the possibility of a broken head or a broken limb down your throat, so to speak, but a way of life and an environment in which, sooner or later, danger blossoms like a flower..."

"Yes, but think of the vast tree *I'm* going to have— one day!"

"All that rushing about they do when they first arrive— the exercises, climbing ropes, swimming in the lake— they're only means to an end ... useful, of course—hardship, pain, the heart lurching—good training, good training.... But it's all a preparation for the grand moments when they come, as come they must—the moment when a boy finds himself up against it in a way he's never experienced before.... Yes, it's then that he learns what he's made of, whether he's capable of *real* decision, *real* action..."

"The creative mind, too, has its peaks and precipices..."

All this time the Reverend "Ronnie" Beddoes had remained absolutely motionless, crouched forward, hands resting on knee, his big lower lip and jaw out-thrust. So still that he did not notice a fly which had settled on his wrist, teetering precariously on the long blond hairs. It had been impossible to tell whether or not he had been listening to the others. Now he too suddenly began to speak, in a powerful baritone voice, but without moving his head or the direction of his faraway blue gaze.

"Of course I'm very industrious too," he began. "I run

a parish as well as dashing to and fro all over the country from one Excelsior chapel to another—not to mention all my other activities and all the committee meetings I have to attend ... *you* know, Tim, what a stickler I am for all the rules and observances...." Captain Truscott nodded absent-mindedly.

"'Conscientious', that's what they used to write on my school reports—and it's quite true. In my own way I too drive myself to the limit.... I'm a good organizer too. At any hour of the day I know exactly what will be happening not only in my own parish, but in every one of the Excelsior Schools..."

"Quite good with a rope," Captain Truscott interrupted.

"Yes, not at all bad am I?"

"Keep yourself fit—you can't see people's souls through layers of fat..."

"True, true, there was a time, as you know, when I used to come to at least one full course a year—mountains one year, sea-rescue the next, and so on.... Too busy now, but I still try and put in a few days..."

"Always welcome—good for the boys..."

"All those chapels—I carry them in my mind's eye, every one of them... I only have to make the slightest effort of will and I can see inside any one I choose—the white chapel at your place, Tim, which always seems to be flooded with the blue water of the tarn, and where the mountains come nudging up to the great east window with its Swedish glass, like inquisitive cattle ... the white chapel like a converted wine-cellar placed on top of the cliffs above Hartland Point ... that odd wooden arrangement like a Pullman carriage up in the Welsh mountains ... the renovated monk's cell on Staffa —and so on.... My own parish church, too, needless to say..."

He suddenly fell silent. Captain Truscott and Edgar stared at him, then resumed their own monologues— but a few minutes later the Reverend "Ronnie" also started speaking again. Hugo's head swivelled from one to the other. Now it was like watching a game of True Tennis, with the ball coming at one from all kinds of unexpected angles. Or better, he thought, it was like an operatic trio in which each of the performers was enclosed in a sound-proof glass cage—and presented with different scores. His preparations for the showing of the film now being complete he amused himself by trying to disentangle the separate motifs, watching them pop up in unexpected places, like porpoises surfacing.

"One moment of shocked experience—just one—and the whole of life takes on a shape, a form ... it's the key, the king-pin ... take it away and it's nothing but a meaningless rubble..."

"It's a long time, I agree—but it's all here, stored away..."

"I take great pains over the interiors ... I've always tried to give any place of worship for which I'm responsible a lived-in atmosphere..."

"Use yourselves, I tell them. Force your body to obey you. You must go on, I tell them, until it feels as if you're breathing barbed wire...."

"Somebody else may have to unlock its secrets ..."

"In my own church there are several devoted ladies —you know the type—they're always doing little things: polishing the brasses, scrubbing the floors, embroidering hassocks and altar cloths, doing the flowers—all that sort of thing: in fact they practically *live* there, and they're not at all keen about going back home in the evening.... You'll see one or two of them (usually they take it in turns) wandering about with a duster still in their hands even after they've got their hat and coat on, giving a last flick here and a last flick there..."

"They're all medically examined, of course, before they come to us. I know exactly how far each boy can go physically—far better than he does himself..."

"Naturally I intend to finish, but it's a gargantuan task.... There have been other family chronicles, of course, but they've all been women's magazine and 'telly serial' stuff...."

"They look quite sad, you know, when the big door slams behind them, and they always go very slowly down the path, and when they get to the lych-gate they always stop for a few moments and look back..."

"This will be the first truly *historical* series of novels—based on *real* research..."

"I never drive a boy: I'm not a hard man. I've had them weeping and pleading that they can't go on—but I've *known* they were wrong, and I've never yet had a boy who collapsed or who wasn't fitter and stronger when he left me than when he arrived..."

"As a matter of fact that last glimpse of the church at night time *is* rather special.... A beautiful church, as you know—Early English, perfect specimen, a slender spire that seems to float up through the tree tops ... and it's an odd thing, but even on quite dark nights whatever light there is hanging about—moon, stars, lights from distant houses or cars going up the hill several miles away—or even, I suppose, the trains right over at Fetlock—seems to collect in one or other of the church windows, just as if it was lighted inside: you know, a warm, red, cosy light..."

"But just think of the sweep of imagination, the sheer creative *nerve* needed to sustain such a project!"

"It's true, of course, that these old biddies all live alone... They couldn't be more helpful: not even in my own church I mean, but in my other work. I tell them all about the Excelsior chapels. I show them plans and photographs.... They study them, oh so carefully, and then give me things for them—bits of furnishing, altar cloths, vases; in fact they even arrange the flowers *in* the vases when I set out for one or other of the chapels, and I take them in the back of the shooting-brake..."

"A lesser man would have quailed long ago.... And even if I die before it is completed, my life won't have been in vain—I shall have been a martyr, a martyr to my Work!"

"You see I always make a point of setting for each one of them a goal just one step beyond what *he* thinks is his limit..."

"You men of action—you haven't a clue..."

"I do my best when I get to the chapels: put the bits and pieces round in the way the old ladies have shown me—but somehow it never seems to work. All these little

127

chapels are cold, of course: their situation and that kind of thing; but it's not that..."

"Cold, yes—no use molly-coddling them..."

"As a matter of fact I spend quite a lot of money of my own on the chapels—mostly on heating (I've a private income, as you know) but it makes no difference. I can't seem to make any of them *glow*..."

"When he's *done* it—something quite small to begin with (a few yards extra in the lake, a few seconds off the timing round the 'assault course')—when he's found he *can* take that other step, that's when he begins to live..."

"Live? I can never make those chapels really live ... no matter how many knick-knacks I cram into them. They're always cold, empty..."

"It's like an oak tree: it has to take proper root before it can begin to grow..."

"I never ask them to do anything I can't do myself. Last Tuesday I timed myself over the course—beat all the other instructors ... I'm fifty-eight next week, but I'm as light on my feet as a cat..."

"I really do try.... I'm pretty High Church, of course, so that there's always plenty going on—plenty of colour and music and incense and all that kind of thing. You'd think that would help, wouldn't you?"

"Fifty-eight next month..."

"Wherever I go I start things—confirmation classes, voluntary confessionals, Youth Clubs and all the rest of it..."

"When Alice and I were children—Sis I always call her—we used to ask each other: 'What shall we do when we grow up?' ... It was the adventurer in us, I suppose..."

"What's going to happen to me in a few years time, I sometimes ask myself..."

"The truth of the matter is—whenever I walk into a house of God, God seems to walk out..."

"All that growing and changing ... getting bigger every day ... developing ... changes, changes—*horrible!*"

"It will end one day, quite suddenly I suppose. I'll die doing something dangerous ... Perhaps my heart will burst—that's what I should like..."

128

"A terrible thing for a priest to say—terrible, terrible..."

"I don't know who hated it most, Sis or me..."

"At one time I used to console myself because my own church always seemed so snug and cosy—lived in, *used*..."

"We were always trying, Sis and I, to remember something.... We didn't know what it was and we never found it ... something we wanted to remember so that we could forget..."

"But then, one winter, by an odd coincidence my old pussies (actually there are only four of them, but it seemed more) all went sick with influenza at once..."

"Some hidden pain ... something disgusting..."

"It mightn't be like that, of course.... I might lose my co-ordination, get twisted up in one of the rope-ladders, say, or miss my footing on the cat-walk..."

"How glad we were when all that changing and growing was over!"

"Something *clumsy* ... twist my body, rupture my spleen..."

"We've always kept on the move ever since—well, one of us has ... first one then the other ... we couldn't do without each other...."

"Or fall off a mountain-top—blood and brains all over the place.... Oh God, may I not die of clumsiness."

"At first it didn't make much difference ... all that lovely lace, and the embroidery—love in every stitch..."

"If I go like that I want it to be doing something impossible ... or something outside my control—fog, a broken rope, an avalanche..."

"Perhaps it was stillness we were frightened of..."

"You can't really be lonely if you use yourself, if you seek the situations that will make you use yourself..."

"So long as the stillness is shared ... turn and turn about..."

"That's what I tell the boys every time we go out on an initiation test (a small pack, a compass, iron rations) or on a rescue into the mountains ... 'Danger binds men together', I tell them ..."

129

"Then after a bit all those damned cloths and all the lace round them seemed to wilt like flowers in the first frost..."

"A small band of men—each individual knowing himself, at last—and yet bound to the man next to him—oh not only by ropes, but by danger, crisis, pain..."

"I saw the flowers myself, by the way ... fresh practically every day ... but there was something funny even about them—the water stank..."

"My adventures, of course, are adventures of the mind..."

"The church grew cold and dark, no matter how many stoves and candles I lit..."

"As I say, the mind has its chasms and precipices too..."

"And at last I realized—it wasn't my church at all! It belonged to my old pussies!"

"Share and share alike, I always say to Sis..."

"'Courage out of fear', I tell the boys. Independence and inter-dependence ... loyalty ... devotion to duty ... make them your guiding-lines. Beyond them there's nothing, *nothing*!"

"'The still centre'—who said that? That's what frightens Sis and me most ... I wonder if that was what we were trying to remember when we were children?"

There was a pause.

"That's what prayer is," Beddoes said suddenly.

"What?"

"An incantation against chaos."

But at that moment the door was flung open with a bang and Dame Alice marched into the room. The three men jumped to their feet (Hugo was already on his, standing behind his projector like a gunner with a fuse) with expressions of intense relief on their faces. They crowded round her, grinning delightedly. Dame Alice greeted her twin brother first, kissing him lightly on the cheek and patting his left shoulder with an elegantly gloved hand, in a gesture that was both affectionate and (inasmuch as it deftly brushed away a scatter of dandruff) utilitarian. To the others she presented a smooth cheek, glowing with health—one of those cheeks which look as if it has been rubbed in snow and which makes the mouth water. Certainly the three men spent an unconscionable time over their comradely kisses, their lips wide and nuzzling, their eyes glittering as if they longed to take a good bite. Dame Alice smiled and shook herself free. She strode into the middle of the room. The cold blues and greens, even the sickly yellows, turned almost mellow in her presence. From top to toe she radiated a benevolent vitality. The honey-coloured hair, coiled on top of her head in loops and braids so neat and regular that they might have been spun off a potter's wheel, glittered as if it had been sprayed with gold-dust. She wore a suit of very soft, silvery grey material, with a strawberry-coloured low-necked blouse, which managed at one and the same time to convey an impression of brisk efficiency and tranquil femininity. The bosom had reached that stage of plump, perfectly moulded maturity that discourages liberties while still inviting the eye— and, if it comes to that, invites the old-fashioned designation "bosom". Her legs in the perfectly fitting nylons might have belonged to a model. The feet were encased in gleaming black patent leather. But it was perhaps the mouth that was the crowning glory—the lips a dewy work of art, the teeth so white and even that they must indeed have been crowned by a dental mechanic who was a master of his craft. Even Hugo found his heart missing a beat when she bestowed upon him one of her snow-and-rose smiles, at the same time slightly raising a delicately arched eyebrow.

A female metamorphosis was even more spectacular than a masculine one, Hugo reflected, as in response to the eyebrow he went over to the windows and drew the curtains—no longer tacky to the touch, though the material had a slightly oily feel as if made of particularly juicy vegetable fibres. When he returned to his place behind the projector Captain Truscott and the Reverend "Ronnie" were seated on a settee facing the screen. Edgar was standing at the lectern, which he had placed to the right of the screen, slightly behind it. It was in darkness apart from a faint glow cast by a strip of neon inserted into the top of the lectern: the Bible was still open:

Edgar's notes presumably were on top of it. Dame Alice was seated in a straight-backed chair to the left of the screen, with a standard lamp beside her, its shade tilted so that only her face was illuminated.

With the uncanny "I have been here before" feeling which he always experienced on these occasions Hugo switched on his projector. Once more the room was filled with a throaty whirring noise; a beam of light probed the darkness; images formed on the screen.

The effect, however, was very different from that produced on the last occasion Hugo had performed his office. Perhaps Dame Alice had a better camera and cameraman; perhaps, too, the fact that Hugo's apparatus had received professional attention in the interval was a contributory factor. This time at any rate there were no jerkings and flickerings and no muddy sepia wash, so that the images were not only visible but recognizable. Indeed they were so large and round and palpable, while the black was so black and the white so white, that the eyes were dazzled and their focus continually thrown into confusion. In addition there were a large number of looming close-ups, which seemed to spill over the edges of the screen and make one flinch, as if cannon balls were being rolled into the room. Everything seemed impossibly rounded and distinct. Round black bosoms, buttocks, cheeks and heads, white sickle grins and disks of eyes combined to create the impression of a cornucopia continually pouring outsize grapes, mangoes, melons, and coconuts into one's lap, but all of them drained of their natural colours and flavours.

Slightly dazed by the bombardment Hugo switched his attention from the screen to Edgar. He was delivering his commentary in a weird, cracked falsetto which no one seemed to find incongruous.

"Here you see me on the little river steamer which will take me upstream as far as Imgidu," he said. "Beside me you see M'tisa—what beautiful devoted eyes she has! Eloquent too—she cannot speak to me, of course; you will remember from my last film that the Zaba rebels had pulled out her tongue when they overran the Mission.... No doubt you also recall that M'tisa was one of the first converts I made in that remote and still dark corner of Africa...." Dame Alice's face assumed an expression of saccharine concern.

The film, now Hugo came to think of it, (and it was strange that the thought should not have struck him on previous occasions) had something of the slow deliberateness of magic-lantern slides, as if Dame Alice or her technicians had discovered a method of animating them. Certainly the pictures—and again he thought it strange that the idea had not occurred to him before—seemed to belong to the era of Livingstone and Stanley rather than to that of corrugated iron, Japanese motorcycles, and intrauterine coils.... He switched his attention back to Edgar's falsetto commentary:

"Here, too, you will see old Y'zugu—he used to be a cannibal: now he cannot keep his eyes off me...." In the circle of light Dame Alice parted her lips and curved them slightly, then raised her hand to them in a deprecatory gesture. Edgar paused: when no response was forthcoming, he cleared his throat angrily, and the others, at last recognizing their cue, broke into obedient laughter. The film continued to unroll, like a black oily river, bearing rounded tree trunks upon its surface.

"The little steamer rounds the bend," Edgar resumed. "The wash disturbs a flock of crane ... a crocodile flops into the water ... a herd of giraffe take fright, streaking along the river bank parallel to the steamer, until wiser counsels prevail (we are, of course, armed) and, wheeling, they make for the bush...." And crane, crocodile and giraffe unpeeled before the eye like pages damp-fresh from the press, oddly devoid of grace or separate identities.

"That smudge you see in the distance, to the left of the clump of palm trees,"—a close-up of the tops of palm trees, like ragged dusters, followed—"yes, that dear little smudge is Imgidu. It is a year since I was there. My heart begins to flutter...." (Dame Alice's hand flew to her bosom, which heaved twice) "How can I express the emotions which sweep over me?" (She shook her head mournfully) "Will the Zaba rebels have destroyed all that I have worked for all these years? Will the little church which we built with our own hands—M'tisa, old Y'zugu, and others like them—will it still be standing? ... Yes, I myself toiled with trowel and mortar in the heat of the African sun, to lay the foundation stone...." (And Dame Alice raised her hands into the circle of light, and slowly opened them so that the pink, beautifully manicured fingers spread out like the petals of an orchid) "And what of the little bungalow," Edgar continued, "which I loved so much—will that be spared?" (Dame Alice's eyes turned piously upwards) "It was a labour of love—and will love be rewarded? ... And now the steamer draws closer ... M'tisa and Y'zugu stand beside me ... I fall on my knees between them—they, of course, are too laden with baggage to follow suit, but you see from their rapt expressions, that they, too, are deep in prayer...." (Dame Alice raised her hands again into the circle of light, and slowly joined them, palm to palm, together) "Yes, we are praying that the Faith has survived this year of trials and tribulations, of massacre, famine, and ahem!" (Dame Alice coughed modestly) "rape.... We pray that the Word still walks among those ancient trees.... We pray that my work shall not have been in vain, that I am not returning to them as a stranger ... and yet, and yet—my flock, perhaps, are scattered, dead?" (She raised her pencilled eyebrows in interrogation) "Or worse, perhaps they have spurned the Gospel and reverted to their savage tribal gods.... How shall I be received? I ask myself (and God too, of course). With tears of gratitude and relief?" (A beatific smile stole across Dame Alice's features) "Or will my second coming be greeted with oaths and howls of pagan execration?" (The features in the arc of light flinched; the head moved from side to side, in sorrow not anger) "The steamer draws closer.... We can see now that a goodly crowd has gathered on the wooden jetty.... Our skipper takes the sensible precaution of uncovering our gun.... The crowd wavers, rallies.... It is clear at any rate that it is an *excited* crowd.... Arms rise and fall, like branches tossing in the breeze.... But are they raised in anger or in love? Do they threaten—in spite of the gun?" (Dame Alice's features quailed) "Or do they open in loving welcome?" (The beatific smile returned) "Closer, closer ... we pray ... we lick our lips.... The gun crew crouch over their weapon ... closer.... I raise my arms to Heaven" (Dame Alice's arms performed a rapid circling movement, like the arabesque of a ballet dancer) "... and now, now praise be to God, I can see ... yes, I can see that the natives are friendly!" (a variety of joyous expressions flowed across Dame Alice's face) "And now, too, I can pick out faces in the crowd, faces I remember! ... Ah, there you see dear old N'aru, and there are Tampo, B'gala and W'zigu—all members of my old congregation! ... And what is this that they hold aloft? It is the cross from our old church! Charred by fire and fretted by machine-gun bullets into a Maltese shape, but unmistakably ours! ... And now as we approach the jetty the assembled crowd began to sing ... and soon we are all singing—those ashore and those on the steamer—myself, M'tisa and old Y'zugu— the skipper on the bridge and the crew behind the gun— singing the hymn I taught my little congregation just before the Zaba rebels interrupted my work—'All things bright and beautiful'—ah with what fervour they sing!" ... There was a close-up of faces, black and white, mouths opening and shutting like those of large, rounded fish. In the arc of light, Dame Alice's head nodded authoritatively. In a cracked, wavering soprano Edgar began to sing the hymn. He frowned in the direction of the Reverend "Ronnie" Beddoes, who gave a guilty start then began singing too, in a deep rumbling bass. Captain Truscott's rusty baritone followed suit. Dame Alice's mouth, too, opened and shut, and though no sound issued from it the passion of her rendering put that of the others to shame. At the end of the first verse, how-ever, her mouth snapped shut and Edgar instantly re-sumed his commentary: the other two, their lungs already inflated for the next verse, subsided reluctantly.

"The gangplank is lowered," Edgar told them. "We hurry down it—as you see" (sternly directing their atten-tion back to the screen) "we hurry down it. The survivors of my flock rush forward. Everybody is laughing, crying, cheering.... Ah, now you see there's a bit of a fracas at the centre of the crowd—a section of it has become too enthusiastic—they are fighting among themselves as to who shall be the first to touch the hem of my ... to touch my person." (Dame Alice lowered her eyes modestly) "So ardent is the competition that the skipper and members of the crew are obliged to lay about them a little with their rifle butts, laughing good-naturedly as they do so, thoroughly entering into the spirit of the occasion.... Now they have cleared a way for me—and also for certain selected members of my congregation, who now hoist me on their shoulders—and at a kind of jog-trot—as you see, there still seems to be some trouble at the centre of the crowd—chanting psalms as they go, tears of joy streaming down their faces, they bear me to safety—or rather, I should say, towards the village.... Here, you see, we have arrived at the outskirts. These by the way are the charred remnants of the huts of the former witch-doctors and the foolish old chief who supported them. They were, of course, expelled and their confiscated property formed a heaven-sent—friends, I use the word in all seriousness—contribution towards the building of our church.... Opinions differ as to whether they perished in the bush or sought refuge with the Zaba terrorists ... and here *is* our little church! Our poor, desecrated church—or, rather, all that re-mains of it—a few charred timbers, as you see, and the lower courses of brick work.... But what is this?" (Dame Alice's face beamed in joyous interrogation) "Praise be to the Lord! My little bungalow still stands!" (Dame Alice's face was transfigured) "Praise be to Him, for He has preserved a dwelling for His sist ... for His stewardess! The upper timbers at this end, you will notice, are a little charred, but by some miracle (for that, surely, is what we must call it) the flames never took a firm hold of the rest of the building (constructed, for the most part, you will see, of a fine stone brought upstream for the purpose).... My faithful flock have patched up most of the gaps in the upper timbers, though here and there are places still fretted with bullet holes.... Triumphantly my bearers—ah, my *disciples* ... ah, my 'chosen few', carry me up the steps of

136

my dear little bungalow and on to the verandah. I stand for a moment and wave my hand." (Dame Alice's right hand appeared in the beam of light, the fingers crooked in apostolic benediction) "The crowd goes mad with joy...." Dame Alice's face was ecstatic: her eyes were filled with tears, glittering like diamanté: she dashed them impatiently away. On the screen, black, rounded shapes rose and fell, as in some frantic psychedelic ballet, indistinguishable not by virtue of obscurity but because of their very distinctness, bearing down on the eyes like Pop Art posters. Captain Truscott and the Reverend "Ronnie" watched transfixed on the edge of the sofa, the one like a small woodland animal, coiled to spring, but uncertain as to direction, the other breathing noisily through wide, hairy nostrils, as if under an anaesthetic. And Hugo was crouched over his projector, like a priest busy with the rituals of a disbanded order at a deserted shrine, himself a projector of shadows and fantasies, in a valedictory, slightly nostalgic frame of mind, aware that soon these observances—these balancing acts and interchanges, these postponements and sequels, these monologues and duets performed by proxy must all be ended. No, not nostalgic, he decided but consumed by that crushing weariness that is the prelude to movement.

The screen had darkened. "And now," Edgar's voice once more penetrated his consciousness, "we are inside the bungalow.... Observe with what loving care my comrades in Christ have striven in order to prepare an abode fit for..." (Edgar hesitated momentarily; Dame Alice modestly lowered her eyes) "fit for their dearly beloved sister.... Freshly woven rush matting on the floor"... the camera obligingly drew back ... "a few pieces of my favourite china, still unbroken" ... a close-up revealed an elegant tea set on a shelf ... "and yes! Even my books, including a Bible! Here you see old N'aru handing them to me. He is explaining that he had hidden them in the bush until the Zabas withdrew. They are still damp and mildewed, but substantially intact...." With a sudden unexpected flurry the first reel came to an end. Edgar switched on an extra standard lamp, so that Hugo could see to insert the second reel. The two watchers relaxed with a long sigh.

"Faith—in action!" the Reverend "Ronnie" Beddoes exclaimed.

"And action—in faith," Captain Truscott added.

"It makes me ashamed..."

"It helps us to understand.... Chaos is waiting for all of us...."

"Except Alice!" Edgar interposed: his voice had suddenly acquired a sharp edge to it. Dame Alice remained, stiff and motionless, her face floating in the faint glow cast by the neon tubing, like a Chinese lantern.

"The second reel!" Edgar demanded, peremptorily.

"The machine has broken," Hugo lied. Captain Truscott and the Reverend "Ronnie" gasped, in shocked disbelief. Hugo quickly gathered up his apparatus. On his way to the door he glanced back over his shoulder. Dame Alice and the two spectators seemed to be slowly subsiding, like punctured succubi. Only Edgar remained on his feet, teetering up and down on his toes, his moustaches inexplicably bristling.

"Poor Alice," Hugo heard him say as he closed the door. "You are tired. Now it is your turn to rest."

6

The Doctor had arrived. A neat and dapper man, with a burnished black head, a sallow complexion, a black, Assyrian beard which succeeded in being both curly and pointed, and sparkling black eyes. The velvet collar of the black knee-length overcoat which he wore summer and winter (only the thickness of the cloth varying with the changing seasons) never displayed even the minutest speck of dandruff—a most unusual feat where a velvet collar is concerned. On the contrary, the Doctor's collar always possessed a spotless sheen, like a seal's back. Its apparent imperviousness to human decay inspired enormous confidence and was one of the reasons why he had so many patients, and why Hugo had taken to him—though it must be admitted that in Hugo's case the Doctor's unpronounceable name and the obviously remote ethnic and racial origins it implied, had had a good deal to do with it.

These considerations had proved as reliable a guide as the more conventional ones, such as medical qualifications. Not that the Doctor did not possess these too in bewildering abundance. In the world of international psychiatry his was a name to conjure with (in more senses than one). He had written a number of very long books and was famous for a body of theory so complex and erudite, so thickly larded with newly-coined scientific terms, so rich in reference and crossreference, so full of words and phrases cited in their original—and mostly obscure—languages, because the incorporated concepts which were unfortunately untranslatable into English (or any other *lingua franca*) that for the past twenty years and more his work had been the centre of fierce debate as to its correct interpretations, and of a considerable academic industry. "Interpretations" in the plural, for a number of bitterly opposed schools and factions had proliferated round his unpronounceable name. As none of these schools—although each claimed to be the sole repository of the truth—had yet decided what exactly the Doctor was getting at—while whatever it was he *did* mean (as a glance at his velvet collar confirmed) could not, obviously, be lightly dismissed, he naturally occupied a position of unparalleled authority in medical, psychiatric and medico-legal circles. This was, of course, most fortunate for Hugo in his somewhat unusual situation, as no one else could have persuaded—or, rather, bewildered—the authorities into accepting it.

When it came to actual cases, moreover, the Doctor was singularly simple, straightforward and practical. As he had explained to Hugo—with whom he was on terms that could only be described as collusive—his only personal guiding-lines were those he had learned from the peasant folk from whom he had originated—a people so utterly cut off by geography, economics and politics from the outside world that they had been forced to rely almost exclusively upon their common sense and humanity. Obliged to flee from his native land for some obscure political reason and also, it was rumoured, in order to escape charges of witchcraft (the "humanity" had its only too human aberrations), the Doctor had also been obliged to adapt himself to his new environment by the methods already indicated (including the black velvet collar), but, he never tired of assuring Hugo, he had since the date of his hurried departure, learned nothing that he could describe as really new as far as the actual practice of his profession as healer was concerned, and was privately convinced (though in this matter he begged Hugo to exercise his discretion) that since prehistoric times there had been no significant advances whatsoever in the treatment of our bodily and mental ills, apart from the evident fact that we had immeasurably increased their number.

As his own treatments were necessarily of a secret nature, and his cures—besides being more numerous than those of his colleagues—of a kind that completely obliterated the memory of the treatments from his patients' minds, so that they would indignantly deny that there had ever been anything wrong with them, or at least that what small maladjustments they had previously suffered from had been corrected by their own efforts or by the natural course of events (a view with which the Doctor in any case heartily concurred, and to the inculcation of which, indeed, he had directed all his efforts) their simplicity and directness never became common knowledge. Instead, he was credited by his colleagues with the discovery of entirely new techniques: some of them bitterly accused him of chicanery in failing to expound them (for the books, while lavish in the description of the ingredients, never revealed the actual recipes); others declared that he was about to do so at any moment; and yet others (the larger part) supplemented their incomes—after all, scantier than those of the Doctor—by writing regular articles and even lengthy tomes about him of an intriguingly speculative nature.

The Doctor's "method" (to use a convenient shorthand term) had one notable disadvantage (as in the case of Hugo's charge) in that it involved a considerable expenditure of time: of money too, of course—though he was absolutely honest when he declared that the fee must be adjusted to the needs of the patient. It seemed only fair, after all, that those who wished to come to him as a way of life, an alternative, say, to buying first editions, hunting to hounds, or wintering in the Bahamas, should pay at a rate commensurate with that of the superceded activities. The same kind of argument might be applied to those who had all their lives been begging to be hurt where it really hurts (i.e., in the pocket), or who had been searching desperately for a cause for anger sufficiently powerful to eliminate the necessity for alcoholism, sexual aberration, or apoplectic fits. And there was a genuine Robin Hood element about the Doctor; he clothed the hungry and fed the meek, so to speak, out of the superfluities that flowed from his couch. If a patient moved him to respect, liking or compassion (not pity—that he reserved for the wealthy

providers of the feast) he was prepared to devote hours
—indeed years—of his time for no payment at all.

One of the outstanding characteristics of the Doctor's
approach, as a matter of fact, was his utter refusal to
admit the revelance of time in such matters. Several of
his most weighty volumes, indeed, had been devoted
(or so, at any rate, the commentators averred) to this
subject, and in particular one entitled: *Serial Time, and
its Application to the Ending of an Analysis*—though
to Hugo he summed it up by a phrase in his native
tongue which, with the help of several visits to the
British Museum to consult the relevant dictionaries,
they had eventually succeeded in translating, to the
delight of both, into the English adage of biblical
origin: "Time is the great healer".

"But it is *exact!*" the Doctor had exclaimed, excitedly
scribbling the phrase into the small black leather-bound
notebook he carried with him in readiness for such
moments of inspiration. "Though one must also remember," he had added, nodding in the direction of the
green baize door with the brass studs that led to Hugo's
"wine-cellar", "that Time takes a longer view of healing
than we do.... It does not think only in terms of the
individual, for one thing. And when it *is* concerned with
the individual, it may just as well be with the last five
minutes of his life as with the three score years or more
that preceded them. In my profession one ought to
(or at any rate *I* do) think about a patient in much the
same way. I am quite satisfied (and what is more to the
point, so is he) if he achieves one single flash of illumina-
tion—or 'salvation', if you prefer it. Indeed, the patient
himself may be dead before the cure is completed. That
does not matter in the slightest. A healthy dead man is
infinitely to be preferred to an unhealthy living one....
And pray do not accuse me of obscurantism or mystification: I have had many patients who have become perfectly well after their deaths: *I* have felt it, and so have
those who loved them.... The tally, so to speak, does not
add up, until it is held at arm's length.... And the healthy
tissue, in small, long forgotten deeds and accomplish-
ments, may suddenly begin to glow with health...."

142

"I am not implying," the Doctor added, intercepting Hugo's stricken look in the direction of the door to the "wine-cellar", "that I don't prefer a live success to a dead one—or that what I have said applies to *our* patient. On the contrary, I think it very likely that I shall shortly be able to tell you that he is quite recovered (it depends on certain delicate negotiations in which I am involved) and that you will be re-united—at ground level I mean."

"Then we must have the house to ourselves?" Hugo asked, part eager, part fearful.

"All in good time," the Doctor said, drawing on his grey doe-skin gloves. "It is no use pushing people out of a house—you must allow it some say in the matter: you must allow it to shake them off, like rotten apples that have clung too long to the branches.... And don't forget," with another nod towards the green baize door, "what I told you at the very beginning, and what I have never tired of repeating, that there is nothing in the least unusual, unexpected, or reprehensible in a young man pushing his invalid mother over a cliff in her wheelchair. It's the most natural thing in the world!"

"Even such a *loving* mother?" Hugo asked.

"Especially so," the Doctor said, carefully inserting the very pearly buttons into the button-holes of his grey gloves. "After all, that means she ought to understand, doesn't it?"

"I hope I have been the right person to ... well, to ..."

"Carry the can?" (The Doctor had been consulting his little notebook.)

"Look after him!" Hugo replied, indignantly.

"That is a most foolish observation—as you know perfectly well. You cannot avoid the situation. You are in it—indeed you *are* it! Who else could be entrusted with this particular responsibility? ... If you recall, I told the Court as much at the time.... Naturally they took my advice then, and have continued to take it since."

"Yes, yes, of course...."

"My advice is never wrong. It may be interpreted incorrectly: at times, I confess, I may even offer it incorrectly—but the advice itself, that is always right."

"Of course... As you say ..."

"It cannot fail to be: I learned it from my own people." The Doctor rolled back the top of his left glove to consult a wafer-thin gold watch (a present from one of the wealthy patients).

"And now I must hurry," he said. "I have an appointment at the American Embassy."

When the Doctor had gone Hugo rubbed his hands, in a sudden glow of excited anticipation. He went over to his wall chart. This was an innovation, an elaborate affair which he had only finished making the day before. It was, in effect, a detailed plan of the house, with each room marked by a square of coloured plastic, which slid neatly into the appropriate grooves. These squares were of five colours: red denoted occupied rooms, whose tenants had so far showed no inclination to quit; green, on the other hand, referred to tenants who were either under notice, or had given it; the yellow squares were those rooms against which Hugo had entered a question mark, either because he didn't like the tenants concerned or thought them unsuitable in some way—or because he didn't know who they were (as in the case of Number One in the upper regions, whose door, apparently, was perpetually locked); the white squares denoted the rooms which Hugo reserved for himself (these, of course, included the "wine-cellar"); and last and most exciting of all—black stood for rooms already evacuated—silent, empty, and sealed like tombs; hence the funereal colour, though this, as far as Hugo was concerned, indicated rejoicing rather than sorrow. A tin of spares, divided into sections (one for each colour), stood on a table beside the chart.

Hugo studied it carefully for several minutes. In the past six months the configuration and colour scheme had undergone considerable modifications, like a landscape responding to the changing seasons. But, Hugo reflected, he was rather in the position of a rook at the top of an elm tree in that only he could see it,—only he knew that the black squares now made an appreciable contribution to the pattern, like patches of earth emerging from the snow. The knowledge gave him a pleasurable thrill of power. The destiny of the whole house, he told himself, was changing under his will, unbeknown to any of the other occupants. Thus, he imagined, a surgeon must feel as he examines an X-ray plate and sees the dark patches which are meaningless to the patient but which, to him, denote the presence of some dreaded disease.... Except, he told himself, in his own case putting up the shutters meant life not death. He dipped his fingers into the tin and took out another of the black squares. His hand hovered for a moment over the chart; then he sighed and returned the black square to its compartment. He could not anticipate the train of events. His power was limited after all. By way of consolation, he replaced several of the red squares by yellow ones: it was not at all difficult to think of tenants against whose names (these of course were neatly inscribed alongside the relevant squares) a question mark was entirely appropriate.

Suddenly he remembered that he had left the tray in the "wine-cellar"—during the Doctor's visits wine was often imbibed there. He went to retrieve it. When he returned, tray in hand, Roger was standing in the middle of the room, staring, almost beside himself with excitement, at the open door leading to the basement. Hugo closed and locked it behind him, cursing himself for not having dropped the latch of the outer door to his apartment, as he usually did: for obvious reasons he did not encourage the tenants to intrude on his privacy.

"You should have knocked," Hugo said. Roger ignored the admonishment.

"Where have you been?" he demanded.

"To the wine-cellar, of course," Hugo replied cheerfully.

"But the tray?"

"These *are* wine-glasses."

"There are more than one."

"I've had a visitor."

"But *three* glasses!"

"Why, so there are!"

Roger burst out laughing. "But I know! And you know I know!"

Hugo too began to laugh. "Of course you do! At your age you haven't had time to forget!"

Still laughing Roger said: "Then it's about time *you* did, isn't it?"

Hugo blushed.

But suddenly Roger stopped laughing. He stood, his head cocked to one side, listening intently. Hugo glanced uneasily at the locked door leading to the "wine-cellar". For a wild moment he thought there might have been an inexplicable relapse down below, or even a cunning and surely premature attempt to force his hand: but then he recalled the Doctor's confident assurances, and realised from the expression on Roger's face and the poise of his head that whatever it was he was listening to so intently must be some distance away.

"They've had a terrible row," Roger said, in a voice at one and the same time dreamy and matter-of-fact. Very faintly Hugo could now catch the sound of a woman's voice. Presumably there were words attached to it, but at this distance all that came through was a jerky, inter-mittent screaming as if someone was jumping up and down on a concertina. There were longer intervals, too, in which Hugo imaginatively deduced rather than actu-ally heard, from a kind of deepening of the atmosphere —and also from the higher pitch with which each fresh burst of screaming began—that a man was speaking.

"They were arguing all night," Roger said. "There was a party at our place. There were a lot of friends—her friends and his friends. *He* wanted to talk about a concert they'd been to, and *she* wanted to talk about antique furniture. They kept interrupting each other (you know how it is). He knows a lot about concerts and she knows a lot about antique furniture, and those who wanted to listen to him got fed up, and those who wanted to listen to her got fed up—and so everybody left early, and they took the drinks that were left over to bed with them, and began quarrelling there—about who started it."

"How do you know?"

"I could hardly help it, could I?" Roger said drily.

"Can you hear what they're saying now?"

"Yes," Roger replied, with the ghost of a grin. "He says he's getting the hell out of it, and she says 'good riddance' "—he tilted his head—"but she won't let him!"

"Does he mean it?"

Roger shrugged his shoulders. "I shouldn't think so."

The screaming grew louder, or perhaps it was that Hugo's ears had become attuned. At any rate he could now pick out, side by side with the screaming the sound of someone trying to start a car that was reluctant to respond.

"He's pulled the choke out too far," Roger observed knowledgeably. "As usual. He always gets the mixture wrong." There was an even louder wail. "Poor Daddy," Roger said. "This *will* be bad for his image!"

"Hadn't we better go and see what's happening?" Hugo said. The Quinceys, after all, were very respectable people and he didn't want them to set his upper regions a bad example.

They hurried out of the house and round to the back of the Annexe, where there was a concreted area containing a number of lock-up garages for the better-off tenants, and a concrete ramp leading to the back entrance. The front of the Quinceys' garage was rolled back, and from the interior came the spluttering and whining of a reluctant engine. Mrs Quincey, unaware of the arrival of Hugo and Roger, stood just outside the entrance to the garage. She was wearing a knee-length housecoat, of elegant patterns and cut, trimmed with pink fur. On her feet, splayed out and looking abnormally large for her petite build, were slippers of the same pattern as the housecoat and also edged with pink fur. In the absence of stockings her shins and ankles appeared thin and sharp, like ivory paper-knives: the skin was flaked and scaly, as if she had been paddling in salty water. Her frizzy hair was unbrushed, disclosing glimpses of yellowish scalp. She had made up her face hurriedly, as if she had been trying to write her feelings on it, the eyebrows angrily arched, the mouth a violent red; the rather dark powder she used was caked round her pursed-up mouth; tiny globules of mascara clung to her lashes.

The car suddenly leaped into life, then subsided with a sigh. A muffled curse came from the interior of the garage. Mrs Quincey took advantage of the lull to give voice again:

147

"If only you'd admit it! That's your trouble—you're pig-headed! You'll never admit it!"

"Admit what?" came from the interior of the garage, the struggle between a desire to yell and the ingrained habit of bland reasonableness made Mr Quincey's voice tremble.

"Admit that you're pig-headed! Admit that you're always slapping me down!"

"Slapping you down! That's a laugh! I can never get a word in edgeways!"

"*You* say that, you of all people!"—Mrs Quincey gave a high-pitched scornful laugh—"You, who're always hogging the conversation!"

"Peace! That's all I want—peace!"

"Peace! What kind of peace do *I* get?"

"Stop yelling like a fishwife! What will the neighbours think?"

"I don't give a damn what the neighbours think! I'm past caring!"

"Well, I'm not! I've my professional standing to consider!"

"To hell with you *and* your profession!"

Mr Quincey's voice from inside the garage turned into a wail: "Oh God! What a way to behave! This isn't like us at all!"

"Isn't it? Isn't it?"

The series of coughs, splutterings and whirrings started again, frantically, as if Mr Quincey were more intent on drowning their voices than starting the car. The effect was to make Mrs Quincey yell louder than ever.

"I suppose you'll be telling me next that you married beneath you!"

The efforts within the garage became positively frenzied. Mrs Quincey laughed exultantly. "Shall we let the precious neighbours know what *you* came from?" she cried.

A strangled yell came from the garage. "*Damn* the car!"

"You've left the choke out," Mrs Quincey replied, in a conversational almost cosy aside, then capped it with a shriek: "As usual!"

"Always know, don't you?" Mr Quincey's voice came in reply. Mrs Quincey took a deep breath, but before she could deliver her riposte the car suddenly gave a healthy roar.

"If you think you're going to walk out on me like this you've got another think coming!" Mrs Quincey yelled at the top of her voice.

"I'm not walking out—I'm driving," Mr Quincey yelled back, and with a jerk the bonnet of the car appeared in the entrance of the garage, Mr Quincey's long, baggy body sagged over the wheel. A smart navy-blue suit, stiff white collar and grey tie, surmounted by a neat charcoal-grey overcoat were in embarrassed occupancy of the body. On the top of his head—in accordance with the latest Whitehall fashion—a curly black Cossack hat perched incongruously; strands of khaki-grey hair fell over his ears. Agitated creases travelled up and down his putty-coloured face. The eyes behind the American-style rimless spectacles glittered, presumably in anger but with an unexpected effect of avuncular benevolence.

As the car moved forward Mrs Quincey let out a piercing scream. Its genuineness made Hugo jump. She dashed forward and threw herself down in front of the oncoming car. The housecoat rucked up as she did so, uncovering the round bony knees. Roger gave a cry and rushed forward. Ignoring the car he knelt down beside his mother and began trying to pull down the skirts of the housecoat. Hugo caught a glimpse of Mr Quincey's horrified face, the jaw sagging, as he brought his foot down—and found the accelerator instead of the brake. Hugo dashed forward, determined if needs be to block the passage of the car with his own body, impelled not by heroism but by anxiety over the correct patterning of his own destiny: for it was not yet time for the Quinceys to leave his house—or not, at any rate, time for Roger who, as its youngest inhabitant, occupied a special place in Hugo's time-scale.

Fortunately at this juncture the car came to a shuddering halt: Mr Quincey had stalled the engine.

He leaped out and came round to the front of the car. The suddenness of the stop had jerked the Cossack hat

149

forward, so that its peak rested on the bridge of his nose. His Adam's apple in the long stringy neck was heaving convulsively, as if he were trying to swallow it, sending wave after wave of creases up and down his face. He knelt down on the other side of his wife. He had, Hugo noted, forgotten to change out of his slippers.

Mrs Quincey still lay on her back, her eyes tightly closed, muttering, "Over my dead body! Over my dead body!" Mr Quincey adjusted his spectacles and peered at her. The front wheels of the car were against her, but she was apparently unhurt.

A moment later her eyelids sprang open, her eyes angrily at the ready. They wavered when the first face they encountered was that of her son, who was still trying to pull the skirts of her housecoat over her knees. A look of horror passed over her face, and she struggled to get to her feet. One of the wide sleeves of her housecoat, however, was caught beneath the left wheel of the car and she could not dislodge it. She made a despairing, whimpering sound. Roger stared in horrified fascination at the sleeve, then he dug his fingers under the wheel of the car and began scrabbling frantically at the cloth. His father leaned forward, gave a hearty tug, and disengaged the sleeve. Mrs Quincey scrambled to her feet. Husband and wife exchanged frightened, bewildered glances. Realizing that his son had not yet got up, Mr Quincey dropped on one knee beside him, and awkwardly laid a big creased hand on his shoulder.

"It's all right, old man!" he said. "No need to take on! You mustn't pay any attention to the antics of us grown-ups, eh?"

The folds of his face fell into the contours of a sickly grin. Mrs Quincey turned her attention to her housecoat; bits of gravel had adhered to it, and she began brushing them away, with each dash of her hand darting a glance from under her eyebrows, part frightened and part curious, first at her son, who was now standing up, very still and stiff, his fists clenched against the sides of his body, then at her husband, who was also on his feet again, his head lolling this way and that as a series of deprecatory smiles crawled over his face and neck. He even ventured a chuckle once or twice, as if inviting any bystanders or any of those unseen spectators who might be avidly twitching at their curtains, to join him in some matrimonial jest. "Just a little domestic contretemps!" the smiles seemed to say, "A little tiff! The normal give-and take, don't you know? A bit of typical female un-reasonableness, eh? Have a good laugh—and forget it, forget it! It's nothing, absolutely nothing at all!"

But the blood had drained from his face, leaving it paler than ever, and for a moment Hugo thought he was going to faint. To his wife he muttered, "We shall have to leave, of course!" She looked at him intently, a half-smile on her lips.

The bystanders, in fact, consisted, apart from Hugo and Roger, of four people. Mr Sturmer and Pat were standing some twenty yards away, staring at the scene with expressions of incredulous horror, as if they had been witnessing some unmentionable atrocity performed by denizens of another planet. Somewhat closer stood Mr Venner and Mrs Bradbury, very quiet, studiously not touching each other, he puffing furiously at his pipe, she with a faraway, pensive look in her eyes.

Mrs Quincey finished brushing her housecoat, then raised her eyes defiantly. She suddenly caught hold of one of Roger's hands and pressed it against her side, and then, letting the hand go just as suddenly, turned to her husband and said, in an oddly compassionate voice, "Shall we go?"

With Hugo bringing up the rear the little party moved towards the house. As they approached Mr Sturmer and Pat, Mr Quincey's head again began to bob up and down. "Good morning, good morning!" he said in his heartiest, most pat-me-on-the-back voice, unfolding his lips from his teeth in the semblance of a smile. "Turned out nice again, hasn't it?"

Mr Sturmer and Pat, arms round each others' shoulders, backed away as if he had the plague, their eyes wide and questioning. As Hugo drew level their expression changed to a kind of humble pleading, as if to say: "What can it be? *Are* such things possible?"

As they drew level with the other couple, Mrs Quincey,

suffering now from reaction, stumbled a little, and Mrs Bradbury darted forward and placed her arm round her shoulder, shaking off Mr Quincey's offer of help. Wriggling, clucking and clicking, he fell back to join Hugo and Mr Venner.

They entered the house and proceeded upstairs to the Quinceys' apartment. Once inside Mrs Quincey sank on to the couch. Her husband, bending his long body, awkwardly patted her knee. "There, there, old girl!" he said, baring his teeth in a series of ghastly smiles. He looked round him wildly, as if searching for inspiration. His eyes alighted on the occasional table where the drinks were laid out. "Ah! *I* know what would do *you* good!" he cried, loping exultantly towards it. An expression of nausea crossed Mrs Quincey's face. "No!" she shouted. Mr Quincey stopped in his tracks as if he had been shot and looked from one to the other in bewilderment.

At this moment Mrs Bradbury returned from the bathroom bearing a tumbler of water and three aspirin tablets. She handed them to Mrs Quincey, who flashed her a grateful look. When she had swallowed the aspirins she leaned back against the cushions with a sigh that turned into a yawn. Mr Quincey, who had remained transfixed in the centre of the room, suddenly jerked back into life. He pulled forward one of the somewhat fragile antique chairs, placed it close to the couch and lowering his large hams gingerly on to it took one of his wife's hands in his. "They'll be all right now," Roger, who had been studying the scene with the judicious air of a doctor on the look out for familiar symptoms, informed the others. Gravely he conducted them into the hall, then retired to his play-room. Hugo and Mrs Bradbury rejoined Mr Venner, who had remained in the corridor, his eyes round, drawing at his pipe in short, desperate puffs as if his life depended on them. Very quietly Hugo closed the door behind him. They stood in the corridor for a moment, listening intently. A few seconds later, above Roger's subdued murmur, they heard Mr Quincey say, in a hoarse, rather cracked voice: "Sorry, old girl!"

"No, dear, *I*'m sorry!" Mrs Quincey's voice replied.

"Oh no, my dear, *I*'m the one who ought to be sorry!"

There was a short pause. Then Mr Quincey spoke again, in a steadier voice. "I've been selfish and thoughtless...."

"No, *I*'ve been selfish and thoughtless!"

"Why, *you* mustn't blame yourself, old girl!"

"Can't I even do that?" the reply came, this time with a touch of asperity.

Mrs Bradbury looked up at Mr Venner with a quizzical, slightly mocking look in her large blue eyes; then the expression changed to one of mingled complicity and tenderness. She took hold of Mr Venner's hand and they began to move along the corridor so fast that Hugo had difficulty in keeping up with them. When they reached their own door they opened it, gave a quick nod to Hugo, and scuttled inside. Mr Venner was puffing at his pipe more frantically than ever as the door slammed to: a blue smoke-ring hung for a moment over the doorway.

At the bend of the corridor Hugo ran into Mr Sturmer and Pat, faces pale, eyes out on cheekbones.

"We've been looking for you!" they cried in unison.

"Those people—and now this!" Pat wailed.

"She just lay there! Terrible!"

"Who lay there?" Hugo asked.

"Those people!" Pat wailed again. "It almost makes me wish you hadn't married us! Does everybody get like that?"

"*He* didn't have the strength," Mr Sturmer went on, "so I had to help...."

"Can married people behave like that?" Pat demanded, her voice turning querulous.

As if in response a series of bangings, followed by shrieks of laughter came from the "upper regions". Hugo winced. Mr Sturmer and Pat glanced quickly upwards, an expression of joyous yearning on their faces.

"*That* and now this!" Pat cried, lowering her eyes with evident reluctance.

"What is it you are trying to tell me?" Hugo asked.

"The old woman," Mr Sturmer said. "She fell down, in the garden.... She was making noises like an animal.... It was *horrible!*"

"Mrs Palfrey? Where is she now?"

"Inside, I told you, the old boy couldn't move her.

I had to help him.... We carried her inside...."

"Her face," Pat said, "it was purple...."

"When we got inside," Mr Sturmer continued in a strangled voice, "the old boy had to open the bedroom door.... I had to carry her by myself ... I took her over to the bed. I don't know why, I just dropped her there and ran! ... She bounced up and down a bit ... the bed made a rattling noise ... I don't know why, but, man, I was scared!"

Another series of bangings and a fresh burst of laughter came from above. Mr Sturmer's eyes glinted hopefully. "There's company!" he said wistfully.

"I'll see to it," Hugo told him.

"See you!" Mr Sturmer said abruptly, and catching hold of Pat's hand set off at the double in the direction of the staircase leading to the "upper regions".

Hugo hurried over to the Palfreys' flat. He entered the bedroom, dominated by the huge double bed with its iron ends, as big as five-barred gates, the corners surmounted by brass knobs the size of coconuts. Mrs Palfrey lay on her back. The old man had managed to take off her apron, blouse and skirt, and to unhook the antiquated corsets, which lay under her hips, the whalebones protruding from the worn covering, like a section of reticulated fencing. The grey bloomers billowed grotesquely above the heavily veined legs in their thick woollen stockings and the black shoes, worn into the shape of clenched fists by corns and bunions. The patchy redness of her forehead was accentuated by the wisps of white hair, stuck to the skin by sweat. The lower part of the face was stiff and heavy, as if injected with cocaine. A low moaning escaped from the purple lips, accompanied by a succession of snorts and grunts which pouted her lips and deposited small bubbles on them, like those on the lips of a baby.

Hugo helped the Sergeant to finish undressing her. They put her into the long yellowish flannel nightgown, and manoeuvered her beneath the bed-clothes.

Sergeant Palfrey was very quiet: the clefts at the side of his mouth had deepened, setting his face, incongruously, into an expression of grim humour. He had not had time to wash his hands, which were caked with garden dirt.

This time he made no objection to Hugo summoning the doctor immediately. He arrived, gave the patient an injection, shook his head and departed, promising to send a nurse and to return himself later in the day. The snorting and grunting from the bed had subsided, but the low moaning continued. The Sergeant went over to the bed and stood looking down at his wife, his thumbs in the arm-holes of his open waistcoat, the various ornaments and medallions on his watch-chain swaying to and fro. Mrs Palfrey's moaning suddenly stopped: something about the carriage of the head told them that she was trying to reach out to them, but all that moved were the eyes, rolling back into a ghastly squint that disclosed the filmy yellow whites. She began moaning again.

The grimace on Sergeant Palfrey's face deepened. "It would be better if she went now," he said suddenly and quite calmly, as if he were discussing the departure of a train.

In his agitation Hugo made the mistake of passing Mr Skidmore's door on his way back to his own quarters. It burst open, almost knocking him down, and a hand seized his shoulder like a vice. Hugo was no weakling, but he was propelled into the room and deposited into a chair before he had even time to brace himself.

"Listen," Mr Skidmore said, in tones of the utmost urgency. "That cat..."

There was an air of suppressed excitement about him: the normally lank moustache seemed to bristle with electricity; there was a reddish glitter in his eyes. Only when he had satisfied himself that Hugo was more or less quiescent did he return to his own chair and sit down.

"I haven't told you yet how Mitzi died, have I?"

Hugo shook his head, resigned.

"Mitzi—she died for *us!*" Mr Skidmore muttered: his eyes flickered uneasily about the room: for a moment he seemed to be listening intently.

"After that last move I was telling you about," he began again, "things started going from bad to worse. Matilda got ill—never been ill before, you know; came as

155

quite a shock—we couldn't believe it at first . . . Well, the doctor gave her some tablets. At first we thought they'd done the trick: she got quite jolly; her face got smoother and pinker than it had ever been before. It was about this time, though, that we noticed that Mitzi was behaving very strangely. She kept running round and round the house from room to room, as if she was looking for something, mewing all the time in a monotonous, plaintive kind of way . . ." Again Mr Skidmore stopped abruptly, and sat on the edge of his chair, his head cocked to one side. . . . Then as Hugo stirred, his eyes fixed on Hugo, daring him to move.

"Sometimes, too," he went on, "she would suddenly jump on to the lap of one or the other of us, without any reason that we could see and start making a tremendous fuss—rubbing her head against us, licking the tips of our noses and purring in a kind of frantic way. . . .

"Well, Matilda suddenly got funny again. She didn't take an interest in anything—just sat about with her hands in her lap, though sometimes I'd suddenly look up from something I was doing and find her looking at me in a kind of steady way, and I'd know she'd been doing it for a long time. . . .

"Then suddenly she *did* start talking (at any rate to me) and that was even worse. I mean, it wasn't as if we were having a conversation or anything like that, and it only happened at nights in our bedroom. You see, she had suddenly got it into her head that she missed our last house, and that moving from it was the cause of all the trouble. She hadn't seemed particularly interested in it before—no more than usual, anyway; in fact I can think of several places she was really much more attached to. But now as soon as we got into bed she would start talking about this last house of ours and blaming me for moving. Well, that's not quite right—she didn't start talking straight away, not out loud, but it was there, if you know what I mean, and I would know it was coming on any minute. I'd lie in my bed and I could *feel* her lying in hers, tense and still, with all the words gathering up inside her—and then, whoosh! out they'd all come! Always the same thing—she hardly varied a word

—on and on, in a flat monotonous voice that made me want to scream! 'If only you hadn't insisted on leaving the old house, I wouldn't be like this now! What did you do it for? Why didn't you ask me what *I* felt about it?' Then a short pause, and off she'd go again: 'If only you hadn't insisted...' and so on, and so on.... At first I tried to answer her questions; I tried to explain, to put *my* point of view. But it was no use. She didn't listen to what I was saying at all; just went on and on, like I was telling you, hour after hour and for hours on end. For all I know she went on all night—for after a bit I got into the habit of falling asleep after it had been going on for two or three hours... There were times, though, when it used to drive me half mad myself... Let's face it, it would have tried the patience of a saint—honest it would ... I used to feel a kind of scream knotting itself up somewhere inside me—but being a man of course I couldn't really let it rip! ... Once, though, once..." Mr Skidmore swallowed, then continued: "Once I couldn't stand it any longer. I got out of bed (for some reason I couldn't get to sleep that night, even though it had been going on for at least four hours) and went over to Matilda's bed. I caught hold of her by the shoulders and shook her. Do you know she didn't stop talking for a second? And she didn't try to resist, just let me go on shaking her as if she were a rag doll, with the same flat voice coming out of it—tired, terribly tired sort of, with a crack in it—though the sounds came out in a jerky, gulping way, because I was shaking her so hard. Somehow that made me even madder, and before I really knew what had happened my hands had slipped down to her throat ... I got my fingers round it ... I didn't really squeeze, you know—no, no it wasn't really like that at all ... But she did stop talking then ... I ... I don't think she could, perhaps, very well, what with my ... hands ... being there ... Yes, she stopped and looked at me in a queer way, and the funny thing is that her eyes were suddenly very bright, even tender ... and when my fingers relaxed she said, very quietly, 'Go on, I don't mind....' Oh God, oh God! I always *liked* her neck, you know—it was very firm and white, and the feel

157

of it under my hands made me want to howl like a baby! Oh God!" Mr Skidmore broke off and banged his fist on the arm of his chair, rocking himself to and fro.

"Well, all this time Mitzi was ailing too—or so we realized later. We didn't really notice it properly then, if you know what I mean. We knew that she was off her feed a bit and that she was moulting rather a lot for the time of year—but as I say, we were so taken up with other things that it didn't sink in properly—though I did occasionally pop one of her conditioning powders into her cat-food. . . .

"Anyway, I came home rather late from work one day and as soon as I pushed open the garden gate I knew that something was wrong. I seemed to *smell* it, you know? Well, sure enough as soon as I got inside the kids came up to me, very quietly, but in a—I don't know *how* to describe it—a kind of 'end of the world' way . . . the girl—Madge—was crying, but without making a sound—you know, in that funny hopeless way kids have when they're really upset and not putting it on—little, heaving gulps but, as I say, no sound . . . my son, Perry . . . poor boy, poor boy . . . his face was as white as a ghost.

"Well, it seems Matilda had been saving her sleeping pills. . . . I suppose I might have guessed it, the way she talked all night!" Mr Skidmore gave a ghastly laugh.

"As soon as the poor kid managed to get it out I was in the car and off to the hospital of course, like a streak of greased lightning. They'd used the stomach pump and all that kind of thing, of course, by the time I got there, and she was just about conscious, though very heavy and lumpish looking, and breathing in a funny way . . . her face was a purplish colour, all mottled. . . . It was very shiny too, and her eyes seemed to have gone very small. . . . Her breath and her sweat stank—that was all the pills, I suppose. . . ."

Hugo sighed and shook his head. He felt weary, depressed. It was next to impossible, it suddenly seemed to him, to shelter his own spark of hope while forced to play the part of lightning-conductor to so many others. He was tired of being shut up inside his house with all these tenants, to whom he belonged, and who belonged to him—belonged, but in no redeeming sense. "I can't go on much longer," he told himself. "I have given them all too much rope, and they use it not to hang themselves, but to bind me tighter every day. I have allowed them to lead their own lives too long. Surely I have paid enough to and for the past. It is time I had the house to myself, and began to let some of my own skeletons out of their cupboards. . . ."

He became aware that Mr Skidmore was watching him, a bitter yet surprisingly patient expression on his face. He even raised an eyebrow inquiringly, as if to say: "Have you come back from wherever it was you were visiting?" And when he began talking again, the first few sentences were uttered in milder tones than usual, and contained a touch of solicitude, and even gentleness.

"Yes, that's right," he said, as if Hugo had read his thoughts. He swallowed once or twice. "Yes, it's nearly over now . . . the pain—I suppose even that ends some time. . . . Anyway, it was touch and go with Matilda for a bit and all that time we hung round the telephone, dreading to hear it go and yet using it ourselves every half hour or so to ring up the hospital. And all the time Mitzi was getting worse and *still* we didn't take it in. . . . It might still have been all right if I'd done something about it on the second day after Matilda . . . after she'd gone into hospital, because Mitzi perked up a little on that day and was particularly affectionate to all of us—wouldn't leave us alone in fact. But that was the day when Matilda was at her worst and I was too put out to do anything. . . . Then on the third day (Matilda was picking up by then) it *did* suddenly come home to me. I'd stooped down to pick Mitzi up—and I noticed the change in her weight. As I told you, she was a small cat under all that fur, but there was usually *some* bulk to her, if you know what I mean. . . . She'd always felt the same when I picked her up—honest, I reckon I could have told you her weight to the nearest milligram—I'd got so used to it, you see. . . . Well, *this* time she came away from the floor as if I was picking up a feather— and I could feel the bones under the fur, and I saw then that her fur had gone all drab and matted. She gave a little whimpering sound, too, as I lifted her up, as if my hand underneath her was hurting her ribs, though when I nestled her in the crook of my arm she began to purr in her usual way.... Well, of course I got the wind up then and the three of us piled into the car, and we took her round to the vet. It was dreadful, you know, the way she mewed when the vet laid her on his table and began poking at her with his finger—she looked up at us with those great yellow eyes as if she was begging us to make him stop. 'I think it's too late,' the vet said, and he forced her mouth open, showing the inside, all white and spongy.... He gave her an injection of course and gave us some tablets to give her, but he said he couldn't hold out much hope.... Well, we got her back home and she settled down at once on her special cushion, on the floor near the french windows that led to the garden. She was as good as gold, and every time we stroked her she purred—a kind of rattling unsteady purr, but very loud, as if she was trying to tell us how glad she was to be back home, and how much she loved us.... She took the tablets, too, as quiet as a lamb, though she gave a plaintive little 'Miaow' when we opened her mouth for them, and she seemed to have difficulty in swallowing—and she started purring again louder than ever when we put her back down, and she could hunch up again on her cushion, all held together, sort of, and the shoulder-blades sticking up under the fur.... The children didn't want to leave her—I had a job even to get them to go into the kitchen for their meals—and so I let them stay up that night. We all stayed there with Mitzi—the kids on the couch and me in the big armchair—we would have liked to have had her on our laps, but somehow that seemed to hurt her, and the kids seemed to understand and let her stay where she was.... Well, about midnight Mitzi got up very suddenly off her cushion, and stood, very stiff, as if she was listening to something. Then she went up to the french windows, walking with her legs still held very stiff and her tail straight up like a poker. At first I thought perhaps she wanted to go into the garden (she was the cleanest cat imaginable, Mitzi was). So I drew back the curtains and opened the french doors. But she didn't go out. She went up to the door-jamb, and stood very close to it ... the kids were wide awake too now and I wish I'd known.... But, you see, I'd never ... never seen it happen before ... I put some brandy in a teaspoon and knelt down beside Mitzi, and I tried to push the spoon between her lips.... She paid no attention ... the brandy spilled down her front—among all that white fur ... and then she leaned hard against the door-jamb, arched her back and let out the most awful wail I've ever heard in my life. Then she dropped with a thud, as if she'd been shot... Oh God, I shall never forget that wailing sound as long as I live! ... Did you know they did that? ... Arched their backs, I mean, and made that noise ... just before they died?"

Hugo shook his head.

"Neither did I, God help me—and I'm supposed to be the one that knows all about animals!"

Mr Skidmore stopped, took out his handkerchief, and blew noisily into it. The red rims round his eyes glistened.

"Matilda came home the very next day... Of course I had to tell her about Mitzi. She gave me a funny look and asked what time it had happened. I told her, and she kind of nodded to herself, as if she knew all about it. It wasn't until several minutes after that she burst into tears. I was worried at first, but then I saw there was something about her crying that was *all right*—if you know what I mean? Anyway, after a bit she suddenly stopped crying, sat up, brushed her hair back and put her handkerchief away in a business-like kind of way. She got better quite quickly after that. Not that she didn't miss Mitzi—we all did. We just couldn't believe that she had gone. We kept thinking we could still hear her miaowing somewhere.... Every time we saw a shadow in the house, every time we heard a bush rustling in the garden, we thought it was her.... But the really funny thing was that miaowing—the whole place seemed to be full of its echoes. I'd be doing some odd job, for example I'd be kneeling down stoking the stove, say, and suddenly I'd stop—that miaow of Mitzi's was in my ears, clear as a bell. Matilda would give me a funny look and get on with the bit of darning or mending she was doing, but a few minutes later *she* would suddenly stop, with the needle in mid-air, and I could tell that she'd heard it too—and I'd give *her* a funny look, then away quickly—you know, we wouldn't admit what was happening.... Well, it went on like that for quite a time (oh, by the way, it was only Matilda and me kept hearing ... I mean *thinking* we heard ... this miaowing). By this time Matilda was quite her old self—very quiet and withdrawn it's true—but then she always was very quiet ... still, she didn't seem at all ill in any way.... And then, suddenly—you'll hardly credit this part of it!—one evening she put down her mending, looked up at me and said: '*We* killed her!'

"I was so taken aback that I blustered a bit. 'What!' I said. '*Me* kill Mitzi? Why, you must be...' I was just going to say, 'You must be out of your mind,' but stopped myself in time. 'Yes,' Matilda said, 'we killed her—and it's all wasted!' ... 'For Christ's sake!' I said, 'What do you mean?' (I couldn't for the life of me see what she was getting at.) 'Don't you see?', Matilda said, very solemn, 'Mitzi *died for us*! And it was wasted!' And with that she put her things down, got up, went into the bedroom, without saying another word, packed her things and left then and there. It was quite late, and I did my best to make her see reason, but she wouldn't listen ... yes, she walked out, just like that! Well, I stayed on in the house for a bit.... Of course at first I expected Matilda to come walking back through the door any minute—didn't really believe she'd stick to it, you know ... but she did.... She stayed with her sister at first, I heard later; then she got herself a job and a little flat somewhere in North London (miles away from any of the areas we'd ever lived in before, by the way). Well, I stuck it for a bit longer, but I kept hearing that damned cat—it seemed to have got right inside me, you know, as if it was part of me, like my blood or something.... The children still heard nothing, thank goodness, but eventually I couldn't stand having them about the place (not that I'd gone off them or anything like that, mind! I'd go through fire and water for those kids!) But when they were about the place I had to pretend that everything was all right—and I wanted to be alone, so that I could sit and *listen*! So I sent Madge and Perry off to my sister-in-law, and as soon as Matilda got properly settled in her flat they went to live with her, and that's where they are now. And after a couple of weeks I sold up and came here...."

Mr Skidmore stopped abruptly. He leaned back in his chair and fixed his eyes on Hugo. The eyes were expressionless, and yet, far back, there was a flicker in them like a question mark. The minutes ticked by. Then slowly Mr Skidmore leaned forward in his chair: his eyes were still fixed unwaveringly on Hugo's face, but his head was now cocked to one side. Further minutes passed. Hugo was aware that something was expected of him. He struggled to concentrate his energies upon the pin-point in Mr Skidmore's eyes. He felt the strength draining from him. He wanted to rest, to sleep. At length, with what seemed to him a stupendous effort, he brought out the two words, "And then?"

"Ah!" said Mr Skidmore, pouncing, "that's the whole point! You see, *I can hear it again*!"

"You can hear what?"

"Come off it!" Mr Skidmore said angrily. "You know very well what I mean! *Mitzi*, of course! It started three days ago—properly, I mean: I used to *imagine* it occasionally before, but that was different.... Yes, I was sitting in this chair, and suddenly I heard Mitzi's miaow, as clear as a bell!"

"Oh come now! There are lots of cats round here!" Hugo pointed out. "It might have been any one of a dozen!"

The blood rushed to Mr Skidmore's face: his eyes bulged. "Do you think I don't know Mitzi when I hear her?" he shouted. "Why, I could distinguish her miaow among a thousand! I tell you, it's Mitzi I've been hearing!"

Mr Skidmore held up his hand in a peremptory gesture. "Listen," he said softly, "there it is again! Do you hear it?"

Hugo strained his ears, and after a few seconds he thought he really could hear a faint caterwauling, some-

163

times sounding very faint and distant, at other times seeming to come very close. He gave his head a violent shake. Yes, there was no doubt about it, he could hear a cat miaowing ... but then, he told himself, there *were* a lot of cats in the neighbourhood. And in any case he was a notoriously obliging sort of man.

"You see?" Mr Skidmore said softly.

At that moment they both jumped as the telephone started ringing. Mr Skidmore regarded it irritably for a moment, then a speculative expression crossed his face. He picked up the receiver. Hugo could hear the sound of a woman's voice at the other end of the line.

"Have I *what*?" Mr Skidmore said. He nodded his head. "Yes, yes, I have.... Yes of course—straight away!" He put down the receiver and turned to face Hugo.

"I'm off!" he said. "I'm packing and leaving—now!"

"But why?"

"Matilda," Mr Skidmore said. "She can hear Mitzi too!"

Back in his own quarters Hugo looked around him. He had a vague feeling that something was not quite right, but he dismissed it. He was glad to be alone. Going over to the wall chart, he took one of the black squares out of the tin, and slid it into the grooves opposite Mr Skidmore's name and number. Immediately the shape of the chart underwent a change. The addition of the small area of black had given the whole an astonishing appearance of symmetry and balance. If the addition had been made at any other place, Hugo reflected, it would have had nothing like the same effect. He was glad, for example, that he had not yet been obliged to fill in the Palfreys' space: that would have spoiled the pattern: it was a space that had to be filled in its own good time, it was true—an area of experience, so to speak, that must wither away, inevitably, and naturally. The other had demanded an effort of exorcism, and he felt pleased with himself, even though he was aware he should have made it long ago.

As he moved away from the wall chart he suddenly realized what was wrong with his room: the projector was no longer in the corner where he had left it.

7

Within a few days the wall chart was again at sixes
and sevens though Hugo hoped that the transitory
appearance of grace had been prophetic. A snatch of one
of the Doctor's monologues came back to him; "*How
can I tell that our patient will recover, in the ripeness
of time? But my dear fellow, that is the easiest part
of the whole treatment! Any healer who is worth his
salt can tell that* at the very first meeting. How else
do you suppose witch-doctors maintain their authority
over the tribe? If they weren't able to prepare the way
for their failures they would soon be out of business!
But, you see, at the outset of every illness, whether of
body or mind, the patient transmits to us a kind of
paradigm of its whole course and final outcome ...
indeed, it is my experience that the patient himself
usually sees it too (for, after all, he is himself the trans-
mitter).... Yes, in a flash it comes to him as he lies on
his bed—or his couch—of pain, in the form of a vision
or a dream or, perhaps—if he is of that disposition—a
particularly satisfying mathematical formula.... The
difference, of course, is that the patient quickly forgets
it: it is obliterated by the fog of his illness—whereas the
healer must keep the sketch constantly before him if he
is to be of any assistance to his patient during his long,
laborious task of pulling down, discarding, and rebuild-
ing, brick by brick, his house of many mansions...."

As far as Hugo's house was concerned, Mr Skidmore's
sudden departure seemed to have had a disruptive effect.
Neighbours who had ignored each other for years became aware of each other's existence, and did not relish

the discovery. Hugo was kept busy trotting from one flat to another, adjudicating between claims and counter-claims, mediating in all kinds of ridiculous quarrels. Some of the tenants gave in their notice; others departed at once, with or without paying their rent. Not all the departures, it is true, were accompanied by acrimony; Mrs Bradbury and Mr Venner, for example, left in the friendliest spirit imaginable, to sit out the protracted divorce proceedings in a cottage in Cornwall. For one reason or another, though, Hugo found himself spending a good deal of time at his wall chart, and its pattern changed from day to day and almost from hour to hour, bulging, narrowing, then bulging again, the black squares now like vengeful, constantly shifting storm clouds.

And the yellow ones perhaps like flashes of lightning waiting to strike? Certainly they were beginning to out-number the black ones. A question mark indeed, hung over the whole of the "upper regions". He could feel in his bones that something was brewing there, but he hadn't a clue as to what it might be. When rent day came he called first on Pat and Mr Sturmer, but they were strangely distant, simmering, it seemed to him, with some suppressed but intensely private excitement.

He made his way to Mr Smith's studio. Mr Smith frowned as he entered. He was hard at work at his easel. The girl was seated on the same stool and in the same posture as on Hugo's previous visit: even the goose-pimples on her thighs seemed the same. All Mr Smith's old paintings had either disappeared or been relegated to his storage cupboard. The new ones, too, were greenish-brown studies of peasant women, but their squat faces now bore some slight resemblance of that of the girl seated on the stool. There was another difference too: previously Mr Smith had preferred to have his peasants draped in shapeless blouses, but these new paint-ings were all nudes, except that the heads were sur-mounted by head-dresses of a vaguely Caucasian pattern. Wherever he looked and at every conceivable angle, even from the floor, Hugo was confronted by gross, lum-pish figures, with legs tucked under them to reveal
166

monstrous balloon-like knees, enormous buttocks and equally enormous breasts, the latter executed with a pernickety attention to detail, the nipples exaggeratedly circular and elongated.

"Still posing!" the girl said, as she caught sight of Hugo. But her lopsided grin lacked its usual perky confidence: she was pale, and her eyes kept glancing at Mr Smith, with an oddly calculating, slightly bewildered expression.

"Is anything wrong?" Hugo asked. The girl looked at him quickly, almost, it seemed to Hugo, hopefully.

Mr Smith turned from his easel, and seated himself on the edge of his high stool: he rested his hands on his bony knees and subjected Hugo to his black, unwinking stare.

"*Wrong*?" he said, angrily.

Hugo, realizing that he had been suspected of criticizing the artist's work, hastened to explain: "Up here, I mean. Something funny seems to be going on, but I don't know what it is...."

Mr Smith got off his stool and taking up his palette returned to his easel.

"How can you expect *me* to know?" he said without turning his head. "Can't you see that I'm in the middle of a new phase?"

The girl, however, slipped from her stool and slipping her arms into a kimono accompanied Hugo to the door. She put out a hand, touched his arm, and frowned, as if searching for something she wanted to say which eluded her. Then with a curt nod she held open the door. Glancing back over his shoulder Hugo saw that Mr Smith was bent over his easel, his eyes close to the canvas, laboriously painting a nipple. Hugo looked at the girl, but she avoided his gaze. He closed the door behind him, and feeling vaguely troubled, as if he had been found wanting in some respect, he continued his rounds of the "upper regions".

It was not a heartening experience. None of the tenants whom he knew could or would pay his rent. Hugo was not of course unused to such eventualities. He was, he used to say with a chuckle, "an accommodating land-

167

lord" (he liked such little jests)—while privately reminding himself, with a rather more rueful chuckle, that
he was not really "a free agent". Even so he was not
prepared for the curt manner in which his mild requests
for settlement were, in most cases, repulsed. But in fact
he found very few tenants he *did* know. Time after time
he would approach a door, his heart warming at the buzz
that came from behind it, only to find when he opened
it that he was confronted by rows of strange faces and
eyes that regarded him in a far from friendly fashion,
while the murmur of earnest voices which had stopped
abruptly at his appearance, started up again as soon as he
had left.

He comforted himself with the reflection that at any
rate the traffic round the windows had stopped ...
perhaps, though, that was because it had now served its
purpose? The afterthought was not at all comforting.

He left the upper regions with his little Gladstone bag
almost empty, and closed the green baize door behind
him with a feeling of relief. For once the fashionable
mauve paintwork of the Quinceys' front door, the expensive rug in front of it and the green fitted carpet of
the hall just visible through the lighted crack at the
bottom of the door, were cosy and reassuring. He paused
for a moment and applied his ear to the door. The
strains of some modish musical composition from Mrs
Quincey's record-player accompanied by the sound of a
B.B.C. third programme discussion on Mr Quincey's
radio, for once blended and soothed.

He paused, too, at the door of the Proudfoot-Lorns'
apartment (at this time of the year they used both
barrels). It had been repainted a yellowish-ochre colour
to match the light-wood motif within: the smell of a
particularly pungent linseed oil came from it. He tried
to work out the exact point the occupants would have
reached in their yearly cycle, but as he could not remember the date, he dismissed the matter from his mind
and hurried on.

The corridor leading past the rooms once occupied by
Mr Skidmore (now locked and empty) was in semi-
darkness. For some reason Hugo found himself hurrying.

A shadow formed, and for one wild moment Hugo had a vision of a dark shape arched against the door-post. As he rounded the corner he could have sworn he heard a faint "miaow" behind him. But no, he told himself: if Mitzi was conducting a serenade anywhere it would be outside the flat in North London now occupied by both Mr and Mrs Skidmore. He hurried on, making a mental note to renew the light bulb in the corridor he had just left, and to purchase some cat repellant: there had been far too many strays about lately.

He heaved a sigh of relief when he reached his own quarters, so cosy and ship-shape. He hesitated a moment before approaching the wall chart. Then, very gingerly, he inserted a black square in the space of the upper regions from which the tenants had absconded with his furniture. It did not improve the pattern, regarding him menacingly like a Cyclops' eye. The feeling of uneasiness persisted: there was a rupture, a fracture somewhere in his house which he could not comprehend: it nagged at him with an obscure ache.

He undressed and climbed into his bunk—bunk, not bed, for he liked to encourage the sea-going aspect of his reputation (though apart from the war his sea-going travels had been confined to the Pas de Calais). Normally he slept the kind of dreamless sleep one would associate with his rotund body and his smooth, unwrinkled face. Tonight he was restless and tormented by nightmares. The bunk on this occasion did in fact heave all night as if he were caught in a storm at sea. He was pursued by leering monsters, in whose features he detected glimpses of most of his tenants, pre-eminent amongst them the Quinceys, the Proudfoot-Lorns and Mr Smith, and by a huge, grinning cat with gigantic whiskers and teeth which somehow bore a resemblance to the Doctor. There was a creaking and a groaning in his ears as if his house were itself a ship that was tugging at its moorings. And when some time later he woke with a start, it was to see that the portrait which he kept on the wall at the foot of his bunk—a large woodcut from some nineteenth-century history of the Austro-Hungarian

Empire which he had persuaded himself was a portrait of Frans Prěserěn (it was in fact of the Emperor Franz Josef as a young man) was hanging askew. As he regarded it, still half-asleep, his heart still thudding from the nightmares, it slowly slid down the wall, with a scrabbling noise like that of a crab, disappeared behind the foot of the bunk and struck the floor with a crash.

As the echoes died away he became aware of another noise, faint and distant but somehow monstrous and horrifying, which nagged at the edges of consciousness. At first he thought it must be one of the echoes that still lingered along the corridors of his nightmares. Then he decided it must be a radio or television set somewhere in the house, broadcasting a spine-chiller of some sort. He put his head under the bed-clothes, trying to cling to one or other of these explanations. But a few moments later the clock of the church round the corner from his house began to chime. He threw back the bed-clothes and sat up, his heart beating painfully as he counted the strokes. It was three o'clock, so it could hardly be a radio play. He got out of bed and, his fingers trembling, put on his slippers and dressing gown. His hand on the door-knob, he paused and listened intently. There was no doubt about it. Somewhere in the house somebody was screaming, persistently and horribly. At the same moment some intuition told him where it came from. He threw open the door and began to run—down corridors, round corners, up stairs—his rotund body balanced on the balls of his toes, astonishingly silent and swift. He was dimly aware, as he raced past, of doors opening, and faces, sleepy, irritable or frightened, staring out at him. And as he drew closer to the upper floors the screaming grew louder and louder. It was screaming of a kind he had never heard before ... except once, perhaps—the thought flashed through his mind—a screaming that must proceed from agony of a particularly unexpected and atrocious nature. It shrilled in his ears with such intensity that he felt his whole frame shudder, on the verge it seemed of fracture or collapse, as if he had touched a high-voltage cable. Somehow he forced himself to run even faster up the staircase leading to the upper regions, and hurled the heavy door open.

Now the screaming almost paralysed him, as when one stands directly under a full, shattering peal of bells: he had difficulty in forcing his legs to keep moving. The corridors were full of people, standing about indecisively, in twos and threes, their mouths open, their eyes wide, staring about them as if mesmerized. The fact that all of them were strangers increased Hugo's sense of horror, as if one of his nightmares had suddenly come to life. They made no effort, either, to move in the direction of the screams, staring into Hugo's eyes with hostile and even accusing expressions as they made way for him, stumbling and tripping over each other as they did so.

But Hugo had never felt so nimble and fleet of foot in his life. Swerving, pushing, leaping over projecting legs, he did not slacken his pace for an instant. Turning the last corner he came to the door of Mr Smith's studio and, without pausing to ask himself whether it was locked or whether he had brought his keys with him, hurled himself against it. The door did not simply burst open, it fell flat before him, with a clang like that of a drawbridge, so that he ran straight over it and into the room, fighting down a spasm of wild laughter in the midst of the deafening screams, at the grotesque intrusion of an effect that might have belonged to the Keystone Cops.

His eyes took in the room—a table overturned, chairs smashed, the easel toppled over, several canvases stove in —and a fraction later the bed flecked with blood and two wildly heaving bodies. One of the girl's breasts was exposed, its centre welling blood, blood dappling the surrounding skin. The other breast was hidden by Mr Smith's head, very still and intent, the teeth clenched. The girl was screaming, screaming....

Hugo caught hold of the long black hair at the nape of Mr Smith's neck and pulled, at the same time driving his knee in the region of the kidneys. Mr Smith jerked upright and stood beside the bed: his white teeth, still clenched, were bared as he fought for breath: a moment later he spat something from between them. There was blood on his upper lip: his eyes were as

171

expressionless as black slate. The girl's screaming was now long-drawn-out, monotonous. She raised her hands and cupped her breasts: blood seeped through her fingers. Mr Smith turned his head sharply. The tip of his tongue came out, delicately, and caught one of the drops of blood on his upper lip: he smiled, dreamily, and made a move back towards the bed. Hugo hit him with all his strength in the pit of the stomach, with a sense of satisfaction that was profound yet somehow disgusting. Mr Smith's eyes were fixed on Hugo with a look of intense astonishment, as, his hand clutching his stomach, he slowly subsided to the floor.

A number of the other tenants were now clustered, pale-faced, in the doorway.

"Well, don't just stand there!" Hugo spoke in tones of unaccustomed authority: but that, too, he found somewhat distasteful.

Hesitantly they entered the room. Hugo gave his orders —to tie up Mr Smith, who was beginning to stir again, with one of the blood-stained sheets; to fetch towels and dressings from the bathroom; to telephone the ambulance and the police. They obeyed him without question, but with strangely sullen, resentful expressions, glancing uneasily at each other and muttering, as if in some way they were blaming Hugo for what had happened. When they turned to the girl, whose screams had now died down into a continuous, despairing moan, their faces were wooden, as if they were determined to withhold from them any sign of either horror or compassion.

The police arrived first, took in the scene, clapped handcuffs on Mr Smith's bony wrists and lifted him to his feet—though it was evident that his ultimate destination would not be a police cell.

Two ambulance men, carrying a stretcher, passed them in the doorway. They lifted the girl onto the stretcher. She was not even moaning now: she lay flat on her back, staring up at the ceiling, her eyes distended. As the ambulance men carried her out Hugo approached the stretcher and tried to take her hand. She snatched it away, and her eyes, turned towards him, shocked, incredulous, and somehow reproachful.

Hugo locked the door of Mr Smith's studio behind him. He made his way towards the head of the stairs. The groups of strangers in the corridors stood aside to let him pass, staring at him with a hostile expression in their eyes. Walking as if in a dream he reached his own quarters and closed the door behind him. His self-command entirely evaporated, he stood for a moment and stretched his arms despairingly in the direction of the green baize door that led to the basement. Then he let them fall to his side, and fighting down a wave of nausea, he sank into a chair in front of his wall chart, placed his elbows on the table and buried his head in his hands. "Oh God," he whispered, "is *that* here too? In *my* house?" His body was shuddering so violently that the box of plastic squares fell off the table and scattered its contents. Suddenly it struck him that this was the first time in years that his body—his own body—had felt shame and horror and fear. With an effort he forced himself to stoop down, pick up one of the black squares from the floor, and with trembling fingers insert it in its appropriate space on the chart.

The Indian Summer was fading. The sun still rose, bright and yellow, but within a few hours it was as weak and pale as a candle behind parchment. As he walked through the gardens Hugo could see only with difficulty; he stumbled over the edges of rockeries; tripped over trails of creepers; found himself running down unexpected slopes with small steps like those of a child. The dim light, however, was due to mist rather than to full-scale fog. There was nothing static about it. On the contrary it was in perpetual motion, coiling in long loops and streamers, or piling up suddenly like sheep crowding at a narrow opening. By the time he had walked from one end of the garden to the other Hugo felt as if he had passed through a thousand different caves and grottoes at a thousand different points in place and time. Some had been in sunlight, some in semi-darkness; some had been pits of velvety blackness, and others mere insubstantial, wavering hollows. As he brushed against plants and bushes, handfuls of moisture were dashed into his face. But the moisture had no real penetrative power, and the earth remained dry and brittle, only slightly darkened by the spray-like drops: there had been no rain, in fact, for weeks and the papers carried warnings of drought. By a similar paradox, the atmosphere was sultry—and yet laced with cold air, so that Hugo found himself sweating and shivering at one and the same time. His breath was the mist: the moisture dashed from the leaves were the drops of his perspiration. The earth heaved about him: the glimpses of reality quivered like a mirage. House, garden, man—all of them seemed to be shifting and changing, fabric, tissue and cell, and it was impossible to tell whether it was an ending or a beginning.

An ending, certainly, for some of Hugo's tenants—though looked at from their point of view of course it might be regarded as a beginning. ... For suddenly as Hugo returned to the front of the house, a furniture van loomed up out of the mist. It was followed closely by another, and another, and yet another. Hugo was so startled that he stopped counting. Startled, not because a number of his tenants were moving: there had been a general exodus among the more respectable since the horror of Mr Smith's studio—though for them the horror had resided chiefly in the arrival of the police—but by the series of coincidences. Not only had all the tenants who were moving this morning apparently chosen the same hour of departure, but they must also have chosen to patronize the same firm of hauliers, while the firm concerned must have been one that believed in precision and uniformity. For the vans that emerged from the mist, proceeding at identical speeds, were identical, too, in size, shape and design. For a moment Hugo thought he must be watching one of those films in which the crime that is plotted is of so breath-taking a nature (such as stealing the gold from Fort Knox, or the Ashes from the Long Room at Lord's) that it depends on a clock-work precision that is of itself sinister and menacing.

Slowly and in perfect unison, as if rehearsal-perfect, the vans swung round in an arc, went into reverse at exactly the same moment, nudged their way towards the various exits (Hugo's house was plentifully endowed with doors and passages—indeed he had an odd feeling that they must have multiplied during the past six months)—and at exactly the same moment came to rest, letting down their rear flaps in one unified clang.

Hugo walked to and fro between the vans. The removals men, by some trick of the light presumably, looked remarkably alike, as if it was also the policy of the firm concerned—or firms in the plural, for none of the vans bore identifying marks—to employ only sets of identical twins. It so happened, moreover, that every time Hugo approached the tail-end of a van, the article of furniture being handed into it bore an astonishing resemblance to that which he had just seen handed into the previous van—and when he reached the next one, the article of furniture that was being handed into it was ... and so on. Hugo had the weird feeling that his house must consist of a series of cuckoo clocks ... or rather (as a coil of mist, yellow, flecked with black, curled round his nostrils with an acrid, metallic tang) cells that exuded the same matter.

He was relieved, when he reached the last of the vans, to find Roger standing by the tail-board, peering into the dark interior—for Mr Quincey had handed in his notice after the "disgraceful episode" on the top floor, which was, he had explained to Hugo amidst a wreath of creased smiles, "bad for his image".

Hugo and Roger exchanged nods and without speaking a word (none, after all, was necessary) set out on a farewell tour of the gardens. Roger first led the way to that recalcitrant zone near the front gate which always inspired him with such revulsion, and which so obstinately resisted Hugo's civilizing efforts. At this time of the year, of course, everything was bedraggled in any case; even so Hugo's heart sank. The rusty tin cans, soiled paper bags and cartons, discarded tyres and other more unmentionable debris, were piled higher than ever, cemented together now by clots of black leaf-mould.

There was no denying, either, that the band had widened considerably since he had last inspected it. From being a mere fringe which collected the normal flotsam and jetsam of the London streets, as a result of topography in conjunction with the prevailing winds of the district, supplemented by the casual offerings of passersby who had just left the tobacconist's, confectioner's, or bus stop, it had grown into a veritable rubbish dump. A sudden break in the mist revealed a wheel-less perambulator, its paint flaking, like grey wood shavings; the torso of an ancient Austin Seven motor car, also without wheels, and a cracked wash-basin, which Hugo uneasily though he recognized as coming from his top floor—not to mention the "unmentionable" articles, which had undoubtedly multiplied alarmingly. When the mist closed in again it curled over the pile like a sulphurous smoke.

Hugo and Roger turned on their heels and made for the orchard. Here the earth was black and tacky from trampled fruit, interspersed with clumps of grey-looking grass which showered drops of moisture on to their shoes, so that the leather quickly darkened, like sodden brown paper. They made their way through the trees, rising out of the mist like opponents in some ghostly game of football, and reached the brick wall. Roger immediately sat down with his back against it, oblivious of the state of the ground. Gingerly Hugo lowered himself beside him. He pressed his back against the wall, and after a while he, too, could feel a grainy pressure which, despite the chill and the damp, called back memories of past summers—and a more painful sensation from one of the spidery, rusty nails that had once held espaliers in place, but which broke off when he wriggled his back.

But though the touch of the brick was still evocative, it no longer conjured up the murmur of summer heat, and he was glad when Roger rose to his feet, and he was able to follow suit. Roger led the way to his favourite apple tree—its branches more like tarred ropes than ever, the few leaves at the branches' ends like dirty dusters. Hugo, proud of his sailor-like agility shinned up the tree after Roger, and together they gazed over the

176

wall at the school. As always it squatted in the square of asphalt that looked like congealed ink, apparently impervious of the changing seasons, like a prehistoric animal preserved in a museum. Emptied of children it looked so completely abandoned that it was impossible now to believe that it had ever housed a living creature: it hunched up with a guilty air about it as if permeated with the smell of ancient sacrifices to a thoroughly discredited god. From this distance the small details, of course, were not visible; but in imagination Hugo ran his fingers along the familiar surfaces of the brick, while his eyes registered every scratch on every door and the minutest flaw in each of the window-panes—and at the same time felt his spirits plunging like a lift down a mine-shaft.

Descending from the apple tree they steered their way back through the orchard, gnarled shapes looming up at them out of the mist. They skirted the yew hedge and entered the dank well of Hugo's kitchen garden. They proceeded down the narrow path beside the greenhouse, through the rockery (now practically bare of plants and more like a miniature lunar landscape than ever) and so round to the back of the house and to the Palfreys' allotment. The base of the water-butt was a mash of dead leaves, squashed cabbage stalks, and the blackened heads of dahlias and chrysanthemums: but the holly-hocks behind it were straight green poles, their leaves as big as elephants' ears. They went up to the window of the shed, rubbed a pane clean, and peered through. The gardening implements were neatly stacked away, under a layer of grease; but on the table, with its oil-cloth covering, the tea-caddy was open and a half-eaten biscuit lay on a plate beside it.

When they returned to the furniture van the men were just fastening the back flaps, and the Quinceys were seated in their Rover impatiently waiting for Roger. They ignored Hugo. Roger gave him a brief nod and climbed in beside his parents (the Quinceys were very proud of the fact that the front seat of their car held three passengers). As Roger bent his head, Hugo noticed for the first time that he had grown considerably during the past six months—and that he was wearing long trousers. He felt a spasm—not so much of irritation as of an undefined distaste.

The feeling remained with him when he reached his own quarters and stood before his wall chart. The departure of the Quinceys had given it a lop-sided shape, as if the whole house was about to topple over. It was not at all as he had planned it: for one thing, Roger should not have gone before the Palfreys; for another, it should have been *he* who gave notice, not the other way round. A new beginning surely demanded that due order of precedence be observed?

The house telephone rang. Hugo picked up the receiver. "Yes?" he asked. There was no reply. "Who is it?" he demanded. This time he heard a heavy, guttural breathing. "Yes, of course," he said, "I will be over immediately."

When he reached the Proudfoot-Lorns' apartment he found the front door ajar. He pushed it open and entered the hall. He looked round him in bewilderment, then remembered the date ... ah yes, it was an in-between time. The walls had been recently repapered—how or when Hugo did not know; certainly he had seen no sign of any workmen. The paper was of a thick, drab chocolate brown colour, on which a greasy patina was already forming. It always puzzled Hugo how the Proudfoot-Lorns achieved this effect so quickly: did they boil puddings in gigantic cauldrons all over the place—or steam countless kippers in greasy frying pans? On the other hand, the woodwork below the wall-paper was much as it had been on his last visit; the light, linseedy effect had not yet been obliterated under layers of thick brown paint.

A good deal of light wood still remained in the living-room too. So did Dame Alice's lectern, with its huge Bible in the purple binding, open at exactly the same page. But her African carvings and most of the other fruits of her missionary labours had been removed, while her religious paintings—one of Christ sheltering children, black, brown or yellow, under his outspread arms, uppermost—were stacked against the wall. In their places

178

were Colonel Arnold's South American trophies, under exactly the same layer of mushroom-grey dust, each phosphorescent streak of decay intact, as if they had been stored all this time in a vacuum. In place, but not yet quite settled: shrunken heads, stuffed animals and birds peered round them, out of glass eyes or sunken sockets, uneasily and watchfully, while the lizards and snakes seemed still to be slithering tentatively along the walls, and the stuffed cayman suspended from the ceiling swayed slightly, as if still seeking its point of equilibrium. At the same time, Edgar's filing cabinet, with its undigested contents, had not yet been removed, though there were several of Eunice's half-empty tins and boxes of chocolates scattered about, and Eunice's smell undoubtedly pervaded the room, subduing even the acrid odours of crumbling scale and feather and stale formalin.

The figures on the couch (Dame Alice's chintz now replaced by Eunice's greasy brocade) were also not quite settled, as if each had got stuck halfway out of its chrysalis. Hugo had little difficulty in recognizing Arnold's brisk little head with the darting bird-like eyes and the bristling white moustache, but the legs were clad in baggy yellow-stained tweed that undoubtedly belonged to Edgar. By the same token, he could hardly mistake Dame Alice's apple cheeks and commanding blue eyes, but Dame Alice's coiffure had collapsed into greasy disarray, while her expensive tailor-made did not have at all the same appearance unsupported by the expensive corset—and there was no getting away from the fact that the shawl across the shoulders, once black, now plum-coloured, covered with stains and scorch marks, the fringes caked with dirt, was Eunice's.

The two figures sat side by side, with a stark, desperate expression in their eyes as if they had been struck by lightning, or one of their most devoted disciples had suddenly and unaccountably spat in their faces. An open letter lay on the lap of Edgar's unmentionable trousers.

"You rang?" Hugo asked politely. Two pairs of eyes switched in his direction; both figures nodded; neither spoke.

"You wished to ... ah, communicate with me?" Hugo

spoke very loudly and clearly, as if he were addressing children of limited intelligence, the slightly deaf, or foreigners from Central Europe who had not yet acquired an adequate command of English. The two heads nodded in unison.

"Something has happened?" Again the two heads nodded.

"Something that does not fit into your ... your, ah, 'grand design'?"

A more vigorous nod.

"*What* has happened?" This time both pairs of eyes swivelled in the direction of Edgar's trousers.

"You wish me to read the letter?" The heads nodded.

Hugo cautiously detached the letter from Edgar's lap, while Arnold's eyes snapped and glittered frantically.

Hugo unfolded the letter. It was headed "B.B.C. Television Service". "My dear Arnold," it began; "Ever Yours" it ended, followed by the signature of the producer of Arnold's film series. Hugo nevertheless addressed himself to the intervening matter. "In accordance with our usual policy of discontinuing a series when it is at the peak of its popularity... As a Public Corporation it is our duty to act as a barometer or seismograph ... we detect a faint lowering of the atmosphere ... that distant tremor indicates that some subtle change is taking place in the public's taste... Better to end with a bang than a whimper... Sure you will agree ... Dr Baxbr, the nature photographer ... a series about the 'secret life' of Britain's sea shore... Admittedly speaks little English ... an unusually thick and difficult accent ... the public will laugh, then feel exasperated and write indignant letters to the press and the 'Keep British Television Clean' movement ... then they will love to hate, and eventually it will be all the rage ... especially as there will be a lot of philosophical bits (the usual Miracle of Life stuff) ... will suddenly appear profound ... You of all people will appreciate that the secret of our success has been to endow the grotesque with the appearance of significance... Duty to the public... Therefore we regret ... funds no longer available ... will surely be in great demand ... your distinguished work for the Science

180

of Anthropology ... in itself a consolation ... Duty to the public...."

Hugo's heart warmed to Dr Baxbr: he made a mental note to look out for his programmes.... For a fleeting moment he even wondered whether he might be in need of lodgings....

He switched his attention back to the couch. The two pairs of eyes regarded him steadily. Carefully he returned the letter to Edgar's trousers and addressed Arnold's face.

"I am sorry," he said. "It must have been a blow— but there are other television companies—other film companies?"

Arnold's moustache bristled in derisory fashion.

"After all this does not effect your, ah scientific work...."

Arnold's shoulders jerked convulsively.

"You have no doubt already planned another expedition?" Mournfully the head nodded.

"The still uncharted forests that lie between Brazil and Venezuela?" Hugo asked, recalling a phrase from the blurb in the *Radio Times* that had accompanied Arnold's last series. Arnold's eyebrows shot up in pained surprise at the stupidity of the question.

"But of course you will go just the same?" The centre of Arnold's moustache shot out as a silent "Tcha!" formed behind it.

"Money?" Hugo asked. Arnold made a circling movement with his shoulders and spread out the palms of his hands, in a gesture which Hugo interpreted as "Yes— and no."

"You could obtain the money easily enough? It is simply a matter of writing to the appropriate bodies? You have plenty of your own in any case?"

Both Arnold and Eunice nodded briefly, gazing down into their laps in a sullen, slightly irritable manner.

"Well, why *don't* you start writing the appropriate letters?"

But at this they both showed unmistakable signs of agitation, twisting and turning this way and that and twitching various portions of their anatomies.

"Ah, well," Hugo said, deciding that heartiness was the best policy, "you can reverse your usual procedure. Your sister" (addressing Arnold) "can go on one of her missionary trips, and by the time she returns" (addressing Eunice) "your brother will no doubt have found other sponsors."

For the first time the two figures on the couch gave voice simultaneously and in unison:

"What sister?" ... "What brother?"

Two pairs of eyes focussed on him with a glitter in them so unmistakably malevolent that Hugo beat a hasty retreat.

To his surprise he found Mr Sturmer and Pat waiting outside his door. He unlocked it and stood aside for them to enter. He was even more surprised at the change in their appearance. They had an odd, pinched waif-like look that reminded him of pictures of the first world war which he had seen as a child. Mr Sturmer's guitar (which, Hugo noticed, now lacked a string) struck an anachronistic note perhaps, but the khaki army great-coat, several sizes too large for him, was exactly in period. He had shaved off his curly side-whiskers, though the wispy moustache and beard remained ... the Russian front, perhaps, Hugo reflected.

Pat was wearing a maxi-coat that reached practically to her insteps. The high collar, wide *revers*, and the fawn drabness of its herring-bone pattern further heightened the impression of faded sepia: Hugo half-expected to see her take out a packet of "Dorothy papers", such as he had seen his female relatives use as a child, tear off one of the fragrant powdery tissues and apply it to her undoubtedly shiny nose. For she was wearing no make-up: without it her face looked pinched and pale, as if she was in a consumption. Gone, too, was the hairdo that had soared above her head like a filigree mobile: instead her hair was flattened under a faded brown felt hat, with a darker band where a ribbon had once been; a few lank looking strands protruded from under the brim and curled round the tiny, child-like ears.

Any minute, Hugo thought, he would see the two of them break into convulsive movement, like a 1918 news-reel. In fact they seemed hesitant and embarrassed.

"Well?" Hugo prompted.

"We're off!" Mr Sturmer announced abruptly.

"We'll send the rent later," Pat added.

"But why?" Hugo asked: he wanted the house to himself, yet he was unhappy to see any of his favourites go. There was a long pause. Mr Sturmer and Pat regarded each other, eyebrows raised.

"We're having a baby for one thing," Pat said at length, then when Hugo made clucking noises of old-fashioned solicitude a look of disgust crossed her face. "Oh not for a long time," she said. "*That's* nothing— it happens all the time!"

"Then why?" Hugo repeated. There was another pause.

"We think it's better..." Mr Sturmer said.

"For the baby," Pat added, then hurriedly, "and of course for us...."

"Under the circumstances," Mr Sturmer said, with peculiar emphasis.

"Where are you going?" Hugo asked.

"Oh not far." Mr Sturmer stooped down (despite the guitar) to pick up his luggage, which Hugo had not noticed before. This too was "in period", consisting of several brown-paper parcels tied to a bulging trunk of basket weave, the two halves kept together by a leather strap. Hugo had not seen such a trunk since his grand-mother died—then remembered that his grandmother's trunk had indeed been stowed away in one of the attics.

Mr Sturmer heaved the trunk on to his shoulder, and he and Pat made for the door. Then suddenly they both halted and turned round.

"You'd better look out," Mr Sturmer said. "You're not our generation—but we're warning you."

8

It did not take Hugo long to discover the import of Mr Sturmer's warning. As he made his way towards the "upper regions" in order to lock the rooms he and Pat had vacated he could hear a murmur which gradually increased in volume as he mounted from one floor to another, and which eventually resolved itself into a series of impassioned harangues interspersed with cheers, yells, laughter and stamping. As he climbed the final flight he saw that the green baize door had been removed and that planks had been nailed across the outside of the doorway. He managed to get his hand through an opening between two of the planks and to insert the key in the lock; it turned easily enough, but the door did not give; obviously some heavy object had been placed against it; a moment later, too, the key leaped out of the lock and clattered at his feet as a nail was driven into the keyhole from the opposite side amid a further burst of triumphant cheering.

Hugo thoughtfully retraced his steps. He decided not to summon the police. He still retained a feeling of responsibility towards all his tenants.

In any case the continuous uproar proceeding from the upper regions had the advantage of dislodging several of the more awkward ones in other parts of the house, thus saving him the trouble of giving them notice, and before long the only "respectable" tenants left in the house (apart, that is, from himself and the mysterious occupant of the basement) were the Palfreys and the Proudfoot-Lorns.

For some reason, however, the tenants—or rather occupants—of the upper regions insisted on regarding themselves as under siege, though in fact there was nothing to prevent them taking down their barricades, unnailing the door, and coming and going as they pleased. Instead they behaved as if it was perilous in the extreme to venture out, though one wild-haired, bare-footed young man (who bore a remarkable resemblance, Hugo thought, to the picture of John the Baptist in the illustrated Bible of his childhood) came shinning down a drain pipe on the second day (ignoring the considerably more solid iron fire-escape), ran across the garden—deserted apart from Hugo—bent double for some extraordinary reason (presumably to avoid an imaginary cross-fire) and made for the shop at the corner, to return a few minutes later bearing a packet of Woodbines amid the rapturous cheers of his companions crowding at the windows of the upper regions. He took the same loping circuitous path across the garden, returning Hugo's look of mild surprise with one of truculent suspicion—though this time, after one rather embarrassing attempt at the drain pipe, he did make use of the fire-escape.

As for food, this was provided by friends and sympathizers of the beleaguered garrison, who would at regular intervals dash across the garden (taking the same puzzling precautions as the young man) to deposit their offerings in the baskets lowered for the purpose, at the ends of ropes or sheets knotted together, from the top floor windows. At first Hugo's appearances on the scene of operations were attended by hostile demonstrations of one sort or another: those placing articles in the basket would adopt a threatening attitude, while those above hurled down oaths and insults, as well as more tangible objects—but these were seldom more lethal than toilet rolls (which unfurled with picturesque effect, like Chinese kites, during their descent) and in any case seldom found their mark, striking friends more frequently than foe—who after all presented only a solitary target. After a while, moreover, a certain camaraderie sprang up between the besieger down below and the beleaguered above. In the absence of the police Hugo, naturally, had to expect the imprecations to continue, but as ingenuity began to flag and monotony intervened, these gradually faded away in number and intensity, until the comparatively mild "exploiter" and "landlord!" took pride of place—to the second of which, at any rate, Hugo could raise no valid objection. The only remaining insult, indeed, that offended him was "tubby", chiefly because at this distance it was difficult to explain that his rotundity was a matter of muscle rather than fat, though every now and then he tried to convey this information by striking himself two or three times in the stomach with his clenched fist.

After a while, indeed, Hugo grew quite fond of the strangers thronging the open windows or the platforms of the fire-escapes (shut off now by rolls of barbed wire). He became concerned about their diet and general welfare, and on several occasions surreptitiously slipped into the siege baskets fresh fruit and vegetables, pieces of good, nourishing stewing steak, bottles of orange juice, tins of halibut oil capsules and so on (as well as toilet rolls).

This state of affairs might have continued indefinitely as far as Hugo was concerned. The police, it is true, did call on one occasion, as the result of complaints by the neighbours—which was a considerable tribute to the volume of noise proceeding from the upper regions, in view of the fact that the nearest house was a good two hundred yards away. Hugo, however, was able to persuade them that the uproar was connected with the betrothal ceremonies of a couple of his tenants who hailed from an obscure corner of the Balkans, where such ceremonies were of an abnormally protracted nature and where the future happiness of the affianced pair depended on the amount of noise the guests could generate, in order to drive away "the spirits of contention and discord". Questioned about the baskets, continually bobbing up and down like cradles on a construction site, Hugo replied that these, too, were part of the antique ritual: for until this reached its climax both betrothed couple and guests must be confirmed in a species of purdah, to the topmost floor of whatever building they might be occupying at the time: in their own country, of course, where one-storeyed huts were the rule, this meant the roof, but that, he was sure the police would agree, was not at all suitable in such an inclement climate as ours. The purpose of this elevation Hugo explained (now waxing eloquent) was to separate them from evil influences, whose natural habitat was on the ground (did not serpents glide upon their bellies?) and—as they happened to be Zoroastrians—to bring them as close as possible to the source of their religious inspiration. But the faithful, even if they were foreigners, must be fed, and so their co-religionists placed gifts of food and other necessities—duly purified in another impressive ritual—into the baskets, with the appropriate prayers and blessings.

The police listened to Hugo's explanation with great politeness, and then went peaceably away. Indeed, one young constable who had received a higher education in the course of which he had been converted to Buddhism, stopped beside one of the baskets on his way out, closed his eyes in silent prayer, and then deposited in the basket a quarter-pound block of chocolate he chanced to have about his person.

Eventually, however, the garrison on the top floor, discovering that a purely imaginary beleaguerment lacked excitement, and despairing of provoking Hugo to any satisfactory show of violence, anger, or even exasperation, sent one of their number shinning down a drain pipe and across No Man's Land: it was raining heavily, but Hugo had thoughtfully placed an umbrella and a pair of Wellingtons in a little lean-to of corrugated iron which he had constructed at the foot of the drain pipe which bore the brunt of the traffic (and which Hugo had now stapled more firmly to the wall). This emissary carried with him a "Revolutionary Manifesto"—which he obligingly allowed Hugo to read, and whose spelling errors Hugo obligingly and innocently corrected in return—proclaiming that "The Witherers"—as this particular anarchical group called itself, in deference presumably to Lenin's famous prognostication of the ultimate destiny of the State—had "taken over" the top floor of Hugo's house as a protest against housing conditions in the area and as a gesture of general defiance, and that although their aims were entirely peaceable they would resist, "by violence if necessary", any show of "naked power" designed to dislodge them.

The emissary carried this Manifesto (with Hugo's pencilled corrections) to the nearest police station (a destination which had certainly not entered into Hugo's calculations) and somehow managed to insert it under the glass of the notice board which was fastened to the wall outside, where the black skull and cross-bones and the red hand dripping blood (which decorated the top and bottom of the Manifesto respectively) added an agreeable touch of colour and drama to the obscure and gloomy "Wanted Persons" photographs, the Meccano-like Identikit pictures, and the warnings about the renewal of gun, broadcasting and dog licences.

Acting on information so unequivocally received, therefore, the police had no alternative but to accept the challenge. They informed Hugo of their intention, suggesting that "undesirable elements" must somehow have mingled with the Wedding Guests, and expressing the hope that the action they were now obliged to take would not seriously incommode the bridal pair. Hugo, who did not seriously think that the beleaguered garrison would carry out its threats of violence, informed one of the scouts as he was returning the umbrella and Wellington boots to their shelter, giving him details as to date and time, for the police had made no attempt to bind him to secrecy.

This information must have been promptly passed on to allies and sympathizers outside, so that when on the appointed day the two elderly policemen who had been deemed sufficient to cope with the original demonstration arrived at the road leading to Hugo's house, it was to find their entrance blocked by a milling and excited crowd. They surveyed the scene stolidly for a minute or two and then withdrew with the same deliberate, unhurried tread with which they had arrived.

Hugo, meanwhile, dismayed by the size of the crowd and suffering from pangs of conscience, had left the house with the intention of acting as mediator. Seeing the police withdraw in good order, and excited by the fairground atmosphere, he stayed on, wandering round from one exhibit to another. The core of the crowd consisted of the "demo" proper—bands of young people bearing such reasonable slogans as "House the Homeless", and "Down with the Police State", and others, such as "Hang the Landlords", which Hugo regarded as rather more provocative. The *bona fide* demonstrators, however, were naturally outnumbered by those who had flocked to the scene activated by curiosity, a desire to support some vaguely defined "good cause", solidarity with their own age group, or simple boredom. Two local politicians, however, had also taken advantage of the captive audience (the road was now sealed off at both ends by police cars) to set up makeshift rostrums, from which they declaimed upon the merits of their respective parties' housing policies, though apart from an occasional perfuntory catcall they aroused little interest.

Proceedings, indeed, were beginning to flag when a stir of excitement ran through the crowd, and Hugo caught the word "skinheads". Although secretly ashamed that he had never heard the term before, Hugo nevertheless experienced a *frisson* of mingled pleasure and horror, as at the memory of some emanation from childhood nightmares, though the pleasurable part of the sensation evaporated when he learned that a band of these mysterious "skinheads" had offered their services to the defenders of his "upper regions" and that the offer had been accepted. This information was imparted to him by Mr Sturmer and Pat, who had suddenly appeared at his side. They showed no surprise at meeting him among a crowd demonstrating outside his own house and, presumably, against his own person, though Mr Sturmer did say, "Nothing against you personally, Hugo—you're merely the Tool of the System", before he and Pat took their places beneath one of the more inflammatory of the banners. No one else knew him, however, and he was accepted tolerantly as some amiable middle-aged do-gooder, anxious to demonstrate that he was still young at heart—a clergyman who rode a motor-bike and scorned a dog-collar, for example, a sociologist collecting material for a thesis, or an unsuccessful retired amateur middle-weight boxer with mild homosexual tendencies which had been long since battered into aquiescence, and who had therefore turned to Youth Club work.

The murmur of excitement provoked by the news of the skinheads had barely died away, when a whistle sounded and the police suddenly appeared, not, as the demonstrators had expected, from either end of the street where the police cars were placed, but seeming as if by magic, to rise out of the ground from behind bush, tree or rubbish heap inside Hugo's garden itself, which they had presumably entered from the rear. They split into two groups. One half ranged themselves behind the gates of Hugo's garden, facing the crowd outside. The other half formed themselves into a column, two abreast, and marched towards the house, each man close to the one in front of him and with the toe-caps of his boots turned outwards, so that the column looked like a cen-tipede or an elongated pantomime horse. As they advanced there was a hoarse roar of mingled rage and defiance from the roof and windows of the house, and the defenders congregated there began to pelt the police with stones, lumps of coal, crockery, kitchen utensils, and (Hugo noticed uneasily) toilet rolls. One of the constables' helmets was removed by an iron saucepan that had found its mark. A lump appeared on his forehead and he turned pale but the column gave no sign that anything untoward had happened and continued on its way without the least variation in pace and rhythm, and a few seconds later disappeared through the front door.

Meanwhile the other file stood stolidly facing the crowd—who, enraged by the success of the police man-oeuvre, now turned and rushed at the gates. Severely restricted for space, however (the street narrowed con-siderably at this point), only a few at a time could approach, and that not entirely of their own volition, but ejected like peas squeezed from a pod, by the pres-sure of those behind them. Unable to return to the matrix that had expelled them, these either rattled in-effectually against the iron gates, which were securely locked and bolted, or in order to save themselves from being crushed, clambered over the breast-high walls, either to be tumbled back over again by the waiting police, or to be escorted (if their protestations of non-violent intention were sufficiently voluble) to a back entrance, known only to the police—and of course, to Hugo.

If he could have extricated himself from the crowd, indeed, Hugo would have sought it out himself, for he earnestly desired to return to his house in order to ascertain what was happening inside. At first this was quite out of the question, but a few minutes later a lucky heave of the crowd smacked him right up against the gates. By another stroke of luck the police sergeant on the other side recognized him and calmly proceeded to unlock the gates: holding one hand majestically aloft as if directing the traffic, he held the gate slightly ajar with the other so that Hugo might squeeze through. This he was unable to do immediately, until Mr Sturmer called out indignantly, "It's his *home!*" at which those nearest to Hugo, their deepest British instincts having been thus triggered (and momentarily forgetting the purpose for which they were assembled) pushed and heaved at those pressing behind them until Hugo was able to slip through the proffered opening. The sergeant, after first saluting Hugo as a representative of the sacred rights of property, locked and bolted the gate again, and resumed his former stance, feet solidly planted, arms behind his back, chewing the ends of his moustache and eyeing the crowd (now anxious to expiate their temporary lapse and therefore for the first time turning really violent) with the wary but half-bored expression of an old sheep-dog.

A moment later, however, he turned and moved un-hurriedly to his left, to a point at which the wall, at that side of the gate, had suddenly collapsed, depositing a jumble of bricks, mortar, and flailing, dust-covered bodies at the feet of the police. The crowd behind, believing that this was the result of heroic action on the part of the vanguard, gave a cheer and surged forward. The sergeant tugged at the end of his moustache and regarded the advancing horde with a critical, calculating air, as if he were making up his mind about the weather: Hugo half-expected him to lick his thumb and hold it aloft. Instead he tut-tutted and shook his head, more, it appeared, in sorrow than in anger. It was indeed now clear to Hugo that words like "column" and "file" —and certainly "force"—which had previously entered his mind in connection with the police presence, were altogether too grandiose for the numbers actually involved. These in fact totalled only a dozen—six of whom had gone into the house. It was the generous dimensions and imperturbable demeanour of the men concerned that had created the illusion of impregnability. The six police officers remaining in the garden, therefore, were hard put to it to cope with this new situation, especially as the scope of their duties had been unexpectedly broadened, as they struggled at one and the same time to clear away the rubble, to hoist the dazed and dusty figures beneath it to their feet, to cast a quick eye over them for signs of serious injury, while every now and then obliged to throw back those members of the advancing crowd who sought to take advantage of the situation by making a break for the house.

Nevertheless, the sergeant detached one of his men to escort Hugo. On the way a stone struck the young constable a sharp blow on the cheek: he paused for a moment to remove his helmet and wipe away the blood, before once more grasping Hugo firmly by the elbow and continuing his unhurried progress. "Sorry about that, sir," he said, as they reached the shelter of the porch. He opened the front door and held it aside for Hugo to enter. "Now in you go! And please, sir, leave this to us. Why don't you shut yourself in your room and make yourself a nice cup of tea?" He saluted, and turned on his heel. Through the glass panels of the door Hugo saw that the tide of masonry and tumbled bodies had advanced far beyond the fringe of filth and debris that had always so disheartened him. The police, reinforced now by the constable who had escorted Hugo, were gradually falling back. Every now and then a member of the crowd—which though noisy and threatening were for the most part extremely wary—would make a sudden dash, to run straight into the linked arms of the six policemen, there to heave convulsively for a moment, with a tremendous show of energy, before being bounced back—as if engaged in a rather rough game of catch-as-catch-can. To Hugo's disappointment these young men were all extremely hairy. The majority of the crowd had now entered the garden, and Hugo could see over their heads that the police cars, which had previously been stationed at either end of the street, together with a Black Maria, had driven up behind the crowd, and were silently disgorging reinforcements, though these, obviously under orders to act strictly as reserves, made no attempt to join in the *mêlée* in front of the house.

Hugo retreated a few steps across the hall. The front door—like all the doors in Hugo's house—was unusually solid, almost obliterating the roar from outside. From somewhere above his head came another series of yells, shrieks, crashings and bangings—but these sounds, too, were strangely muted. The rooms on the ground floor (apart from his own of course) had by now all been vacated, and their emptiness spread through the whole area like a slowly rising tide. The hallway, despite the distant uproar, was a well of peace: Hugo found himself loving it with a passion that startled him: there was nothing he would have liked better than to retire to his own rooms, lock the door, and make himself the nice cup of tea the young constable had recommended. At that moment, however, there was a particularly heavy bang from above, which even at this distance caused the chandelier over his head to lurch alarmingly. Hugo sighed; he hurried to his rooms, collected his old A.R.P. helmet from the capacious cupboard, and reluctantly made his way to the upper regions.

When he arrived he saw that the planks which had been nailed across the entrance, the door itself, and the packing cases which had been piled up against the door on the inside had all been removed. Inside a furious struggle was in progress, both in the main corridor and in the passageways opening off it, as the police attempted to get behind the squatters and so drive them out of the upper regions and down the stairs.

As Hugo entered, a chamber-pot spinning in a low, swooping trajectory, like a flying saucer, struck his tin hat with a clang. Various other hostile objects, among them coins, bottles, and potatoes stuck with razor-blades, were also hurtling through the air, and most of the police had cuts, bumps or bruises on their faces and foreheads. Underfoot it was slippery with miscellaneous filth: the stench was overpowering.

Turning into one of the passageways, Hugo saw a young constable, unnoticed by his colleagues, slowly subsiding to the ground under the weight of assailants: he had lost his helmet and his hair was clotted to his forehead with blood. Hugo's heart skipped a beat. At last he had found the skinheads: four naked scalps, mottled and bristly, faced him: he thrilled to the memory of horror films with bald-headed monsters, and of savage adventure films with sadistic Huns and ferocious Mongols (to both of which he was secretly addicted). For a moment he was too terrified to think of going to the aid of the young constable. But at that moment the latter twisted round, in an effort to regain his feet, and Hugo got a closer view of the assailants. Instead of the barrel-chested giants he had imagined, he saw four pimply lads in their teens whose "bovver boots" accentuated the skinniness of their legs, like unwieldy club-feet. The absence of hair on their foreheads (which were, admittedly, of no remarkable depth) had the effect of narrowing their faces, so that they looked like those of mice or stoats: the glint of tiny teeth as they grinned in triumph when the policeman finally sank to the ground, heightened the impression. The rims of their eyes—also very naked looking, so that it seemed to Hugo that they must have shaved their eyelashes and eyebrows as well as their scalps— were abnormally red; their nostrils and upper lips, too, had a red, puffy look. Perhaps, Hugo thought, the police had been using tear gas. For a moment he felt quite indignant, until he realized that the skinheads were equipped with knuckle-dusters (elaborately embossed to resemble signet rings) and that the "bovver boots" were tipped with steel—and that they were using both to belabour the constable (who had curled himself up into

194

a ball) while the little teeth at the sides of their mouths glistened like tubers on a potato or miniature boar's tusks. At this Hugo seized the nearest of the skinheads by the arms, just below the elbows, and spun him round, with the intention of addressing to him a few words of gentle admonishment, but he was so startled by the stringy condition of the limbs he was gripping, that he paused—and in that moment the youth brought his shaven head down on to the bridge of Hugo's nose. His own eyes watering now, Hugo let go of the stringy arms and, in one of his rare moments of pique, hit the youth on the point of the chin—though still sufficiently in control of himself to pull his punch, in view of the fragility of his opponent's physique. The youth collapsed against the skirting-board, moaning. Hugo turned his attention, more cautiously this time, to another of the skinheads: he had thrown away the truncheon—with a pang, for he had long dreamed of putting it to use, but it hardly seemed fair play to apply it to scalps so reminiscent of those of newly born infants. This skinhead too, he deposited against the skirting-board, with a certain degree of roughness. A massive sergeant, shaking off attackers as a cart-horse shakes off flies, approached.

"Now then, what's all this?" he said gruffly. He bent down over the moaning youths. "Shouldn't have done that, sir," he told Hugo sternly, as he straightened his huge bulk. "Against the law, that is." He twisted his shoulders once or twice as the other skinheads hurled themselves at him—to bounce off again like drops of water on a hot plate. In the meantime the young constable on the floor uncurled himself, retrieved his helmet, clapped it on his head, and rose a little unsteadily to his feet. He shook his head from side to side, like a swimmer emerging from water, then turned to the recumbent skinhead, satisfied himself that he was mobile, hauled him to his feet and passed him over to the massive sergeant, who in his turn passed him back to another colleague, and so on until he reached the door, where several of the newly arrived police were waiting to escort him downstairs, and so into the Black Maria.

The sergeant wagged his finger at Hugo. "Thank you for your help, sir," he said, "but you must leave this kind of thing to us!"—and then sternly, over his shoulder, as he once more turned towards the other skinheads, "just see that it doesn't happen again!"

Perhaps it was the schoolmasterly tone of the reproof, or perhaps it was that his susceptibilities had been sharpened by the smarting of his own eyes and the soreness of his nose (which, though not seriously damaged, had suffered minor abrasions from its contact with the bristly scalp of his recent assailant) but Hugo now began to feel a little sorry for the skinheads. He suddenly realized that the redness round their eyes and nostrils had a very simple explanation: they were the result of colds in the head. It hardly seemed fair to treat them so unceremoniously when they must be debilitated in this way, and (Hugo reflected indignantly) no doubt by constant bouts of neuralgia as well. He wished they would decide to confine their activities to warmer weather: their present condition was obviously quite unsuited to an English November. Or would Nature, he wondered, in due course provide the tops of their heads with protective layers of fat, as she had done in the case of mini-skirted thighs?

By now the police had cleared the main corridor, and despatched the more violent of the defenders by the same route as the skinheads. They now turned into another corridor to be greeted by a fusillade of missiles, directed with considerably more venom and accuracy than before: indeed Hugo, who had tagged on behind the police, but at a respectful distance, only just nipped back in time to save his nose from further damage. Much more cautious now (and carefully tilting his A.R.P. helmet over the bridge of his nose) he peered round the corner. The missiles came from behind a barricade of bedding and upturned furniture, which was manned by a group very different in appearance and demeanour from either the skinheads or any of the other defenders: solid, morose-looking men, none of them under thirty, dressed in business-like overalls, the legs tucked into white Wellington-type boots, and crash-helmets buckled under

196

the chin, and with that air of professional phlegm one sees in mercenary soldiers. The police paused for a moment: obviously they recognized these new opponents, and a look of determination oddly mingled with something approaching respect passed between the two parties. For the first time the police drew their batons, and advanced on the barricade. Hugo, recognizing a chair of which he was rather fond as one of its components, also moved forward, to be sternly and decisively pushed back by the giant sergeant. At the same moment he noticed a line of light coming from under one of the bathroom doors on his left.

He tried the door, found it unlocked, and entered. He was nearly driven back by the overpowering stench. The lavatory, its lid torn off for some reason and thrown into the corner, was crammed to overflowing with faeces, sanitary towels and filthy sheets of newspaper. The floor was slippery with a yellowish-brown liquid: slumped against the bath—filled to the brim in the same manner as the lavatory—was a young girl, dressed in something resembling a Red Indian costume, and apparently unconscious. A boy of about the same age was half-lying, half-sitting against the lavatory pan; his left sleeve was rolled up and a piece of elastic was twisted round the arm, just above the elbow: a trickle of blood, brown rather than red, curved down the inside of his arm, very white and smooth, like that of an infant. A tin, which had once contained the components of a geometry set, lay beside him, filled with wads of dirty cotton wool and small glass phials: a syringe had fallen out of the tin and lay almost covered by the surrounding filth.

The boy looked up at Hugo with brilliant but mournful eyes: he nodded in the direction of the girl, gave a thin little smile, and said in a thick, lisping voice, as if his gums were swollen, "Freaked out!" Hugo went over to the girl and shook her by the shoulder: she moved her head and muttered: her face was deathly pale. He turned his attention to the boy (he could not have been more than fifteen) and tried to lift him to his feet, but the body sagged, the heels sliding on the slippery floor. Hugo tried again. This time the boy feebly pushed his hands aside. "No, no," he said, "leave me alone," then began laughing in a gentle, protesting way, as if Hugo was tickling him.

Hugo abandoned the attempt. He stood pondering for a moment, and then, deciding that neither he nor the girl was in imminent danger—or at any rate that it was better under the circumstances to take the risk—he left them where they were, locking the door behind him with his master key.

He returned to the corridor in time to see six fresh police officers, presumably summoned from outside by radio, join in the assault. Only four of the defenders, themselves armed with truncheons very similar to those of the police, were still standing: the others were draped unconscious over the barricade. The blows exchanged on both sides were brutal and business-like, but curiously free from rancour. The struggle, however, was quickly over, with another of the defenders lying on his back— his face deathly white against the black crash-helmet, which was half wrenched off his head, and breathing in a hoarse, rasping way—and those still standing hand-cuffed and led away.

Hugo made his way down the stairs and out of the house. An ambulance and two Black Marias were now drawn up outside the entrance. At either end of the gravel path in front of the house a police car was stationed, each with an arc lamp mounted on the roof. The November dusk was thickening, and as Hugo descended the steps both these arc lights were switched on, flooding the whole front of the house in a brilliant light, suddenly endowing the clusters of cars and figures with a festive air, as if some fashionable reception were taking place. Hugo, his rotund figure high-lighted, found himself descending the last few steps with a baronial gait: he was half-persuaded that the trampled grass, trodden flower beds and broken masonry, dim and mysterious beyond the rim of light, had been caused by nothing more reprehensible than an amiable stampede of sight-seers or fans, and as a matter of fact the crowd had for the most part regressed to the mood of onlookers, standing excited but obedient beyond the half-circle of police

198

and craning their necks to get a better view.

The police meanwhile were busy sorting out the sheep from the goats. The hard core that had manned the barricade were dealt with first. It was they who provided the only stretcher cases. The police handled them with the same cold hostility tinged with professional punctilio that they had displayed during the fight itself. Three of them were still unconscious. The fourth, his arm in an improvised sling, was half-sitting, half-lying on his stretcher. One of the older constables approached him, felt in the pockets of his overall, produced a packet of cigarettes, extracted one, lit it and placed it between the lips of the injured man, who held it with his free hand and sucked at it greedily. The faces of both remained wooden.

The remaining "professionals"—the only ones to be handcuffed—were conducted to the first of the Black Marias. One of them paused at the door and turned to face the crowd. The constables on either side also paused. Throwing his voice with the expertise of long experience the man began to address the crowd.

"Once again," he shouted, "you have seen the realities beneath the surface of our so-called affluent society. Once again you have seen that a capitalist state is inevitably a police state. My comrades and I have nothing against the police as individuals: they are merely the tools of a frightened and therefore brutal capitalism. Each demonstration of the kind you have witnessed and participated in is a further proof of the violence inherent, behind all the fine phrases and all the fine talk about 'democracy' and 'civilization' in the decaying capitalist system. . . ."

He stopped and glanced quickly at the police standing on either side of him, as if to ascertain whether he had received his quota of free speech. He opened his mouth again, but his escorts, deciding that the conventions had been decently observed, hustled him into the van. When it had been driven away, the police turned their attention to those of their prisoners who were most obviously below the age of consent (at any rate as far as this kind of activity was concerned). They were either returned— hang-dog or sullen—to weeping mothers and scowling

199

fathers, or simply let loose with a shove. The others were herded into the remaining Black Maria. Some went docilely; others at the last moment put up a show of violent resistance, wriggling, kicking, heaving and bucking, trying to jump over the backs of the police like cattle crowded into a pen, and earning a few desultory cheers from the spectators.

One of them, a tall, emaciated young man, with unkempt hair down to his shoulders and wearing a long, sleeveless coat fringed with dirty wool, such as Persian shepherds wear, and a very large pair of down-at-heel suède shoes with abnormally wide welts which looked as if they had just been dug out of a grey bog, and who apparently regarded himself as one of the leaders of the squatters also began to harangue the crowd in a frayed, jerky voice.

"Comrades, as you have just heard, our purpose is to expose the viciousness of the System under which we live... A police state, yes... Every time we force the police to show us what they really are we are showing the System up for what it really is... Yes, and to show you the iniquities that still go on... Profiteering... The homeless... The rent racket... Yes, there are certain slum landlords ... we do not have to look far for an example..."

Ragged booing and hissing broke from the crowd. Hugo looked round him eagerly to see at whom it was directed, suddenly became aware that the young man's eyes were fixed—though with an oddly pleading expression as if begging for a response, even if it was only forgiveness—on himself. Hugo blushed and looked down at his toe-caps.

"Balls!" a voice came booming out of the crowd—a voice which Hugo recognized with gratitude as belonging to Mr Sturmer. Somebody shouted something back which Hugo could not catch.

"He said 'Balls!'," a shrill voice rang out in reply—a voice which Hugo recognized with even greater gratitude as belonging to Pat, and which continued, rather inconsequentially, "And that makes two of us!"

A further burst of cheering followed, though Hugo

could not be sure whether this was in agreement with the underlying sentiment as it related to himself, or in acknowledgment of the choice of epithet. But to his relief the police were now hustling the young man in the Persian shepherd's surtout towards the Black Maria.

It was now the turn of the skinheads (the police apparently preferred to keep their categories separate). The one who had butted Hugo on the nose put up a vigorous resistance, in spite of his chilled condition, kicking, biting, and scratching, until he was picked up by the gigantic sergeant, who held him poised in his arms, feet pointing towards the back of the Black Maria. Perhaps it was the uncomfortable angle of his carriage, or perhaps the ignominy of his situation as he writhed helplessly in the blue serge grip, or perhaps simply the effects of the chronic coryza, but suddenly Hugo saw that the irritable little eyes were filling with tears, while the shaven scalp began to throb like that of a baby before the skull has knitted together. Hugo felt a stab of pity. He dashed back into the house and into his own room: he rummaged for a moment in the store cupboard, then extracted the old khaki Balaclava helmet which he some-times wore when he was shovelling snow. When he got back the sergeant was passing his captive, still feet first, into the back of the Black Maria, like a baker sliding a loaf into a bread van. As the skinhead scrambled to his feet, a dew drop now prominently suspended from his nose, Hugo offered him the Balaclava helmet. He darted a look at Hugo, startled, venomous, puzzled, then sus-piciously grateful, hesitated, sneezed violently, then snatched the Balaclava helmet from Hugo's fingers just as the doors of the Black Maria clanged to.

The giant sergeant watched it disappear, then turned to Hugo and saluted.

"Will that be all, sir?" he said.

Hugo nodded and mounted the steps leading to his front door. At the top he turned and looked back. The crowd outside his house, which had already been split in two by the passage of the Black Maria, seemed to sway hesitantly like a tide on the turn. Then someone began to walk away in a great hurry as if he had an urgent appointment or had just remembered that he had left the gas on under the kettle. Somebody followed his example; then another and another jerked into motion and darted off in this direction or that. It was as if a deep-freeze had suddenly thawed, throwing the mass once again into its individual components. The trickle grew into a flood. Within a few minutes the whole of the crowd had melted away. The remaining police, who had been standing side by side, very quietly, as if recognizing a familiar phenomenon, and observing extreme caution in case any sudden movement on their part might arrest the process, formed themselves into a squad and marched off. The street and the trampled garden of Hugo's house, littered with bricks and mortar, were still and deserted.

Hugo opened the front door, entered, and closed it softly behind him. He stood in the hall, closed his eyes and breathed deeply as if savouring the ozone at his favourite seaside resort. His house had passed through a crisis. Now it was practically his again; now he and it were nearly coterminous. But suddenly a puzzled, disappointed expression crossed his face. In part, no doubt, this arose from the fact that the stench from the upper regions, which had begun to reach down to him even here, quickly dispelled any briny illusions. But in addition he could hear a number of people moving about above him and voices raised in inquiry and exasperation. Was there a pocket of resistance the police had overlooked? The thought also reminded him of the couple he had left locked in the bathroom: something would have to be done about them.

Warily he made his way upstairs. As he approached the mezzanine the voices sorted themselves out into male and female, young and middle-aged, educated and refined, and, above all, puzzled and indignant. Rounding the corner of the corridor he saw two little groups assembled outside the Proudfoot-Lorns' apartment, like rival diplomatic missions or the two halves of a family before the reading of the last will and testament. To the right stood Mrs Vaisey—pince-nez glittering, tailor-made edges snapping like razor blades, Susan—plump, pink and soluble like a strawberry sundae—and Hardiman, his mahogany forehead, white hair and blue eyes apparently detached from his body, floating above some imaginary cloud line. To the left stood Captain Truscott—paler and more fragile-looking than ever, arms bent at the elbows, fingers crooked, poised on the balls of his feet as if about to launch himself at an invisible rope, and the Reverend "Ronnie" Beddoes—nutty-brown and blond, chunky, and tobacco-stained.

Hugo, who sometimes took a perverse delight in the social contretemps of his tenants, stood and listened for a moment without announcing his presence.

"I cannot understand it..."

"We heard there was some sort of disturbance..."

"So did we..."

"Our friends might need help..."

"So might ours..."

"Well, this is where they live...."

"This is where *they* live..."

"We are rather special friends and colleagues..."

"So are we..."

"*Our* friend, you know, is a rather distinguished personage..."

"Well, so is ours..."

"He always invites us to a preview of his film..."

"What an odd coincidence! *She* always invites us to a preview of *hers!*"

"Obviously there is some mistake..."

"Undoubtedly..."

"A most distinguished explorer..."

"You could call her that..."

"Her? You mean him..."

"Him? You mean her..."

"Brother and sister..."

"Sister and brother..."

"Twins..."

"Twins!"

"Colonel and Eunice Proudfoot..."

"No, Dame Alice and Edgar Lorn..."

"There must be some mistake..."

"No, there is no mistake," Hugo said, coming forward.

Both parties fell on him, as if he were the potentate at the diplomatic levee, or the lawyer bearing the will.

"The landlord!"

"Thank God!"

"He will sort it out!"

"He will know what is happening in his own house!"

"Presumably...."

"My dear fellow!" Hardiman cried, clasping Hugo's arm and bringing his head down to earth, as if it were an Indian rope trick that had gone wrong. "I'm glad you are still at your post! You can sort out this muddle for us.... Would you be so good as to tell these two fellows that they've come to the wrong house?"

"But we haven't!" the Reverend "Ronnie" protested. He nodded at Hugo and Hugo nodded back.

"What! You know each other?" Hardiman demanded.

"We are tenants!" Captain Truscott said, his forehead flushing, "We have a *pied à terre*..."

"Impossible!"

"There is no mistake," Hugo assured them, taking out his pass key. "You have come to the right house, the right flat, the right people—and the right landlord." He flung open the door, and stood aside for them to enter. They were greeted by a stench like that emanating from a jungle swamp or unburied corpses. Hugo, whose nostrils were naturally attuned to every odour of his house, immediately recognized the new and distinctive smell as the product of two blended sources. The others looked at each other, a horrible suspicion dilating their eyes—but a rattling, whirring noise, apparently proceeding from the living-room, reassured them, and the look of alarm was replaced by one of bewilderment. They went up to the walls and peered at them: the light wood panels were now reduced to the same chocolate-brown greasiness as the wall-paper; a layer of grime covered stuffed animals, shrunken heads, religious pictures and crucifix alike. With Hugo in the lead, they advanced along the corridor. Two pin-points of light suddenly emerged from the gloom. They stopped. The points of light appeared to be moving towards them. Susan screamed: the others fell back. But the points of light still pursued them. They seemed, however, to be veering to the left. Suddenly there was a faint metallic noise and one of them disappeared through the open doorway. The other—as they pressed themselves against the greasy wall—passed close to and they saw that it was an aluminium film container. It, too, rolled on through the door—and as if endowed with volition continued along the corridor towards the head of the stairs. A moment later they heard a twin bumping as the two containers descended the stairs. Where they went to Hugo never discovered.

The whirring noise grew louder as they approached the living-room. As Hugo opened the door a puff of hot, putrid air greeted them, as if a boa constrictor had opened its jaws and yawned in their faces after a heavy meal. The curtains, their thick, greasy velvet more flesh-like than ever, were drawn so that they admitted only a pencil of light. But a faint, phosphorescent glow appeared to encompass the long couch and the two dim figures crouched at either end of it. It took them several seconds to realize that this, together with the mysterious whirring noise, proceeded from a film projector—which, a moment later, Hugo recognized as his own, and which had mysteriously disappeared from his store cupboard some time before. No film had been inserted in the machine, however, and there was no screen: on the other hand the whirring noise was strangely reminiscent of the jungle chorus of insects, birds, frogs, monkeys and other small animals.

The carpet was tacky with grease and scraps of food, except in the place where their feet crunched on spilled sugar, corn flakes, and potato crisps. Half-consumed tins and packets of food, mixed up with bits of bone, feather, cloth, pottery and desiccated, crumbling flesh, were also scattered about. The glass cases which had once housed Arnold's more precious South American trophies were shattered. The lizards and snakes that had once slithered over the walls, hung askew, suspended by a tail-tip or a single claw. The cayman, too, had become detached from its fastenings and hung, head downwards, like a grotesque bell rope. Stacked against the walls were heaps of fur, feather, corpses of birds and animals that looked as if they had been gnawed by rats, broken pots and baskets, and shrunken heads, like squashed figs, that had obviously been savagely trampled under foot—all mixed up with chipped ebony heads, shattered crucifixes, broken glass and picture-frames and the torn scraps of the religious pictures they had contained. Each heap was studded with torn and crumpled scraps of paper, creating the impression of a demolished jakes. In one corner lay Dame Alice's lectern, thrown on its side and smashed, and in another lay Edgar's filing cabinet, the drawers pulled out, the contents scattered, and the solid steel side stove in with kicks that must have had the force of a sledge hammer.

The visitors advanced cautiously through the gloom, stench and debris to the couch, paused, split into two groups, one opposite each of the seated figures, paused again, changed places, then mingled in confusion.

"There must be some mistake...." Hardiman ventured at last, his voice shaky—and indeed even Hugo (who prided himself on his ability to adapt himself with lightning-like agility to the smallest or most bizarre of his tenants' vagaries) was hard put to it to unscramble the two images that confronted him: the verb was singularly apt, he reflected, because they really did look like two eggs, broken side by side in the same pan, after the first few turns of the whisk or flicks of the fork. It was still possible, at any rate to Hugo, to discern Dame Alice's apple-cheeks beneath Eunice's congealed *coiffure*, and Arnold's jaunty head on Edgar's dirty and raddled neck. But further identification was confused by the fact that whereas the upper half of one of the figures was draped in a linen jacket which though crumpled and stained undeniably suggested Arnold, the lower half was attired in Eunice's unmentionable skirt—while the upper half of the other figure wore a blouse which still retained something of Dame Alice's crispness at the same time that the lower half displayed Edgar's equally unmentionable trousers.

"Arnold, old man," Hardiman ventured at last, addressing the couch rather than its occupants.

"Dame Alice—my dear," the Reverend "Ronnie" Beddoes followed suit, casting his voice, shocked into a frayed rumble, in the same general direction.

Unfortunately they spoke simultaneously, thereby evoking two simultaneous nods of the head.

"It *is* Arnold? Colonel Arnold Proudfoot?" Mrs Vaisey tried, in a quavering voice, "and ... and his sister Eunice?" Again both heads jerked up and down simultaneously.

"No, no!" Captain Truscott cried, "It is Dame Alice Lorn—and, of course her brother Edgar—is ... is it not?" Once again the two heads nodded in unison. The movement was particularly disconcerting because the bodies, propped up at either end of the couch, remained completely flaccid: it was as if the head-pieces of two dummies continued to function after the ventriloquists had withdrawn their sustaining fingers—and the bodies looked even more puppet-like by virtue of the fact that each had an arm twisted behind its back.

They stood in the semi-darkness, their nerves tingling. Suddenly Susan broke from the group and flinging herself on her knees before the figure in the left-hand corner of the couch, seized its free hand. "Arnold!" she cried, "what has she done to you?" The face above her remained motionless, the eyes staring fixedly over her head. But a moment later the head at the right hand extremity of the couch jerked several times, and a faint ruffling movement such as one might expect from the puffing of a moustache, was discernible on the upper lip. Susan dropped the hand she was holding as if it was red hot and began to scream. Still screaming, she scrambled to her feet and, eyes dilated and fixed on the couch, began to back away towards the door. White and trembling now, the others followed her, almost at the double; Hardiman first, the aloof expression entirely vanished, then Mrs Vaisey, her face suddenly lined and elderly; Captain Truscott also seemed to have aged, his shoulders hunched, his arms folded across his chest as if he were holding his ribs together and a pinched look round his mouth as if it were filled with alum; the Reverend "Ronnie" came last, throwing glances over his shoulder and murmuring over and over again: "Alice, Alice, Alice...."

Hugo himself, poised between panic and hilarity, with difficulty restrained himself from warbling " 'Where art thou?' " as he shepherded the visitors out of the room. Before he closed the door, however, he became aware of an odd, regular movement behind him. He forced himself to turn round and look back. The two figures were still propped against the two ends of the couch, but they no longer had the right arms twisted behind their backs, and in the right hand of each was a round-ish object which Hugo at first took for a rubber ball. They began to throw these objects to each other, back-wards and forwards, slowly and deliberately and taking great care not to let them collide in mid-air. After a few attempts they became more expert, settling quickly into a rhythm that chimed exactly with the whirring of the empty projector. A puff of wind from the windows momentarily stirred one of the curtains, widening the sliver of light. Hugo saw that the two objects passing rhythmically to and fro were shrunken heads. At the same time the two figures began to sing: the words were indistinguishable, but there was some vague resemblance to a nursery rhyme: both voices were in a high-pitched falsetto. Hugo jumped back and slammed the door be-hind him. The others had already trooped down the hall and into the corridor beyond, where they stood in a tense, silent group. Hurriedly Hugo joined them. He locked the main door of the flat and pocketed the key. Still in silence they descended the stairs. Hugo found that his shoulders were shaking, but whether with hysterical fear or hysterical mirth he could not deter-mine.

When he reached his own rooms he was astonished to find the Doctor there, sitting calmly in front of the wall chart, re-arranged the plastic pieces—with un-canny accuracy, it seemed to Hugo from a cursory glance. The Doctor gave a curt nod when he heard the door open, finished his task, then swivelled round to face him. "An interesting game of solitaire," he said. He was as neat and dapper as ever, the black velvet collar of his overcoat gleaming like patent-leather. He was however, Hugo thought, a trifle plumper and more florid, and the black Assyrian beard fractionally longer and more curly.

"Clearing-up time, eh?" he said, crossing his immaculately trousered legs and encircling a slim ankle between finger and thumb. Hugo continued to stare at him, his eyes rounder than ever in the presence of this remarkably timely advent. The Doctor frowned.

"No," he said, "I have *not* dropped out of the clouds. Really, you must check these random romanticisms: they are enervating, like nocturnal emissions."

"But," Hugo mumbled, "How ... what. ... ?"

"You forget that it is one of the techniques of my profession—or 'tricks of the trade' if you prefer it—to startle by sudden and unexpected intervention. If you were sufficiently rational to cast your mind back over the past four or five years without all kinds of sentimental distortions, you would realize that there have been a number of them. Some you were too absorbed in yourself to notice, others you had the vanity to ascribe to old-world courtesy or even personal liking—considerations which may be valid in other contexts, but not in this, for all were professionally calculated (as you would see if I allowed you to examine my appointments book). But sooner or later over such a period of time one of these interventions was bound to appear as miraculous..."

"But," Hugo tried to interrupt, only to be quailed by the Doctor's stern black eyes as he continued without a pause:

"A reputation as a miracle-maker may, it is true, be useful in my profession—but mostly with patients of limited intelligence or quite unusual immaturity (and, of course, with one's colleagues)—but in your case, my dear Hugo, it is not at all applicable. Nevertheless, it is clear that my arrival is opportune—and we in my profession are nothing if not opportunists. So pray explain the circumstances: there are, I take it, several minor matters you wish me to attend to before I get down to the main purpose of this visit—which, incidentally, I

209

had decided upon two days ago."

Hugo explained. Then he conducted the Doctor to the upper regions. At the foot of the stairway leading to the shattered door the Doctor paused, sniffed, then drew from the inside pocket of his overcoat a soft-leather case, no larger than a note-case. This zipped open to reveal a folded pair of galoshes, which the Doctor proceeded to fasten carefully over his patent-leather shoes. Thus prepared, he followed Hugo up the stairs, down the corridor, littered with broken furniture, and to the bathroom where Hugo had left the boy and girl. He unlocked the door. Stepping delicately through the various obstacles the Doctor approached them. They were lying in exactly the same position, the girl still breathing heavily, the boy with an idiotically beatific smile on his face. The Doctor stood for a moment looking down at them, stroking his beard. With a pained expression he pointed to the floor. Hugo promptly produced a clean towel which he had surreptitiously brought with him. The Doctor pursed his lips, rounded his eyes and nodded his head up and down very slowly in approval, then spreading the towel on the floor knelt down beside the girl. He felt her pulse, pulled down an eyelid and examined the pupil with the aid of a pencil-torch. Then he opened his neat little bag, extracted a syringe and deftly applied it to the girl's forearm. He waited for a moment, nodded his head, and turned his attention to the boy. A few seconds later both of them stirred, muttered, opened their eyes and stared round them peevishly, though they showed no inclination for further activity.

The Doctor packed up his instruments and stood up, dusting the knee of his trousers. His hands and clothing were in fact as immaculate as ever—a remarkable achievement, Hugo reflected, in view of the condition of the bathroom. He was reminded of a famous television gourmet who demonstrated the most complicated and messy recipes in full evening dress.

"An ambulance here," the Doctor said curtly. "Next?"

Hugo led the way out of the upper regions. At the foot of the stairway the Doctor stopped, removed his galoshes, cleaned them thoroughly with pieces of tissue, returned them to their case and slipped the case back into the inside pocket of his overcoat.

They came to the Proudfoot-Lorns' apartment. Again Hugo unlocked the door. Again the Doctor sniffed. He glanced sharply at Hugo, who was staring innocently at the ceiling, secretly pleased at having thus stolen a march.

"Aha," said the Doctor, wagging a finger before once more unbuttoning his overcoat. "We progress, do we not? We progress!" He smiled benignly as once more he donned the galoshes. Blushing slightly Hugo led the way along the corridor and opened the door of the living-room. The Doctor stood for a moment on the threshold watching the shrunken heads passing to and fro, his own turning from side to side as if he were watching a slow-motion tennis tournament.

"A plain van here," he announced, shutting the door behind him.

While the Doctor busied himself with his several phone calls Hugo hurried round to the local police station. The sergeant behind the desk recognized him.

"You have come to lay charges?" he asked eagerly.

"Oh no, not at all!" Hugo replied.

"But they are squatters ... *trespassers!*" the sergeant protested.

"Oh no, that is what I wanted to explain," Hugo said, his round face bland and innocent. "They are tenants."

"Tenants, *all* of them?"

"Why, yes...."

"A likely tale!"

"If they were beneath my roof, then they were my tenants!" Hugo said indignantly.

"But they broke up your property sir! Defaced your walls! Deposited all manner of objects!"

Patiently Hugo explained about the betrothal celebrations.

"Wedding guests!" the sergeant pounced. "Guests aren't tenants!"

"But these applied for tenancy," Hugo insisted, "and I accepted them."

The sergeant regarded him glumly and suspiciously. When Hugo had finished his long and extremely circumstantial explanation, he took up a pencil and pad.

"Names?" he said softly, simulating an absent-minded air. Hugo thought rapidly. "Palfrey," he said, mentioning the first name that came to mind. The sergeant wrote it down to Hugo's dictation, then looked up at him. chewing the ends of his moustache, pencil poised.

"Quincey, Skidmore, Smith, Venner, Bradbury, Sturmer, Proudfoot ... er ... Lorn ..." he rattled the names off.

"Just a moment, sir! Not so fast!" Hugo waited while he laboriously wrote down the names. "H'm," said the sergeant when they had finished, surveying the list of names lugubriously. "The numbers seem to tally ... Needless to say the young so-and-sos wouldn't give us their names themselves ... Thank you for your co-operation sir ... Just a minute, though! You're one short!"

For a moment Hugo's mind went blank. Frantically he cast about for another name. Then, gulping with a sense of betrayal, he murmured, "Prěserěn ..."

"Eh?" the sergeant said, startled.

Hugo repeated the name in a faint voice.

"Oh—a foreigner! How do you spell it, sir?" Hugo told him. When the sergeant had written it down he leaned over the desk, took the pencil from the sergeant's hand, and inserted the cuticles above the relevant vowels. He felt as if he were laying a pair of wreaths.

Nevertheless he felt rather pleased with himself as he hurried back home. In some cases no doubt other charges would be laid (such as assaulting the police and resisting arrest) but the more innocent of the squatters would probably be spared a good deal of inconvenience. He felt as if he had made some small act of expiation.

As he rounded the corner of the street leading to his own house an ambulance passed him. It was followed a few minutes later by a plain van. When he entered his garden he was surprised to see that another ambulance was drawn up outside the front door. He stopped in the gateway (the gate itself had been torn off its hinges and tossed on top of one of the piles of masonry and debris) and regarded his house for several minutes. A full moon hung behind two tall chimneys, motionless, it seemed, as if it had been nailed to them: it had the pale gold one finds on the haloes of ancient Russian ikons. The light welled over on to the sloping roofs, appeared to slide down them, very slowly like an in-coming tide over an expanse of flat beach, and then to drip down over the eaves and gutterings. It trickled down the walls, losing momentum as it went, sent out a few yellow tongues across the paths and over the stones of the terraces and rockeries, and then disappeared, apart from an occasional flicker, among the tangled and trodden undergrowth. It gave the house, with its smashed upper windows—from some of which sheets and ropes with baskets attached to them still dangled—a mel-ancholy, decaying appearance—but at the same time a remarkably Gothic one which warmed the cockles of Hugo's heart and stilled some of the pangs of conscience that had assailed him for taking Prěseřěn's name in vain.

Inside the house, Hugo found the door of his office open; just inside stood Sergeant Palfrey, talking earnestly with the Doctor. The old man was wearing his Sunday suit, which smelt strongly of moth balls and lavender. It was of an antique cut, with very high *revers*, and made—constructed, rather—of some black material which was so stiff and thick that Hugo had the fancy that it must have been cut in sections with a blowlamp. With it went a striped flannel shirt surmounted by a stiff wing-collar the colour of old ivory: it stood out round his neck like a halter, throwing into relief the folds of yellow, stringy skin, like that of a tortoise. The Sergeant's whole body, indeed, seemed to have under-gone a further process of reduction, shrunken back in-side its carapace. The hairy, sinewy wrists with their blue tattoo marks stuck out from the stiff white cuffs as if they had been screwed in: the splayed, calloused fingers were outspread as if groping for support: the Adam's apple looked enormous, wobbling up and down like a buoy in rough water. The seamed and sunken cheeks, freshly scraped by a cut-throat razor, were the colour and texture of pumice stone; a scrap of blood-flecked cotton-wool adhered to the point of his chin. He had, however, allowed himself to leave the buttons of the waistcoat un-done, though the edges protruded as if they were the parts of a breast-plate, and the Albert, with its dangling cluster of medallions, mementoes and gadgets, had difficulty in bridging the gap.

In spite of the constrictions of his garments he man-aged to straighten himself when Hugo entered and to greet him with the usual sidelong twist of the mouth and his customary ironic salute.

"I came to tell you about the missus," he said. "It's happened again..." Hugo remembered the other ambulance standing outside the house. The Sergeant read his mind. "Yes," he said, "a bad one...."

A wave of nausea and panic swept over Hugo. "But you mustn't send her away!" he cried. "You can keep her here!"

Very slowly Sergeant Palfrey shook his head. "Not this time, poor old girl. This time it's the Union...."

"But we can get nurses! I will help you! We'll manage somehow!" Hugo's heart was thumping painfully. He had no idea he was so attached to the Palfreys, but suddenly the thought of their leaving was unbearable. "I don't want them to go," he thought, "especially I don't want *her* to go.... They are the last! When they've gone the house will be empty... I shall be alone, alone with..."

"But what about the allotment?" he asked.

The Sergeant's mouth twitched. " 'Earth to earth, ashes to ashes'," he quoted surprisingly.

"But has the Doctor here seen her?" Hugo cried, seized with a wild hope.

"I have," the Doctor himself spoke for the first time, fixing Hugo with a long, level look.

"Don't you worry about us, sir," the Sergeant said. "I don't feel quite as bad about it now—I've had a chat with the doctor gentleman here. We speak the same lingo, him and me!" and Sergeant Palfrey and the Doctor exchanged a look of almost comradely complicity:

Hugo had, indeed, never seen the Doctor so natural and relaxed: on the other hand, the eye which he once more turned on Hugo was professionally cold and calculating.

"But *you* don't have to go!" Hugo made one last appeal.

"Yes, I'm going to my niece for a bit," Sergeant Palfrey replied, glancing down ruefully at the Sunday suiting that encased him. "She lives near the hospital. No," he added, shaking his head as Hugo started to speak, "we ... I ... shan't be coming back." He was silent for a moment: then he wiped his moustache with the back of his hand, first one side then the other, as if he had just downed a tankard of ale: with a quick, almost jaunty movement he straightened his back, gave Hugo another ironic salute, turned on his heel and made for the door. With his hand on the knob he hesitated.

"Would you like to see her before she goes?" he said, in a low voice, and added almost slyly, "for the last time, like... ?"

Hugo envisaged the bloated body inside the ambulance; the swollen, mis-shapen legs; the feet with their bunions, hammer-toes and lemon-coloured soles; the purple face with its stiff left cheek and down-drooping mouth; the sparse, frizzy grey hair—and the eyes, above all the eyes, hurt, puzzled, frightened, and crooked, yet still tender and alive. He felt his own eyes, round like those of a lemur in the round babyish face, filling with tears, but to his astonishment he heard himself reply, in quiet, almost matter-of-fact tones: "Remember me to her—but no thank you I don't want to see her again." He was equally surprised when the Sergeant clasped his hand and wrung it heartily, looking into his eyes with a simple, man-to-man expression.

"That's right," he said, "better that way, much better!" A moment later he had left the room.

"Excellent!" the Doctor exclaimed when he had gone. "There is no doubt about it—you are making progress! It was necessary, not only for your own sake but also because..."

But before he could finish the sentence there was an

exclamation from outside the door. Someone had apparently collided with Sergeant Palfrey on his way out. A moment later Roger Quincey burst into the room.

"Just in time!" he gasped.

"Just in time for what?" Hugo asked, rubbing his hands without much conviction, feeling that he ought to be elated by Roger's apt reappearance.

"Why, to see the mess!" Roger cried. "Somebody told us about the riot. 'They' were having one of their parties, so I slipped out and ran round here! The garden's in a terrible state, and the orchard—everywhere in fact! I went round it all with my torch before I came in—all the places where I used to play—smashed up! It's a mess everywhere now—not just that bit by the gate!"

He had grown even faster since Hugo had last seen him and seemed to be several inches taller. There was a faint downy smudge on his upper lip, as if he had just been drinking soup.

"Can I see the damage upstairs too?" he asked.

"No, you can't!" Hugo replied, with unaccustomed tartness. It has been a long day and he was feeling tired. He regarded Roger morosely, as if he might, indeed, be the Spirit of Christmas Past—but of a Christmas which, after all, he had no particular wish to remember.... Yes, it pleased his sense of pattern that the last of his tenants to abandon the premises would be the oldest and youngest: the two ends of his life joined together, so to speak ... desirable, perhaps, before he could begin a new life in his own house, independent of them... But why did the thought bring him so little pleasure?

Roger gave him a faint smile. "I expect you're anxious to open up now," he said. "The wine-cellar, I mean," darting a knowing look at Hugo. He went over to the door leading to the basement and tried it.

"Can I meet him?" he asked, in a mocking tone of voice. But Hugo was not to be caught out so easily after all this time. He knew that Roger knew; and he knew that Roger knew that he knew. That too, no doubt, had its rightness; but so did respect for the

216

preservation of his own mystery. So he merely replied, in the same tone of mockery: "You know you're still much too young to drink."

Roger laughed. "All right," he said, "I can take a hint. As a matter of fact I wish I hadn't come. I've just realized that I'm bored by it all. I didn't think I would be when I decided to come, but I am. I don't want to meet *him*." He jerked his thumb in the direction of the door leading to the basement. "I'm so bored I think I shall forget all about him soon...."

He stood silent for a moment, an expression half-sullen, half cunning stealing over his face. Then he looked up from under his eyebrows.

"As a matter of fact," he said quietly, "I'm bored with you too!"

"Bored!" Hugo exclaimed indignantly, and then a moment later, "bored!" in tones of delighted relief. "Why, do you think I'm not bored with *you*, cropping up enigmatically all over the place like that wretched kid in *'Waiting for Godot'*?"

Roger's expression darkened. "And what about you?" he said in a jeering voice. "Pad-padding all over the place with your fat bum and your fat, padded fingers!"

"How dare you!" Hugo shouted.

"How dare *you*! How dare *you*!" Roger chanted. "Wouldn't you just have liked to put those padded fingers on my knee? But you didn't dare! You didn't da ... are!"

"But I would never *dream...*!" Hugo protested, deeply shocked.

"Oh yes, we all know you! You haven't got any spunk in you!"

"And you have, I suppose?"

"Yes I ha ... ave! Yes I ha ... ave!" Roger cried, prancing round the room, and adding in the same sing-song voice, "Pad-pad-pad! Pad-pad-pad!"

"Get out you little perisher!" Hugo said.

Immediately Roger stopped his prancing. "Well, I must be off," he said, in a perfectly normal tone of voice. "So long!" and with a cheery wave of the hand he hurried out.

217

"Bored?" Hugo said to himself, but of course! Why hadn't he realized it before? If his tenants had done with him he had certainly done with them. They had played out their tenancies and they had played out themselves. It was his house at last.

He was aroused from his reverie by a faint click, and turning round he saw that the Doctor had just inserted the last of the plastic squares into its niche: the chart now presented the appearance of the sky on a cloudy night: black everywhere except for one small cluster of white against those sections of his house which Hugo had never surrendered.

"Excellent!" the Doctor exclaimed abruptly, sitting down again. "You have not only made progress—you have arrived. And this brings me to the main object of my visit which I have not yet had an opportunity of explaining to you. I have decided, you see, that our patient should now be released."

Hugo could not at once take this in. "I don't understand," he temporized. "I mean, you haven't even seen him since your last visit, have you?"

"What on earth," the Doctor exclaimed, "has that to do with it?" His eyes were fully open in astonishment, for the first time since Hugo had known him.

"I still don't follow you," he said. "Last time you were here you didn't think he *was* ready—ah, to emerge. And now you suddenly say that he is! Is that consistent?"

The Doctor regarded him with even greater astonishment. "But in my profession one *must* be inconsistent!" he cried.

"Well, has anything happened since you were last here to make you change your mind?"

"But naturally!"

"Oh ... then perhaps you called on him one day when I was out?"

"Certainly not."

"But you said 'something had happened'..."

"It happened to *me*!" the Doctor exclaimed, tugging at his curly beard in exasperation. "Why *must* you always arrogate everything to yourself? Do you imagine I have

218

no life of my own? Really! The self-centredness of you people—it's the main drawback of my profession!"

"I beg your pardon," Hugo said, timidly but suddenly revealing a buried streak of obstinacy. "But I don't see how something that has happened to *you* can make you suddenly come to this sort of conclusion about a patient. How can it affect *him*?" And he nodded towards the door leading to the basement.

"Why, very materially," the Doctor replied calmly. "I'm going away!"

"But ... but," Hugo spluttered. The Doctor, however, was walking up and down the room, his head slightly bowed, his hands tucked under the tails of his immaculate overcoat, talking volubly.

"It will renew me!" he cried. "It will renew me completely, but completely! I, too, was getting bored, stale—this foggy climate of yours, and your foggy fellow countrymen, and all my foggy patients! And then, of course, there's the financial side of it ... I've long had my eyes on an estate in my own country, and now I shall be able to buy it several times over ... ah! to live among my own folk again! To hear some sense talked at last! I shall make an ideal landlord too! Where I shall differ from the usual feudal-minded landlord is that while *I* have forgotten nothing I have learned everything! Besides, my countrymen have always had a special regard for the prodigal son of lowly origins who returns to lord it over his neighbours—provided he knows how to temper hauteur with benevolence—and you must admit, my profession provides an excellent training ground for that rare but estimable combination of qualities!"

"But going away? ... Just going ... going where?" Hugo managed to interrupt.

"You should never interfere with a man in my profession when he is absorbed in himself," the Doctor told him, without the least change in the tempo of his pacing or his voice. "It may do him irreparable harm. On the other hand, it may also be interpreted as an infallible sign that one of his patients has won through and set him free in the process... Just think of it! A prolonged lecture tour of the United States—at astronomical fees, needless to say! Did I say 'prolonged'? Self-perpetuating, rather, for I shall lecture to them on my books, and that, of course, means that I shall mystify them further—so that *another* course of lectures will be necessary to explicate the mystification—and then another to explicate the mystification of the explanation, and so on *ad infinitum*! ... Well, there will be a finish, of course—when I've collected sufficient dollars for my purpose (perhaps it would be a good idea to buy the neighbouring estate too? ... Or would it be better to marry the daughter?) ... And then, home for good! How we shall laugh over all this nonsense back home! ... My cronies and I in the cafés, at those little brown-veined, marble-topped tables with their curly iron legs and the old newspapers on brass rods! ... Ah, yes and with the peasants too in the taverns on market days! *How* they will laugh! ... Yes, and eventually I shall become quite a big man—a figure in a simple legend made by simple folk...."

"So your patients count for nothing?" Hugo succeeded in interrupting again.

"On the contrary, they count for everything I am prepared to give them, and for everything they are prepared to take!"

It was rarely that Hugo attempted a sneer, but he managed one now.

"Is that an example of your peasant virtues?" he asked.

"Pray do not be facetious with me," the Doctor replied, as if he were addressing a sulky schoolboy.

"So you just drop your patients when it suits you?" Hugo persisted.

"No, only when it suits me *enough*! If there is something *I* want to do so badly that I am prepared to abandon my patients, then clearly it is time that they *were* abandoned. Obviously they will get nothing more from me, and if we are no longer of mutual benefit to each other what would be the point of continuing?"

"This isn't just 'patients', 'a patient', 'any old patient'!" Hugo cried. "It is my own flesh and blood! And you yourself have always referred to him as 'our patient'..."

The Doctor stopped his pacing and laid his hand on Hugo's arm: when he spoke his voice was unexpectedly gentle: "Then you must be thankful that my selfishness and greed are powerful enough to force the issue! All these years you have been secretly longing for the one, unique shock that would be the key to your fetters. You did not know it, and I did not know it—and now the fallibility of human nature (even *my* nature!) has found that key for you! ... And now I must go. I shall, of course, send you a picture postcard from time to time—though when I return to my own country they may arrive at rather infrequent intervals (the communications system, thank God, is antediluvian!)" He smoothed the collar of his overcoat with long, elegant fingers. "The key of which I spoke," he added, "is hanging beside your wall chart." He nodded briskly and hurried out.

Hugo pulled forward his favourite wing-chair: he placed its companion on the other side of the fire-place. Then he sat quite still for several minutes. At length he got up, took the key from its hook beside the wall chart, and unlocked the door leading to the basement.

"You can come up now, Kurt!" he called out. His voice was steady and matter-of-fact. He returned to his armchair and waited. He could hear Kurt moving about below, collecting his papers and humming softly to himself. A few minutes later he heard him climbing the stairs. Halfway up he stumbled and swore. When he emerged he blinked round him for a moment, then made straight for the other wing-chair, settled himself comfortably in it, and still humming, put on his spectacles and began to examine the papers he had brought with him. It was not until half an hour later that he looked over the top of his spectacles, smiled at Hugo and said, "Hello!"

He was astonishingly like his twin brother. He had exactly the same rotund build; the same short, muscular arms and legs; the same barrel chest; the same round blue eyes, and the same round, moon-like face. There was a difference, though. Whereas Hugo's face was completely unmarked—smooth, and round and silvery like a moon devoid of geographical features—Kurt's looked as if it had been scored over and over again, not so much with wrinkles as with innumerable tiny stencilled lines, which gave his face the appearance of a mahogany table-top which bears the scratch marks of a half a dozen genera-tions, or of an autumn leaf of three years ago, which has grown wafer-thin in the process of survival. When he smiled these tiny lines flickered across his face like sun-beams through half-closed eyelashes. What was remark-able was that the lines extended above the brow, mingling with the rather scanty hair, like ribbed sand disappearing among clumps of scrub. In view of the fact that he had spent so many years in seclusion, apart from the visitations of Hugo and the Doctor, his com-plexion was naturally somewhat pallid, but otherwise he looked in remarkably good health: like Hugo he was rather tubby, but not in the least flaccid: his body had the same springy carriage and his eyes were just as bright. Apart from the lines on his face, indeed, he conveyed exactly the same appearance of unused in-nocence: but there was no gainsaying the lines: they spoke of pain and guilt enough for two.

They sat in this cosy, companionable manner for some time longer, savouring their reunion, their aloneness and their freedom. It did not occur to either of them to discuss the past, or even the Doctor's unexpected decision.

At the end of an hour or so, however, Hugo got to his feet.

"Shall we go?" he said.

Kurt smiled and gathered up his papers. Together they made their way through the silent, deserted house. It was not a simple emptiness of which they were aware, but rather a whole series of emptinesses, as if each room, separately sealed and isolated, drew in upon itself. Where-as in the past Hugo had felt that the breathing of his house, though that of a single organism, was nevertheless made up of many different respirations, each at its own tempo and pressure, so now he could feel the separate silences all over the house—intense, concentrated silences, like those of dying animals retreating to their

222

last corners. It was thus, he reflected, that the separate cells of a honeycomb must die, cut off from each other yet parts of a whole, and therefore affecting the whole.

Hugo, as a prudent landlord, had acquired an economical turn of mind and he was careful, as they left each room or corridor, to switch off the lights. Light, in consequence, seemed to be continually springing up before them or dying away behind them, like blood drawn in and out of veins. Light ran like blood, too, along the tops of the walls in the Music Room, which was their ultimate destination. Hugo had installed the wall lighting himself, along with the central-heating which kept the room at exactly the right temperature for the Bechstein grand piano, which stood in the centre of the room, so highly polished that it glowed as if it were itself an atomic core that provided light and heat.

Hugo took out his keys, chose the one for the piano and held it up for Kurt to see. They exchanged that look of delighted complicity which had been special to them since infancy. Hugo unlocked the piano. Kurt put his papers on top of it and then seated himself on the stool. He pulled at his fingers, as if taking off skin-tight gloves, then massaged them for a few minutes. Suddenly he let one hand fall on the keys, as if absent-mindedly: he raised it: the fingers of both hands hovered over the keys like butterflies: and then notes of such detached purity rose from the instrument that it did not seem possible that they could have been produced by either human or mechanical agency.

Kurt smiled and nodded approvingly. "Good! Good!" he said. Hugo felt as pleased as if he had tuned the piano with his own hands and ears. Kurt took one of the sheafs of paper from the top of the piano and propped it up on the stand. Hugo, who could read music, stood beside him, ready to turn the pages. But Kurt played only a few bars, frowned, took the music from the stand, tore it up and threw the scraps into the waste-paper basket. He took down another sheaf, which he treated in the same manner. Hugo looked at his brother with raised eyebrows: Kurt gave him a gentle deprecating smile. He continued to place the sheets of music on the stand.

In some cases he played through a whole section; in others he played only a few bars or even notes; and in yet others merely stared closely at the music and then with a sigh and a shake of the head took it down and tore it up. On each occasion he and Hugo smiled sadly and affectionately at each other, and Hugo patted his twin's arm encouragingly. As the pile on top of the piano gradually subsided, however, Hugo began to look anxious, and then it was only Kurt who smiled, shaking his head as if to say: "Wait—wait—don't lose heart!"

When he was nearly at the bottom of the manuscripts he took down a sheaf consisting of only a few pages and placed it with a thoughtful expression on the stand. He sat back on his stool for a few moments, regarding the music from a distance. Hugo watched him eagerly. Kurt leaned forward, bringing his nose almost within touching distance of the music. He stared at it for several minutes.

He drew back and began massaging his fingers again: they trembled slightly. He hummed a few bars, very softly. "Yes?" Hugo's eyes said. Kurt smiled and began to play. "Ah!" Hugo's eyes said a few seconds later. Kurt gave him a slow, confident smile and went on playing. The notes rose and circled round the room like sunlight. Every few seconds Hugo and Kurt exchanged excited glances. The piece lasted just under five minutes. At the end of it Kurt and Hugo sat very still. Then Kurt swept the few remaining sheets off the top of the piano and deposited them in the waste-paper basket.

"Well, there it is!" he said, staring at the piece of music in front of him, dropping his hands at his sides in pleasurable exhaustion. "It's all right!"

"It's wonderful!" Hugo said.

"It is our best..."

"The years haven't been wasted..."

"It's very little, of course..."

"It's enough!"

"It's certainly better than nothing!"

"And, after all, it may only be another beginning!"